Sherlock Holmes through the Microscope

Carl L. Heifetz

Paperback ISBN 978-1-78705-307-6
ePub ISBN 978-1-78705-308-3
PDF ISBN 978-1-78705-309-0

Published in the UK by MX Publishing
335 Princess Park Manor, Royal Drive,
London, N11 3GX
www.mxpublishing.com

Cover layout and construction by
Brian Belanger

Sherlock Holmes: Master Of Espionage

Published in *The Whitechapel Gazette* Issue No. 4, Mid-1994; p 21-8; T*he Hounds Collection* Vol. 3, 1998, p 40-5; *Baker Street West* 1 Vol. 13, No. 3, Winter 2007, p 12-18; Coppola, Joseph A. Ed.), ...*Occasionally the British Government*, August 2000, The Mycroft Holmes Society Press, Fayetteville, NY, p 109-19; the *Communication* of the Pleasant Places of Florida, #299, 2010, p 2-3: Practice Notes, The Friends of Dr. John H. Watson, Feb. 2013, pages 2-7.

The life and career of Mr. Sherlock Holmes have inspired the interest of many of the brightest intellects in the world. They have expended great efforts to penetrate beyond the glimpses afforded us in the 60 published adventures -- to detect the real underlying character of "the best and the wisest man" Dr. Watson has ever known (*The Final Problem* by A. C. Doyle). To the hundreds of past and present day Sherlockians, Holmesians, Doyeleans, we owe a great deal of gratitude for helping to shred the veil which has been created to obfuscate the real character of our remarkable hero: from the sainted Christopher Morley and Vincent Starrett; to the renowned commentators Ronald A. Knox, William S. Baring-Gould, Edgar W. Smith, Sydney C. Roberts, Michael Harrison, Michael Hardwick, and many others too numerous to mention. Commentators have included bookmen, journalists and essayists, physicians, psychiatrists and pathologists, chemists, monsignors and vicars, barristers and solicitors, and automobile executives. All have brought their intelligence, unique perspectives, and, most of all, a very desperate need for knowledge to this quest, their labor of love. With great humility but stout heart, I feel highly motivated, even obligated, to attempt to add my voice to this ongoing effort.

As a microbiologist, I hope to bring a different perspective to these studies. I am used to dealing with very minute objects that produce consequences much greater than their size would indicate. Is not this obsession with minutiae the perfect training and background for one who feels the need to participate in Sherlockian studies? I do hope that this makes me somewhat qualified to join in this important area of scholarly research.

All of us have been haunted by the same questions over and over and over again. They have disturbed our sleeping dreams and our daytime thoughts. Why was Sherlock Holmes so reticent to reveal his complete lineage, even to his long-term confidential comrade John H. Watson, M.D? Was he protecting relatives from some anticipated danger? Why did Mr. Holmes never allow records of his participation in the successful pursuit of justice to ever appear in the newspapers? Why did he not permit Dr. Watson to reveal the real location of his practice, rather than giving one which had never existed? Why did he make sure that he was never photographed, and why are there so many different illustrations of his visage, so that we may never know what he really looked like? Why, indeed, did he refuse to accept the offer of knighthood? Is this the way of a private consulting detective who has nothing to hide and who is seeking commercial success? It is true that a Victorian gentleman and professional man would never countenance advertising in newspapers or handing out leaflets, as is the accepted practice among some lady and gentleman professionals of today, but to hide his true identity and place of business is surely beyond the pale. He could, at least, have eventually installed a telephone and been listed in the directory, but no such record exists.

And what about his mysterious brother Mycroft? He "audited the books in some of the government departments, but in actuality, in Sherlock's words, Mycroft occasionally was the British government" (Jack Tracy's *The*

2

Encyclopaedia Sherlockiana, a marvelous treasure trove of Sherlockian lore).

A scientist's first effort must be to review whatever primary evidence is available. In this case, the original source of truth is the Canon itself. Following this, the investigations and opinions of other seekers of knowledge must be consulted for their insight. Then, a working hypothesis must be reached and a model constructed to fit all of the available facts. Unable to follow my instincts to don my tattered and stained lab coat and to perform marvelously constructed, controlled experiments to test my hypotheses, I was forced to enter foreign territory and apply the strange (to me) methods utilized by scientists in the fields of geology, anthropology, and archaeology. I was required to pick my way through the fossil traces of a previous epoch to seek support for my conjectures. The theory easily fell into place. Following the lead of my predecessors, who are much more experienced and skilled in such explorations, it seemed logical to me that Mr. Holmes' main business was that of a super-secret agent for the British government, and that Mycroft, his older brother, was the first and original director of the very first and very, very underground British secret service. Their machinations in this regard were so well covered-up that only Her Majesty the Queen, her Prime Minister, and the Foreign Office were privy to these activities. His detective practice was an excellent cover for his more underground activities. As a detective he could perform most of the functions of a spy without revealing the true nature of his quarry. He could go anywhere day or night, follow people and keep track of their comings and goings, delve into classified official documents, and pursue many other practices which are common to both of these careers.

What is the basis for refuting Mr. Sherlock Holmes' publicly professed practice as that of a private consulting detective as his only profession? Why should we instead insist on characterizing him as a master, undercover espionage agent? Let us first explore some of the evidence available in the Canon. In only four published accounts did Mr. Holmes perform services for the British government.

In three of his earlier cases, Mr. Holmes admitted that he provided services to Her Majesty's government. Although they required some knowledge of foreign agents and their activities, they were, as far as has been revealed, more in the line of his publicly acknowledged profession and revolved around the retrieval of highly important stolen documents (*The Bruce-Partington Plans, The Naval Treaty,* and *The Second Stain* by A. C. Doyle). Had these exploits been published after WWI, I am certain that Mr. Holmes would be portrayed, as is his due, as a much more active participant in these and related activities. In only one case, *His Last Bow* (published in 1917), was Mr. Holmes finally able to reveal his true calling, divest himself of the mantle of detective and tell the public how, in this particular instance, he served his government in the capacity of an undercover secret agent.

Also in the Canon, it is acknowledged that, during the Great Hiatus, Mr. Holmes traveled vast distances to far off exotic locations, at great risk to life and limb, to provide services to the British government. Acting undercover as the Norwegian explorer Sigerson, he said that he "paid a short but interesting visit to the Khalifa at Khartoum, the results of which I have communicated to the Foreign Office" (*The Empty House* by A. C. Doyle).

The post-canonical apocrypha is well marked with suggestions which also lead to the same conclusions. For example, in his stirring account, *Sherlock Holmes My Life and Crimes*, Mr. Michael Hardwick proposed an interesting theory of the activities that took place during these famous travels. He suggested that the great detective and his foremost adversary Professor Moriarty jointly penetrated the secret German electromagnetic wave research facility. Although, unlike the Canon, this is a work of fiction, the story does help lend credence to the idea that espionage was Mr. Holmes' main occupation during his career. Even Huret, the boulevard assassin and French anarchist, fell prey to the activities of Mr. Sherlock Holmes, acting in his capacity as a foreign agent ("Huret the Anarchists, and Sherlock Holmes" by Derek Hinrich in *France in the Blood*, 1993). In addition, in another exciting work of fiction, *Son of Holmes*, the admirable Mr. John T. Lescroart proposed the interesting concept that Mycroft Holmes "...ran the British government single-handedly, especially during World War I. As head of the secret service, among other things, he is known as 'M,' a title which I'm sure is familiar to all of you. His initials became the title for the head of British Intelligence." I am not at all convinced that the elder Holmes sibling actually ran the British government. If he had, the British would have been much better prepared to fight off the German onslaught during that horrendous encounter. However, the supposition that Mycroft Holmes was the head of the original British Intelligence Service is very attractive. No doubt this heavy responsibility dates back before the time of *The Greek Interpreter* (A. C. Doyle). This would place these events as far back as 1888, if one accepts the chronological investigations provided by the meticulous work of Mr. William S. Baring-Gould and others (*The Annotated Sherlock Holmes*). Even the popular motion picture series featuring Basil Rathbone and Nigel Bruce seemed to pursue the right path. Although commencing with a Hollywoodized version of the authentic Doylean drama *Hound of the Baskervilles*, they quickly became a variety of adventures featuring Mr. Holmes, with the "assistance" of a bumbling Watson, serving as espionage agents against the Nazi cause. Did the authors of these World War II films have secret information which contained a germ of truth about Mr. Holmes' real vocation? Would a search of studio records turn-up authentic information about this, or has this data also been relegated to carbon dioxide, water and ash as have all other traces of our hero?

As I previously stated, in order to test a hypothesis, scientists need to construct a working model. Then, they attempt to fit the available facts into the model to support it, or failing that, construct a model which is in better agreement with their theories. Since I have no experience in the world of espionage, I was happy to find an available published device to test the theory that Sherlock Holmes had the characteristics necessary to be a professional spy.

In a very interesting book by Michael Kurlan titled *The Spymaster's Handbook* (Facts on File Publications, New York, 1988), is a "Self Test for Spies." If one were to design a secret agent, Sherlock Holmes would serve as the foremost example in almost every respect. This, of course, should come as no surprise. Since this profession is based on Dr. Doyle's characterization of Sherlock Holmes in the Canon, our favorite detective passes with flying colors. Mr. Holmes, without a doubt, would get high marks for his brilliant intelligence and the fact that he is fluent in many languages. Other outstanding attributes would include: being a leader and not a follower, having a strong but unconventional sense of morality based on his own readings and beliefs, and his ability to keep a secret if required. His Olympic character physical condition and the fact that he enjoys individual sports rather than team sports is an important feature, along with the fact that he is proficient (black belt or equivalent) in martial arts (baritsu for example), as well as being exceptionally skilled in boxing, swordsmanship, and single sticks. There is also evidence that he enjoys horseback riding, golf, swimming, bicycling, and fishing. His physical strength is heroic; he was even able to bend a fireplace poker back to its original shape, a much more difficult task than that of bending it out of shape in the first place (*The Speckled Band*). His interest in practice shooting and skill with the revolver is attested to by his "adorning the wall of the Baker Street sitting room with a patriotic V. R. done in bullet-pocks" (*The Musgrave Ritual*). Other attributes which mark him as an excellent secret agent are as follows: he reads many newspapers every day (but we do not know if he reads any magazines other than his biographer's stories in *Strand*); he likes to regularly go to such entertainments as the opera, plays, and concerts; he has visited many places more than 100 miles from home (including such exotic locales as Tibet and Khartoum, *The Empty House*); he has a vast knowledge of history (especially criminal), poisons, weapons (including air rifles), cartology, science, trigonometry, linguistics, exploration (as Sigerson, for example), foreign secret agents and their organizations, ciphers and decoding. He is particularly adept at following people undetected. This is exemplified by the verbal exchange between Messrs. Sterndale and Holmes in *The Devil's Foot*, "I followed you." "I saw no one." "That is what you may expect to see when I follow you." Thus, there is no doubt that when following someone, Sherlock Holmes would be able to remain undetected while at the same time discovering the person's name, occupation, home, and business address. In addition to the listed requirements for a successful spy, add Mr. Holmes' skill as a second-story man, master safe-cracker, and burglar. Also very useful to his cause are his myriad disguises, acting skills, and his uncanny ability to mix with all levels of British society on an equal footing.

There is only one characteristic of Holmes that will prevent his scoring a perfect grade in the quiz: He cannot possibly be able to claim an average appearance. Any reading of the Canon will support this: tall, thin, penetrating eyes, hawk like nose, dominating presence. This incomplete characterization will help explain his obvious desire to never be photographed or appear as a drawing in the popular press, and why illustrations of his image have been made to vary so considerably over the years. Once viewed, he will never be forgotten.

Why it is that of more than 1,000 recorded cases, only sixty have been allowed to be brought to the public's attention? Why it is that Mr. Holmes' true address has never been revealed to the public, and why he eventually left London to an even more secret location. To quote Dr. Watson "... he has definitely retired from London and betaken himself to study and beefarming on the Sussex Downs, notoriety has become hateful to him, and he has peremptorily requested that his wishes in this matter should be strictly observed" (*The Second Stain*). How can we explain why he never allowed accounts of his adventures to appear in the newspapers (preferring instead to allow the official police to take credit for his successes), and why so many different versions of his appearance been published, preventing his true physiognomy from being recognized. Is this the attitude of someone who is trying to establish a going business enterprise? No! All of these subterfuges were necessary to enable him to follow his true secret profession as the world's first and preeminent master spy. Would it not be exciting to know the true nature of his enterprises during the time of his false retirement, how he worked endlessly and tirelessly on behalf of the Crown, freedom, and the British way?

Two additional reasons come to mind which also help explain the highly secretive nature of Mr. Holmes: personal pride and personal safety. First, as stated by Mr. Kurla, "Spies have been praised, but mostly they have been reviled; they have been thanked, but mostly they have been ignored; they have been rewarded, but mostly they have been disowned." How would the proud descendent of British country squires and elegant French artists respond to having his name reviled as a spy, especially in the era before espionage became considered as a glamorous and worthy occupation. However, I must defer to the opinions of those qualified in psychology to define whether such a revelation would have had a profound effect on his psyche. In my opinion, only a very loyal and patriotic person would undertake such a great personal risk as this occupation entails. It is sad indeed that he was not even able to accept the richly deserved knighthood offered by his grateful sovereign as a reward for his services to the state. This public announcement would have blown his cover. Another reason for avoiding the spotlight and remaining hidden was the ever-increasing effort on behalf of his adversaries to eliminate him from the secret struggle as world conflict became more inevitable. The bravery of Mr. Holmes has never been in doubt. But, a dead hero is of no value to the cause.

The great prolific writer, Dr. Arthur Conan Doyle (later Sir Arthur), introduced the world to the first private consulting detective in the now famous story *Study in Scarlet*. By way of these writings he also created the very paradigm of a highly successful secret agent and a secret service organization. All of the wonderful tools that Mr. Holmes the detective was given to fight crime and solve mysteries can be equally applied to the business of espionage and counterespionage. Later, in 1893, in *The Greek Interpreter*, Dr. Doyle introduced the shadowy figure of Sherlock Holmes' older brother Mycroft. Thus, he completed the stage setting for the introduction of the now famous British secret services MI5 and MI6 which were not to appear until sixteen years later in 1909. How much the development of the science of espionage we owe to the mind and skills of Sir Arthur will never be fully known. However, his contributions, as expressed via his alter egos Messrs. Sherlock and Mycroft Holmes and Dr. John H. Watson must surely have contributed greatly to the allied intelligence services which were essential to the successful conclusion of the two global wars.

Sherlock Holmes - Typical Research Chemist

Published in *The Holmes Front*, Issue #5 August 1999

In the recent edition of the Baker Street Journal, the eminent scholars Wayne and Francine Swift provided a very interesting and well researched article defining the characteristics of the various "Associates of Sherlock Holmes."(1) Although I generally agree with their analyses of Sherlock Holmes' contemporaries, I regret that I must thoroughly disagree with their contention that Mr. Holmes was a physician. Looking at the table provided on page 30 of their essay, they submit as their only proof the evidence that they have extracted from a prior work by Dr. Gideon Hill. Indicated therein are Dr. Hill's interpretations of the various steps that Sherlock Holmes uses in solving the problems that are presented to him. These are listed as "Making the appointment, Patient's statement of medical history and present situation, Physical examination by the physician, the diagnosis, Physician explains to the patient, and Lab studies ordered."

I contend that this is a serious misinterpretation of Mr. Holmes' mode of operation, and I would like to counter with evidence that clearly demonstrate that in personality traits and modus operandi Mr. Holmes was a prototypical research chemist. I will support my thesis with evidence regarding the fact that he was trained as a research chemist, had the peculiar lifestyle of a research chemist, and finally, approached the solution to mysteries using the methods of a research chemist.

Let us first regard his training. In the beginning of *Study in Scarlet*, while discussing his proposed new apartment mate with Mr. Stamford, Watson queries: "A medical student, I suppose?" To which Stamford clearly replies: "No - I have no idea what he intends to go in for. I believe that he is well up in anatomy, and he is a first-class chemist." I reiterate: When asked if Holmes was a medical student, Stamford didn't say "maybe" or "I'm not sure." Stamford said "No." That's good enough for me. Why would he lie or try to cover up the possibility that Sherlock Holmes was a medical student when he clearly had no reason to?

Now let us look briefly at Sherlock Holmes personality. In my opinion, nobody acts the way Sherlock acts except for research chemists. Believe me, I know. I have worked with many chemists in my more than 28 years in the pharmaceutical industry, and nobody acts the way they do - crazy, just like Sherlock Holmes. Once they have an idea for a chemical series, they work night, day, and weekends on their syntheses. I can still see them clearly, their stained and tattered laboratory garments half engulfed in their safety hoods watching crystals form, filtering, stirring, centrifuging, distilling, adding smelly and mysterious ingredients to their flasks, making photographs of thin layer chromatographic plates, and scribbling illegible entries, into their laboratory notebooks. Finally, they hand deliver small vials of their product to be evaluated for biological activity, along with handwritten copies of their submission forms. Then they come back the next day asking for results of tests that they have been informed over and over again will take at least two weeks to complete and report out. In the interim, they brood. They sit in desultory fashion reading journals, writing patents, filing piles of accumulated data sheets, all the while waiting impatiently to determine whether their new side chains are worthy of further pursuit or not. Not for them the orderly life of the microbiologist: working through the day to set up the cultures that, thankfully, must be left to their own devices in overnight incubation before any readings can be made. Not for them the way of the biochemist who sets up reagents or extractions for overnight processing in a beta scintillation counter or sample changer. No, they will work tirelessly to produce their products and undergo serious ennui until they are finally informed of the results obtained with their precious products. Can anything be more reminiscent of Sherlock Holmes actions?

Finally, let us refute the thesis of the Swifts and Dr. Hill that Sherlock Holmes used the methodology of a physician. I believe that over the years I have provided sufficient detailed evidence to support my contention that Mr. Holmes used the methods of scientists to solve his cases (2). The steps that make up the "method of scientists" are summarized as follows: (I) Clearly state the **PROBLEM** in its simplest form. (II) Gather all of the **DATA** that you can find on the subject. (III) Be very diligent to **OBSERVE** everything, no matter how unrelated it may appear at the time. (IV) Read and master all of the available **KNOWLEDGE** on the subject to see what data has previously been reported. (V) Sift through all of the data, current and reported, and attempt to **DEDUCE A TENTATIVE HYPOTHESIS** and **WORKING MODEL** that reasonably fits all of the available information. (VI) List further needed information, observations, and experiments that may refute or support your hypotheses. Seek **EXPERIMENTAL PROOF** and **ADDITIONAL OBSERVATIONS** and determine if the results fit or point a reformulation of the hypothesis. (VII) With all data in hand, **PUBLISH** your observations, results, hypotheses, and conclusions in an appropriate format for others to read, challenge, and confirm. To the lay observer, these processes appear identical to those listed in the first paragraph supporting the view that Sherlock Holmes acted as a physician. And, in many cases they are indeed virtually identical. Physicians apply all of their observations to define a previously described medical condition. The scientific researcher, on the other hand, explores and defines the unknown. Thus, unlike the last step in the Swift/Hill sequence (Lab studies ordered), research scientists such as Sherlock Holmes are actually performing experiments to test or reject the validity of their hypotheses.

In the spirit of scientific inquiry, I would welcome any attempts by the readers of this thesis to provide any solid evidence to refute the excellent evidence provided herein.

(1) Swift, Wayne and Francine. "The Associates of Sherlock Holmes" BSJ (NS), vol. 49, no. 1 (Mar 1999)
(2) Heifetz, C. L. "Staying Focused," *Communication* (a publication of the Pleasant Places of Florida), No. 173 New Series, Volume 1, Issue 5, pages 3-4; Heifetz, C.L. 1998. The Scientific Detective Solves the Sign of Four. *The Wigmore Street Post Office*, Issue Number 11, Spring 1998, p 3-9; Heifetz, C.L. 1998. A Study in Scarlet Yields to the Methods of Sherlock Holmes, Scientist *The Wigmore Street Post Office*, Issue Number 12, Summer 1998, p 18-21,24;Heifetz, C. L., Sherlock Holmes Scientist Solves A Case of Identity, *The Wigmore Street Post Office* in press.

A *Study in Scarlet* Yields to the Methods of Sherlock Holmes, Scientist

Published in the *Wigmore Street Post Office,* Issue Number 12, Summer 1998, p 18-21,24; Published in *The Hounds Collection* Vol. 5, April 2000, p 13-17.

Can anyone doubt that Sherlock Holmes is, both in personality and methods of operation, the quintessential research scientist? I have supported these contentions in two prior articles in a general way, and in more detail in my discussion of the case *Sign of Four* 1, 2. For further exemplification of these points, I have selected *A Study in Scarlet* as my Canonical text 3. What better place can there be to examine those qualities of Mr. Sherlock Holmes persona than this very first account of his activities? Here is where it all began! In this narrative we are introduced to the world's first scientific detective, Mr. Sherlock Holmes, as lovingly detailed by his biographer and friend Dr. John H. Watson. Not only are his *modus operandi* and personality quirks further revealed, but, unlike all other accounts, we are given information regarding his scientific training.

As is my custom, I will not attempt to analyze the psychological profile of Mr. Sherlock Holmes. I prefer to leave that aspect to individuals who are more appropriately trained in psychology. Let them postulate that Sherlock Holmes is afflicted with bipolar depression or other psychological disorders. Personally, I do not believe it for a minute! However, I am only a microbiologist not used to studying the functioning of macro cellular beings. As I have discussed previously, my view is that Mr. Holmes has the personality idiosyncrasies expected in a typical well-adjusted monomaniacal and obsessive compulsive research scientist1, 2.

Before going further, let us set the stage by briefly reviewing the methods that scientists currently apply. Then, we can see how well Sherlock Holmes used these means to carry out his particular researches. The steps that make up the "method of scientists" are summarized as follows: (1) Clearly state the **PROBLEM** in its simplest form. (2) Gather all of the **DATA** that you can find on the subject. (3) Be very diligent to **OBSERVE** everything, no matter how unrelated it may appear at the time. (4) Read and master all of the available **KNOWLEDGE** on the subject to see what data has previously been reported. (5) Sift through all of the data, current and reported, and attempt to **DEDUCE** A **TENTATIVE HYPOTHESIS** and **WORKING MODEL** that reasonably fits all of the available information. (6) List further needed information, observations, and experiments that may refute or support your hypotheses. Seek **EXPERIMENTAL PROOF** and **ADDITIONAL OBSERVATIONS** and determine if the results fit or point a reformulation of the hypothesis. (7) With all data in hand, **PUBLISH** your observations, results, hypotheses, and conclusions in an appropriate format for others to read, challenge, and confirm.

Uniquely, *Study in Scarlet* documents the scientific education that prepared Sherlock Holmes for his lifelong career. Young Stamford, who appears briefly only to disappear forever after that, utters the very first descriptions of Mr. Sherlock Holmes. Stamford tells us that Sherlock Holmes is "a little queer in his ideas -- an enthusiast in some branches of science." Additionally, "He is well up in anatomy, and he is a first-class chemist; but as far as I know, he has never taken out any systematic medical classes. His studies are desultory and eccentric, but he has amassed a lot of out-of-the-way knowledge which would astonish his professors." And, Sherlock Holmes "beat the subjects in the dissecting-rooms with a stick ... to verify how far bruises may be produced after death." Here we have a young man, who, we will eventually learn many cases later, has attended, and maybe graduated from, one or the other of England's two most prestigious universities 4. Currently, we find him at a medical school, not studying medicine but pursuing a variety of scientific disciplines that we will find out later, will prepare him to approach the solution of criminal activities in a scientific manner. Clearly, Sherlock Holmes was a man ahead of his time. What seemed odd then is very common now. Basic science departments in medical schools, in addition to providing professional education for future physicians, supply academic graduate and postdoctoral training to research scientists leading to a Ph.D. degree or equivalent. In fact, most of the research funding in such departments supports the work of graduate students and postdoctoral fellows. The innovative academic program that Sherlock Holmes created for himself in the Victorian era is not unlike that received by scientists in toxicology and forensic science.

The **observational** skills that mark a great scientist were displayed by Sherlock Holmes in his very first greeting to Dr. Watson: "You have been in Afghanistan, I perceive." This is akin to the sharp eyes that modern scientists display as they note that extra little wispy precipitin line on a double diffusion plate or an extra DNA band on a mini-gel.

But Watson's prior locale was not Sherlock Holmes' major point of interest. Completely ignoring Watson's astonished query regarding his perception concerning Afghanistan, Holmes carried on at length about his great new "Sherlock Holmes test" to detect minute quantities of human hemoglobin. This is typical of a dedicated research scientist. Nothing can be more important than a discovery of this order. Social amenities and business can be addressed later, as they were in this first conversation. That the "Sherlock Holmes test" was never accepted and implemented by police departments probably reflects a deep reticence by authorities to accept a scientific approach to the solution of crimes. The lack of recognition on the part of the faculty at St. Bart's may, as I have previously postulated, led to Sherlock Holmes eventually leaving that institution and continuing his researches elsewhere, either in his own quarters or briefly in Montpellier 6,7.

As in the prior case studied, *Sign of Four*, the title of the second chapter in *A Study in Scarlet* -- The Science of Deduction -- clearly announces the purpose of Watson's exposition. He wanted to make sure that the reader was fully aware of Sherlock Holmes' mastery of deductive reasoning. Also, Watson makes it clear that Sherlock Holmes was consumed by his scientific training and researches. As Watson narrates: "Sometimes he spent his days at the chemical laboratory, sometimes in the dissecting rooms." And further, "His hands were invariably blotted with ink and stained with chemicals, yet he was possessed of extraordinary delicacy of touch, as I frequently had occasion to observe when I watched him manipulating his fragile philosophical instruments." During this time, Watson became ever more curious and confused about the goals of Sherlock Holmes' self-directed scientific education. Watson was especially astonished when Mr. Holmes indicated that he neither knew the workings of the solar system nor cared about it, since it had no bearing on his craft. Also in this chapter, Watson provides us with the famous list of "Sherlock Holmes-his limits." Of special importance are those items bearing on those aspects that would further Mr. Holmes' abilities to pursue criminal investigations. These include item "5. Botany.--Variable. Well up on belladonna, opium, and poisons generally." Also, "6. Knowledge of Geology.--Practical but limited. Tells at a glance different soils from each other. After walks has shown me splashes upon his trousers, and told me by their colour and consistence in what part of London he had received them." In addition we have item "7. Knowledge of chemistry.--Profound. 8. Knowledge of anatomy.-- Accurate but unsystematic. And Sensational Literature.-

Immense." Can there be any doubt that Mr. Holmes was establishing a great deal of knowledge concerning those subjects that would enable him to further his scientific objectives fulfilling point (4) Knowledge in my above-listed methods that scientist use to answer the questions that are presented to them.

Now that everyone is convinced, by all of the data discussed herein that Mr. Sherlock Holmes possesses, in great measure, the personality, training, and skills required to be a successful research scientist, let us examine how the attributes enabled Mr. Holmes to resolve the complex events delineated in *A Study in Scarlet*.

The action begins in Chapter 3: The Lauriston Garden Mystery. It starts slowly with another demonstration of Mr. Holmes' **observational** and **deductive** skills as he deduces the prior military service of the Commissionaire, who delivers the note that brings the pair onto the scene of their very first case together.

Upon reaching the crime scene, Sherlock Holmes did not immediately interview the official detectives but began, instead, a painstaking accumulation of **data.** He slowly walked up the path leading to the house, very carefully **observing** all of the marks on the ground and along the pavement. Then, Mr. Holmes examined the room in which the murder took place and the body identified as the remains of Enoch J. Drebber lying therein. Unlike the police, Mr. Holmes questioned the presence of blood near the body since there was none emanating from the victim. In doing so, Mr. Holmes alluded to a previously published case, demonstrating how he consulted available criminal literature, as would a scientist who reviews the work of fellow researchers. The appearance of the victim's face clearly pointed to a case of alkaloid poisoning, a fact easily discerned by anyone who was "well up on belladonna, opium, and poisons generally." The presence of a wedding ring in the victim's hand immediately convinced Lestrade, one of the two official police at the scene, that a woman had been present. Then, Lestrade jumps to another conclusion, assuming that the word "RACHE" printed on the wall in blood is the name "RACHEL." After Sherlock Holmes provides an alternative explanation for this cryptic message, he proceeds to examine every inch of the room with a "tape measure and a large round magnifying glass." Holmes examined and measured all of the marks in the room the way a molecular biologist would quantify the DNA traces on a gel-electrophoresis plate or an immunologist would examine the wisps of cloudy precipitate on a double-diffusion plate. Finally, he "gathered up a little pile of gray dust from the floor, and packed it away in an envelope," no doubt to subject it to his "Knowledge of Geology.--Practical but limited." Finally, before leaving the scene, Sherlock Holmes provided the incredulous detectives, Gregson and Lestrade, and the equally befuddled Dr. Watson, with a complete description of the hypothetical murderer: his greater than six-feet in height, florid face, Trichonopoly cigar, and his mode of arrival, with the victim, in a four-wheeled cab drawn by a horse with three old shoes and new one in his off fore-leg. All of these assumptions were based on painstaking observations and their synthesis into a working hypothesis.

How Sherlock Holmes wove his observations into his experimental model is provided by an exposition at the beginning of Chapter 4, in a conversation between Mr. Holmes and Dr. Watson, who is motivated to state: "...you have brought detection as near an exact science as it ever will be brought in this world." Following this, Sherlock Holmes extended the narrative of his reconstruction of the events that took place between the participants in the deadly drama, "patent-leathers and square-toes," based on an interpretation of the foot prints in the dust. Later, Holmes confronts the constable, John Rance, who had unwittingly stumbled onto the murderer returning to the scene of the crime. Holmes astonishes the policeman with a detailed scenario of his actions based on an examination of the foot marks that had been left by the policeman at the scene. John Rance's description of the "drunk" confirms and embellishes Sherlock Holmes' knowledge of the murderer's appearance, and convinces Holmes that the ring left at the scene must be very important to him. Unfortunately, as we see in Chapter 5, an attempt to use the ring as bait to draw out the criminal fails to achieve the desired result. The villain proves too wily for such a trap to work.

The mystery deepens in Chapter 6, as another victim, the dead man's companion Joseph Stangerson, is also found murdered. Although, as we see in Chapter 7, it was obvious that Stangerson's death was due to a stab wound rather than poisoning, the two murders were tied together by finding the word "RACHE" repeated at the second site. An eye witness had observed a man matching the description of Drebber's assassin descending a ladder from the room in which Stangerson had been murdered, confirming that the same man had perpetrated both crimes. Unlike the other witnesses, Sherlock Holmes realized the import of the small pills in the ointment box that was sitting, in an unusual location, on the window sill. Seeking an explanation, Sherlock Holmes performed an experiment in toxicology. He demonstrated, with the unwitting assistance of a small terrier, that some of these pills were poisonous, and produced symptoms that were similar to those observed in the first murder victim. And then, we have the exciting denouement that we have come to expect in these adventures. The street Arab Wiggins escorts, into the steel handcuffs of Sherlock Holmes, the perpetrator of these crimes. Who can forget this exciting moment when Sherlock Holmes introduced the assemblage "to ...Mr. Jefferson Hope, the murderer of Enoch Drebber and of Joseph Stangerson."

How is it possible that Sherlock Holmes, seemingly out of thin air, is able to identify the name of the man that they have sought through this adventure? What secret clues did he use to determine this? Skipping past the interior prologue referred to as Part 2, The Country of the Saints, we resume our deliberations in the final chapter. In this chapter, Sherlock Holmes lays out all of the scientific steps that he took to solve the crime: How he assembled all of the available evidence and formulated a tentative hypothesis. How he revised and extended his hypotheses into a working model using each piece of information that he had analyzed to synthesize a final theorem to test. Armed with this hypothesis, he predicted a prior relationship between the victim and the murderer associated with the mysterious wedding ring. He was then able to determine, via a telegram to the authorities in Cleveland, that Enoch Drebber had previously sought protection against a man named Jefferson Hope at this previous location. The evidence from the first crime scene indicated that the murderer had driven a cab to the site. Sherlock Holmes located a cab driver named Jefferson Hope, using the "Baker Street Irregulars" as his technical assistants. These "Irregulars" led Hope into the arms of Sherlock Holmes and the police, providing an exciting conclusion to the action of this first reminiscence of John H. Watson, M.D.

1 For a previous, more general discussion, please see my article "Staying Focused" which appeared in *Communication* (a publication of the Pleasant Places of Florida), No. 173 New Series, Volume 1, Issue 5, pages 3-4.
2 Heifetz, C.L. 1998. The Scientific Detective Solves the Sign of Four. The Wigmore Street Post Office, Issue Number 11, Spring 1998.
3 Doyle, A. C. The "Gloria Scott" and The Musgrave Ritual, pp 373-385 and 386-397 In: *The Complete Sherlock Holmes* by Arthur Conan Doyle, with a preface by Christopher Morley, Doubleday and Company, Garden City, New York, single volume, 1988.

4 Heifetz, C. L. Sherlock Holmes and the Magic Bullet. *The Whitechapel Gazette* (spring 1995 issue no. 6) and *The Hounds Collection* (Volume 1, first edition, April, 1996).

5 Doyle, A. C. The Adventure of the Empty House In: *The Complete Sherlock Holmes* by Arthur Conan Doyle, with a preface by Christopher Morley, Doubleday and Company, Garden City, New York, single volume, 1988.

The Scientific Detective, Sherlock Holmes, Solves the Case of the *Sign of Four*

(Published in *The Wigmore Street Post Office* Issue No. 11, Spring 1998, p 3-9; Published in *The Hounds Collection* Vol. 4, April 1999, p 5-12; Proceedings of Lippincott's legacy Conference Omaha, Nebraska on May 29-30, 2015.)

It has long been my stated belief that Sherlock Holmes embodies, in both his methods of operation and his personality, the aspects most often associated with a dedicated and monomaniacal research scientist.[1] Perhaps no account of his activities best displays these traits than the narrative entitled *Sign of Four*, in which Dr. Watson clearly delineated these attributes. Throughout, I will refer to the most available collection of Sherlock Holmes adventures -- the Doubleday Edition -- as my reference source so that we can all be "on the same page."[2]

I will attempt to show that Mr. Holmes' personality, as depicted in the Watsonian account, is typical of a dedicated research scientist. My lack of training in the areas of psychiatry and psychology force me to limit such observations to a relatively superficial level. However, since Dr. Watson went to great lengths to explore this facet of Sherlock Holmes' persona, it would be very negligent of me to ignore them completely. This is especially true since his later writings have shown that Dr. Watson was quite interested in psychological manifestations including *idée fixe* and catalepsy.[3,4] He even read Dr. Percy Trevelyan's limited distribution monograph on obscure nervous lesions. I will take this opportunity to reiterate my personal, though not scientifically supported, beliefs regarding the personality of Mr. Sherlock Holmes. His vast mood swings and changes in energy levels are legendary. Sometimes he is up and sometimes he is down in the dumps. Sometimes he sits around playing his violin or having philosophical discussions with Dr. Watson, and demonstrates a hearty appetite for good food and entertainment. Alternatively, he sometimes is seen running hither and yon, night and day, without a word to Watson or a bite to eat. He requires a difficult problem to keep him from being bored. Several respected Holmesian scholars have concluded that these personality changes are the clinical manifestations of bipolar disorder, and that the actor who best exemplifies this condition in Sherlock Holmes is Jeremy Brett. Although I believe that Brett gives a very good picture of this condition in his interpretation of Sherlock Holmes, I tend to disagree that it is entirely accurate.

Also, I believe that if Sherlock Holmes suffered a serious psychological disorder, Dr. Watson would have noticed it after their many years of intimate friendship, and discussed it candidly. After all, Watson tells us about many other private aspects of Sherlock Holmes bohemian habits, especially his abuse of cocaine in his early years. In my opinion, as one who has dealt very closely with scientific researchers over many years, Mr. Holmes extreme behavior mirrors in a somewhat exaggerated manner the personality characters that are encountered among that community. The need for mental stimulation, the absolute single-mindedness to a scientific goal, the lack of interest in physical comfort during investigative activity may all be manifested, in one way or another, in the descriptions of such noted individuals as Albert Einstein, Louis Pasteur, Paul Ehrlich, and many others.

Of course, scientists do not always display all of the outrageous attributes we have come to recognize in Sherlock Holmes. They usually seem to be fairly normal people. Some even dress well. But, I can guarantee you that they all possess some of these attributes in one way or another. I have previously stated that my choice for demonstrating the Sherlockian persona is the often overlooked actor Ronald Howard. But, enough of this. Let's go on to a more tangible exploration of Sherlock Holmes actions as a research scientist who has turned his training and inclination toward the solution of crimes and other puzzles that are presented to him.

After 36 years of dealing with research scientists both as a graduate student and fellow researcher, I feel much better equipped to comment on Mr. Holmes scientific methods of problem solving, rather than his personality. During this essay, I will avoid the use of the term "Scientific Method" since that often implies carefully spelled-out rules of logic. Its implementation varies among different schools of philosophy, a field of which I have little understanding. The "methods of scientists," which evolved over several recent generations, have served the research community well in the search for scientific truth and the development of our modern technological culture.

Before attempting an evaluation of Sherlock Holmes problem-solving methodology, it would be useful to outline the methods that scientists use to answer the questions that are presented to them. Briefly, they may be summarized as follows:

(1) **Problem.** Clearly state the problem in its simplest form. Research requires the step-by-step solution of each problem on the path to an ultimate overall objective. For example, an overall scientific goal may be to find out how food is turned into energy. However, a research problem may require a group of scientists to work years on one step in the process, for example how sugar is absorbed into the blood stream or how sugar is split into glucose and fructose.

(2) **Data.** Gather all of the information that you can find on the subject. Use any method available to acquire the needed data. For example, glance at some else's lab photos (Watson and Crick), crawl in the mud looking for cigarette

butts (Holmes) or human skeletons (several Leakeys). Scientists often talk to each other to gather information that will be helpful to them. Such activity has been expanded by the availability of the Internet.

(3) **Observation.** Be very diligent to observe everything, no matter how unrelated it may appear at the time. Sherlock Holmes often makes use of the differences between seeing something and observing it. Many microbiologists had no doubt **seen** the effects of fungi on staphylococci in an agar culture. It was not until Alexander Fleming's **observations** that anyone realized that the fungus was possibly producing a substance -- penicillin -- that retarded the growth of the staphylococci.

(4) **Knowledge.** Read and master all of the available literature on the subject to see what data has previously been reported. Pay more attention to the data than to the conclusions of the person reporting the information.

(5) **Deduction.** Sift through all of the data, current and reported, and attempt to formulate a tentative hypothesis and working model that reasonably fits all of the available information. Much has been made of Sherlock Holmes' use of the term deductive logic. Working scientists don't worry about the use of such terms. They use deductive and inductive reasoning as the need arises. They are analytical and synthetic, whatever works at the time. As we will see, so does Sherlock Holmes. Albert Einstein's theory of relativity is probably the best known working model that is still under experimental validation. Mr. Holmes' researches are generally less encompassing but still illustrative of the method of research scientists.

(6) **Experimental Proof.** List further needed information, observations, and experiments that may refute or support your hypotheses. Carry out these necessary observations and experiments and see how the results fit, or require a reformulation of the hypothesis.

26

(7) **Publish.** With all data in hand, report your observations, results, hypotheses, and conclusions in an appropriate format for others to read, challenge, and confirm. Also, of course, if you do not publish enough papers, you won't get that professorship or promotion.

Now, let us see how these steps apply to the Sherlockian discourse under consideration: *The Sign of Four*. What could be more instructive than the initial chapter titles themselves? I'm certain that their choice was not arbitrary. Let us list them: *Chapter 1 THE SCIENCE OF DEDUCTION*; *Chapter 2 THE STATEMENT OF THE CASE*; and *Chapter 3 IN QUEST OF A SOLUTION*. Is there any doubt that Dr. Watson was presenting this as a scientific exposition?

Now let's look at the first chapter as we begin to analyze Sherlock Holmes' methods of problem solution, and how they relate to the method used by research scientists. Sherlock Holmes is quoted as stating, on the second page of this adventure, in reference to Dr. Watson's prior report of his activities regarding *Study in Scarlet*: "Detection is, or ought to be, an exact science and should be treated in the same cold and unemotional manner." Here we have the underlying premise. Detection is a science. It should be treated as a science, without emotion interfering with reason and logic. As Sherlock Holmes later stated: "The only point in the case (*Study in Scarlet*) which deserved mention was the curious analytical reasoning from effects to causes, by which I succeeded in unraveling it."

On the next page, when referring to the French detective François le Villard, Mr. Holmes says: "He possesses two out of the three qualities necessary for the ideal detective. He has the power of observation and that of deduction. He is only wanting in knowledge, and that may occur in time. He is now translating my small works into French." This is a reiteration of items (3), (5), (4), (7) in that order: **observation,** **deduction,**

knowledge, and **publication**. The latter is supported again by Mr. Holmes' reference to "several monographs ... on technical subjects." Following that statement is a listing of several other monographs published by Sherlock Holmes on "tracing of footsteps," and "influence of trade upon the form of the hand." These are examples of the data gathering and publishing that research scientists do, not necessarily in pursuit of a specific problem, but to accumulate and disseminate information that will facilitate problem-solving in the future. New methods of chemical and biochemical analysis are clear examples, such as Sherlock Holmes' novel method to detect human blood revealed in the earlier account *Study in Scarlet*. What follows, in the text, are two startling accounts of Holmes' observational and deductive skills. One is the simpler deduction that Watson was at the Wigmore Street Post Office that morning. This is followed by the sad account of Watson's older brother that is based on Sherlock Holmes' magnificent analysis of the clues embodied in Dr. Watson's old watch. At the conclusion of this examination, Sherlock Holmes states another premise of scientific logic: "No, no: I never guess. It is a shocking habit -- destructive to the logical faculty." This is a rule often followed by scientists that has always driven lawyers and politicians crazy. Scientists usually refuse to guess. If they give an opinion based on available evidence, they always couch it in language such as "it is likely" or "it is possible," with the addition of "but, on the other hand ..." Members of the press and the legal profession are always looking for "one handed scientists" to avoid such difficulties. It is also a characteristic of Sherlock Holmes that he rarely reveals a hypothesis until the final curtain. Although this appears to be a means of providing a surprise ending to the adventures, it has scientific precedence.

In Chapter 2, we initiate the specific scientific examination that begins this adventure, the problem presented by Ms. Mary Morstan. Note how calmly and precisely Sherlock Holmes questioned Ms. Morstan. Although Watson let his emotions and infatuation creep into his narrative, Sherlock Holmes coldly stuck to the investigation at hand. Would other scientists note Ms. Morstan's attractiveness? Probably. I would. But, once started, they would still be able to concentrate on business, unlike Watson who was never able to separate facts from the person stating them. During a particularly trying time for Ms. Morstan, as she began to sob, Sherlock Holmes coldly asked: "The date?" This was followed by a series of additional queries, asked without regard to her emotional state. He was cold and calculating when it suited his purposes. His need to obtain information predominated. Throughout the interview, Sherlock Holmes very carefully sought all of the facts from Ms. Morstan and carefully examined the physical evidence available -- the handwriting on the envelope, the letters, and the box that held the pearls. Dr. Watson chastised Sherlock Holmes by calling him an "automaton -- a calculating machine." Holmes replied: "It is of first importance not to allow your judgment to be biased by personal qualities. A client is to me a mere unit, a factor in a problem." Contrast this with members of the press or legal profession who first ask about the mental state and credibility of the witness, and seem to regard a search for motivation to dominate. As the chapter closes, Sherlock Holmes has already started to feel the wisps of a tentative hypothesis, but he will not reveal it until he has the opportunity to go out and seek additional information.

At the beginning of Chapter 3, we begin *IN QUEST OF A SOLUTION*. Sherlock Holmes has returned from gathering more data from the back files of the *Times*. He has started to reach an inference concerning the confluence of events: "Look at it this way, then. Captain Morstan disappears. The only person in London whom he could have visited is Major Sholto. Major Sholto denies having heard that he was in London. Four years later Sholto dies. Within a week of his death, Captain Morstan's daughter receives a valuable present, which is repeated from year to year and now cumulates in a letter which describes her as a wronged woman. What wrong can it refer to except this deprivation of her father? And why should the presents begin immediately after Sholto's death unless it is that Sholto's heir knows something of the mystery and desires to make compensation? Have you any alternative theory which will meet the facts?" Later, Sherlock Holmes admits: "There are difficulties, there are certain difficulties ... but our expedition of tonight will solve them all." So we have Sherlock Holmes taking all of the available information that derived from his interview with Ms. Morstan coupled with that obtained from his later readings. He deduced from them a tentative hypothesis that fits the available facts, with the acknowledgment that further exploration will be required to complete the picture.

Thus begins the mysterious and exciting series of events that produce additional data and a further set of problems for Mr. Sherlock Holmes to unravel. In Chapter 4, we at least have a verbal confirmation, from Thaddeus Sholto, of Mr. Holmes hypothesis that Major Sholto had been involved in the mysterious disappearance of Captain Morstan, and events related to the death of the former led to the annual shipment of pearls to Ms. Morstan. Apparently Thaddeus Sholto's brother also had some degree of analytical ability, enabling him to deduce the location of the missing treasure by determining the inside and outside measurements of the rooms of his father's house. But that skill only led to his death, as we see in Chapter 5, and the disappearance again of the of the jewels after only a brief time in the hands of Major Sholto's sons.

Occasionally during a scientific investigation, new findings reveal a major new research initiative that needs to be followed up. Generally, the primary researchers will gather additional information to confirm the validity of their new discovery. Satisfied with this, they then assign available staff to provide temporary help to carry on the additional assignments while awaiting the approval of a new research grant to support required supplementary staff and equipment. At a major university laboratory, this phase is easily handled by giving more work to the available personnel at the school -- graduate students, postdocs, teaching assistants, junior faculty, etc. Since Sherlock Holmes did not have such a built-in supply of indentured labor, he had to make do with the staff currently available to him. He commissioned Dr. Watson to obtain a scent detector, otherwise known as Toby the dog. Then, he later assigned his available junior associates, the street urchins known as the "Baker Street Irregulars" to assist him further. How this came about is discussed below.

Discovered in Chapter 5 is the dead Bartholomew Sholto. His face bore the obvious signs of alkaloid poisoning and the delivery instrument, a thorn, was found "stuck in the skin just above the ear." Near the body was a primitive stone axe and at the foot of the steps was a coil of rope. Fortuitously, in the corner was a carboy from which was leaking a dark-colored liquid with a pungent odor. A note bearing the words "The sign of the four" completed the mysterious scene. Already, Sherlock Holmes' sharp mind was beginning to formulate a hypothesis.

In Chapter 6, Sherlock Holmes quickly completes his investigation to gather all of the evidence before the official police disrupt the crime scene. Marks on the floor of the chamber revealed to Mr. Holmes that one of the villains was a club footed man who came in through the window, climbing up the side of the house with the assistance of the rope. Tiny footprints on the floor in the secret chamber above showed the identity of his ally as a small man who came in through a trap door in the roof. Sherlock Holmes explained all of these theories to Dr. Watson, following which a minute investigation of the area provided a break that would enable them to expand their investigations further. The small-footed man had stepped into the pool of creosote that had seeped from the leaking container. Before leaving the field to Inspector Althelney Jones, Sherlock Holmes reveals the prime suspect in the murder, Jonathon Small, and describes his appearance to the inspector. How did Sherlock Holmes know who the stump-footed man was? He called upon his observational skills to achieve a description of the home jewel thief and then tied it together with his vast knowledge of members of the criminal class. Thus, Sherlock Holmes brought to bear items (2), (3), and (4), from my list of methods used by scientists to solve their research problems: **Data,** **Observation, Knowledge,** and **Deduction**.

In Chapter 7, Sherlock Holmes and his medical companion use the molecular detecting skills of their new instrument, the dog Toby, to track the creosote-scented foot of Jonathon Small's ally to, as revealed in Chapter 8, Moredcai Smith's boat launch at the edge of the river. It is in Chapter 7 that Sherlock Holmes explains the elucidation of his hypothesis that Jonathon Small was the criminal that they seek, and explained his theory regarding the sequence of events leading up to their adventure that night. All of the evidence was revealed during the interviews with Mary Morstan and Thaddeus Sholto, but only the reasoning skill of Sherlock Holmes could tie all of the loose ends together into a working hypothesis. This is discussed at length on pages 119-121. This passage is well worth rereading since it demonstrates the reasoning skills that Sherlock Holmes applied to resolve all of the many clues that were clear to both him and opaque to Dr. Watson. It would not be appropriate to reiterate the long conversation between Dr. Watson and Mr. Holmes, in which the latter narrates his hypothesis and explains the many steps used in its derivation. The data appear to support Mr. Holmes' thesis that Jonathon Small made a deal with Captain Morstan and

Major Sholto to find the treasure, using a map drawn and signed by Small. Sholto probably double-crossed them and took the treasure to England where he feared a wooden-legged man. The arrival of this man and the shock of seeing him led to the death of Major Sholto. After Small found out that Sholto's older son Bartholomew had finally deduced the location of the treasure, he went after it. His small companion climbed to the roof, went into the chamber below, and dropped down a rope to allow Small to climb up. The companion killed Sholto's son, and they then fled with the treasure to the river's edge where the hunt continues.

In Chapter 8, Sherlock Holmes determines, by skillful questioning, that the villainous pair chartered the steam launch *Aurora* of Mordecai Smith to make their escape. He mobilized his available resources -- his Baker Street Irregulars -- to locate the missing boat. While awaiting word of the boat's appearance in their Baker Street quarters, Sherlock Holmes reveals to Watson his hypothesis regarding the Andaman Island origin of the small-footed, club-wielding, poison dart-shooting companion of Jonathon Small. Sherlock Holmes deduces that the ethnicity of the murderer using the **data** derived from his **observation** at the crime scene, the stated location of the convict prison where Jonathon Small was incarcerated under the control of Captain Morstan and Major Sholto, and the **knowledge** that he gained by reading about the tiny primitives in his gazetteer.

There is no further movement until Chapter 10 when Sherlock Holmes reveals to Dr. Watson and Inspector Jones that he has deduced the location of the missing steam launch. Since the Baker Street Irregulars have not located it, Sherlock Holmes figured that it had been hidden away in a repair yard. Dressed as an old seaman, he went from yard to yard until he found where the boat had been installed by a wooden-legged man for spurious repairs. Learning that the launch was to leave at 8 p.m. Sherlock Holmes and his companions lay in wait for the boat to come out. This was followed by an exciting chase scene that, although full of adventure, revealed nothing about Sherlock Holmes prowess as a scientific detective. As a result of this chase, the Andaman Islander is killed and Small captured. Incidentally, as we see in Chapter 11, the treasure had been ditched in the river by Small. Emboldened by her sudden change in fortune, Dr. Watson was now able to court Mary Morstan.

Finally, the denouement comes in Chapter 12, in which the captured Jonathon Small narrates the true story of getting the treasure and the succeeding events. It is very remarkable how very near the truth Sherlock Holmes was able to come by his deductions. This is a tribute to his skills in the application of the methods applied by research scientists.

[1] For a previous, more general discussion, please see my article "Staying Focused" which appeared in *Communication* (a publication of the Pleasant Places of Florida), No. 173 New Series, Volume 1, Issue 5, pages 3-4.
[2] *The Complete Sherlock Holmes* by Arthur Conan Doyle, with a preface by Christopher Morley, Doubleday and Company, Garden City, New York, single volume, 1122 pages.
[3] The Adventure of the Six Napoleons in *The Complete Sherlock Holmes* by Arthur Conan Doyle, with a preface by Christopher Morley, Doubleday and Company, Garden City, New York, single volume, pages 582-595.
[4] The Resident Patient in *The Complete Sherlock Holmes* by Arthur Conan Doyle, with a preface by Christopher Morley, Doubleday and Company, Garden City, New York, single volume, pages 422-434.

Scientific Lesson Learned from "The Yellow Face"

Published in *Holmes & Watson Report*, 8 (1): 33-36,
(March) 2004

Research scientists do not always have all of the information that they require to reach a valid hypothesis. They may believe that everything is in hand, but occasionally the available facts point in a wrong direction. Often, more information is required to derive an appropriate conclusion. That is why scientific papers use the word "likely" so often, as in "this is likely to be the case" or "this antibiotic will likely be useful in treating" a particular infection.

Let me give an example of how this can happen from personal experience. Research scientists often need to perform mundane, repetitive tasks during an investigation. Nothing could be more humdrum than performing microbiological disk-agar diffusion assays to determine the concentrations of an orally administered sulfonamide in the body fluids of dogs sampled at different time intervals after they receive oral doses of medication. The samples are received from the administering pharmacologists, diluted in the appropriate buffer, and quantitatively measured onto 6.25 mm. filter paper disks. These are then placed on agar plates seeded with the standardized inoculum of test bacterium. After incubation and a standardized growth temperature and time interval, the circular zones of inhibition , the diameters of which are proportional to the logarithm of the concentration of drug in the sample, are carefully measured, and converted to mcg. per ml. by means of a standard linear regression line. This method is so routine that its basic aspects have been described in the *Code of Federal Regulations*. During the experiment in question, samples of plasma and urine provided drug concentration that were predicable from prior experience with other drugs of this class as well as the results of pharmacokinetic studies in mice. Can you imagine the surprise that was generated by the apparent discovery that concentrations in biliary fluids were enormous? The diameters of the inhibition zones resulting from even the most highly diluted samples were far outside of the range of all expected values. There were three possible explanations that immediately suggested themselves: (1) this particular sulfa drug was more highly concentrated in the liver than any other member of the class, (2) it was metabolized in the livers of dogs to a new drug with remarkable activity, or (3) someone screwed up the assay. When several replicate assays revealed reproducible data, the third option was eliminated. Then, my experienced supervisor suggested a fourth possibility that had not occurred to the rest of us: there might be something wrong with the experimental design. He suggested that I check out the protocol. I did and there it was! To prevent infection, the investigators who processed the samples always administered penicillin when cannulating the bile ducts of dogs! Wow! Eureka! This is something that a microbiologist would never do, so it never occurred to us that anyone else would do it. Bingo, this one little piece of information resolved our dilemma and a simple procedure, adding penicillinase to the biliary samples, obviated the need to repeat the animal phase of the procedure. And verification that the inhibition zones now resulted only from the sulfa drug was shown by demonstrating elimination of the activity with para-amino benzoic acid, a competitive inhibitor of sulfonamides.

What has this to do with Sherlock Holmes and the Watsonian narrative published as "The Yellow Face" in *Memoirs of Sherlock Holmes?*[1] Well, just about everything.

Let us summarize the mysterious events concerning this mystery. Very suspicious things were going on in the Munro household. First of all, Mrs. Effie Hebron, a city-bred 25 year old American woman agreed to marry Mr. Grant

Munro, an older bachelor, and move with him to a "countrified" environment, after only a few weeks courtship. This, by itself, is not conclusive, but it is suggestive of ulterior motives to those with a cynical outlook. Then enigmatic things began to take place. First, Effie asked her husband for a hundred pounds while refusing to tell him what she wanted it for. Next, there was the very unfriendly meeting between Munro and the secretive occupant in the previously empty cottage next door. His suspicions were further heightened by the strange yellow face peering out of the window. This was followed by Effie sneaking out in the middle of the night. On another occasion, she was spied emerging from that cottage in the day time, when she thought that Munro was away on business, and refused him entry into the cottage next door or to explain her actions. Further, she appeared to violate her promise never to go there again. Evidence indicated that she had slunk over again when he unexpectedly returned early from London to find the cottage deserted. When he immediately checked the now empty house out, he was surprised and dismayed to find a large picture of his wife. This demonstrated that one of the inhabitants knew her very well. Since Effie had stated that her only child and her husband were dead, who could be secluded next door that she felt so impelled to hide and to visit? Fearing the worst, Mr. Munro consulted the scientific detective, Mr. Sherlock Holmes.

Putting all the available evidence together, and using the method applied by scientists that I have reiterated in other entries of this series -- Sherlock Holmes, Scientist -- Mr. Holmes developed a tentative hypothesis [2]. In response to Watson's query: "You have a theory?" Sherlock Holmes replied: "Yes, a provisional one. But I shall be surprised if it does not turn out to be correct. This woman's first husband is in that cottage." And then, he goes on to lay out his interpretation of all of the preceding events that had led to the development of his hypothesis.

What a surprise was in store for Sherlock Holmes, Dr. Watson, and Grant Munro when they uninvitedly rushed into the cottage. Yes, there was an inhabitant who knew Effie very well -- her still-living daughter, a delightful little black girl whose identity was kept secret and whose visage was unnecessarily hidden behind the yellow mask. As the reader of this story will note, "all's well that ends well."

No evaluation of the available data would have predicted this occurrence, and there was no way possible to obtain this fact without the final phase of their investigation. They needed to get all of the facts, just as we needed to ascertain them in the more recent past.

Let us forgive Mr. Holmes for his rush to judgment. After all, the case took place early in his career, perhaps even before the events documented in *The Sign of Four*. Happily, Mr. Holmes learned his lesson from these events, something that all scientists need to adhere to. Sherlock Holmes summed it up with the following statement: "Watson," said he, "if it should ever strike you that I am getting a little overconfident in my powers, or giving less pains to a case than it deserves, kindly whisper 'Norbury' in my ear, and I shall be infinitely obliged to you." This is a Sherlock Holmes story that all scientists should be assigned to read as part of their training.

[1] Doyle, A. C. "The Red-Headed League" In: *The Complete Sherlock Holmes* by Arthur Conan Doyle, with a preface by Christopher Morley, Doubleday and Company, Garden City, New York, single volume, 1988, p176.

[2] Heifetz, C. L. 1997. Staying Focused. *Communication* (a publication of the Pleasant Places of Florida), No. 173 New Series, Volume 1, Issue 5, pages 3-4; Heifetz, C.L. 1998. The Scientific Detective Solves the Sign of Four. *The Wigmore Street Post Office*, Issue Number 11, Spring 1998, p 3-9; Heifetz, C.L. 1998. A Study in Scarlet Yields to the Methods of Sherlock Holmes, Scientist. *The Wigmore Street*

Post Office, Issue Number 12, Summer 1998, p 18-21,24; Heifetz, C. L. Sherlock Holmes Crosses a Thor Bridge to Scientific Inspiration. *Holmes & Watson* Report, Vol.3, No. 4, September 1999, p 13-5; Heifetz, C. L. A "Second Stain" Saves the Day. *Holmes & Watson* Report, Vol.3, No. 6, January 2000, p 36-9; Heifetz, C. L. Keep Digging until You Find It. *Holmes & Watson Report* Vol. 6, No. 3, July 2002, p 27-31. Heifetz, C. L. Sherlock Holmes Scientist Solves A Case of Identity. *The Hounds Collection* Vol. 8, April 2003, p 13-15, *.Holmes & Watson Report* Vol. 8 In Print.

Sherlock Holmes Crosses a Thor Bridge to Scientific Inspiration

Published in *Holmes & Watson Report*,Vol.3, No. 4, September 1999, p 13-5; *Communication* of the Pleasant Places of Florida, #257 New Series Vol. 9, Issue 9, Special Issue - 30th Annual Fall Gathering 2005 p 10-11; *The Baker Street Picayune* II:1, 2006, p 1-2 .

The 20th century has been characterized by virtually boundless scientific advances. From obtaining an enhanced understanding of subatomic particles to a study of the vast reaches of space, scientists have used the methods so diligently developed during the Victorian era to methodically answer mankind's deepest quest for knowledge of our universe. Biologists and chemists have applied these principles to systematically decipher the genetic code and develop newer and better drugs to fight the ever expanding spectrum of infectious diseases. There can be no doubt that these approaches were utilized by Sherlock Holmes when he developed the "Sherlock Holmes test" for specifically identifying human blood[1]. And, there is ample evidence that Mr. Holmes also applied these very same precepts of scientific investigation to solve many of the cases that have been previously explored in this light [2,3,4,5]. The steps that make up the "method of scientists" may be summarized as follows: (1) Clearly state the **PROBLEM** in its simplest form. (2) Gather all of the **DATA** that you can find on the subject. (3) Be very diligent to **OBSERVE** everything, no matter how unrelated it may appear at the time. (4) Read and master all of the available **KNOWLEDGE** on the subject to see what data has previously been reported. (5) Sift through all of the data, current and reported, and attempt to **DEDUCE** **A** **TENTATIVE** **HYPOTHESIS** and **WORKING MODEL** that reasonably fits all of the available information. (6) List further needed information, observations, and experiments that may refute or support your hypotheses. Seek **EXPERIMENTAL PROOF** and **ADDITIONAL   OBSERVATIONS** and determine if the results fit or point to a reformulation of the hypothesis.   (7) With all data in hand, **PUBLISH** your observations, results, hypotheses, and conclusions in an appropriate format for others to read, challenge, and confirm.

Another important aspect that experienced scientists bring to bear on their researches is a healthy dose of skepticism. An excellent example of this attribute may be found in the annals of Arthur Conan Doyle, M.D., the physician who has been credited by some as the author of several of the accounts of Sherlock Holmes' adventures. However you may feel about this, it is worthy to note that Dr. Doyle deserves credit as one of the few people who were rightly skeptical of the tuberculosis cure proposed by the eminent German physician Robert Koch 6.

Occasionally, by a fortuitous coupling of experience and imagination, an especially inspired researcher has been capable of astounding his colleagues by leaping beyond the limits of the available evidence to reach new levels of understanding. This was very likely the situation that led to Prof. Moriarty's ability to fathom the "Dynamics of an Asteroid," and his struggles with the scientific establishment that led him away from the halls of academe to turn his genius to a life of crime 7. Similarly, it was clearly this ability that led Dr. Paul Ehrlich to devise the specific receptor theory of biochemical interactions -- combining his knowledge of antigen-antibody interaction with his interest in the specific colouration of biological cells by a variety of coal tar derivatives8.

Sherlock Holmes demonstrated his propensities in both of these areas -- skepticism and creative genius -- in the investigation published by Dr. John H. Watson, M.D., as "The Problem of Thor Bridge" 9. The case appeared to be cut and dried. The evidence against Miss Dunbar, as a murderess, fulfilled the trite mantra of means, motive, and opportunity that continuously repeats itself in fictional crime accounts. A note in the hand of the victim, the murdered wife of the "Gold King" Neil Gibson, clearly indicated that Miss Dunbar lured her to the murder site where she was shot in the temple. There was no pistol at that location, but a likely murder weapon was found hidden in Miss Dunbar's wardrobe. And, after all, here was a beautiful young woman living with a wealthy man who was obviously tired of his wife and attendant to her. This seemed good enough for the official police, as well, and also loomed as a possibility to Sherlock Holmes on first glance. However, the ever-skeptical scientific detective was not satisfied. He smelled a rat and suspected a frame-up. The convenient location of the "murder weapon" in Miss Dunbar's wardrobe and the incriminating note clutched in the hand of the victim seemed too pat. Sherlock Holmes insisted, as usual, on a very careful evaluation of the crime scene. There he made a remarkable discovery. There was a fresh chip mark on the ledge of the bridge, one that had not been seen prior to the fatal event, and one that took a great deal of force to produce. This was a fact that only a genius like Sherlock Holmes could insert into the chain of events leading to the death of Mrs. Gibson. As with all great discoveries, the whole thing seemed obviously simple once Mr. Holmes made his demonstration, showing that the rapid flight of a heavy revolver, assisted by a rope attached to a rock, would make a similar chip when hitting the same ledge on its way into the water. Finding the original revolver, rope, and rock in the water below the bridge was evidence enough of how the death of Mrs. Dunbar took place, as a well-planned suicide by a very jealous woman who intended to take revenge on the young lady who had attracted the attention of her husband.

1 Doyle, A. C. "Study in Scarlet" In: *The Complete Sherlock Holmes* by Arthur Conan Doyle, with a preface by Christopher Morley, Doubleday and Company, Garden City, New York, single volume, 1988, p18.

2 Heifetz, C. L. 1997. Staying Focused. *Communication* (a publication of the Pleasant Places of Florida), No. 173 New Series, Volume 1, Issue 5, pages 3-4.

3 Heifetz, C.L. 1998. The Scientific Detective Solves the Sign of Four. *The Wigmore Street Post Office*, Issue Number 11, Spring 1998, p 3-9.

4Heifetz, C.L. 1998. A Study in Scarlet Yields to the Methods of Sherlock Holmes, Scientist. *The Wigmore Street Post Office*, Issue Number 12, Summer 1998, p 18-21,24.

5 Heifetz, C. L. Sherlock Holmes Scientist Solves A Case of Identity. *The Wigmore Street Post Office*, in press.

6 Rodin, A. E. and Key, J. D. Chap. 2 Medical Writings in: Medical Casebook of Doctor Arthur Conan Doyle, Robert E. Krieger Publishing Company, Inc., Malabar, FL 32950, 1984, p 105-9.

7 Doyle, A. C. "The Valley of Fear" In: *The Complete Sherlock Holmes* by Arthur Conan Doyle, with a preface by Christopher Morley, Doubleday and Company, Garden City, New York, single volume, 1988.

8 Heifetz, C. L. 1995 Sherlock Holmes and the Magic Bullet. *The Whitechapel Gazette* (spring 1995 issue no. 6) and Reprinted in *The Hounds Collection* (Volume 1, first edition, April, 1996)

9 Doyle, A. C. "The Problem of Thor Bridge" In: *The Complete Sherlock Holmes* by Arthur Conan Doyle, with a preface by Christopher Morley, Doubleday and Company, Garden City, New York, single volume, 1988.

Sherlock Holmes, Scientific Detective: Solves The Silver Blaze Horse-Napping Case

Presented at the 27th Spring Gathering of the Pleasant Places of Florida, "Watson's Pump," At. Armand's Circle, Sarasota, Florida, May 4, 2002, published in the *Communication* of the Pleasant Places of Florida, #222 New Series, Vol. 6, No. 4, May/June 2002; Published in *Holmes & Watson Report*, 8 (3): 22-25, (July) 2004.

As I have stated many times before, Sherlock Holmes was a trained research scientist who used the methods of research scientists to solve many cases in his long and illustrious career [1]. As a trained researcher, he followed these basic steps: (1) Clearly state the **PROBLEM** in its simplest form. (2) Gather all of the **DATA** that you can find on the subject. (3) Be very diligent to **OBSERVE** everything, no matter how unrelated it may appear at the time. (4) Read and master all of the available **KNOWLEDGE** on the subject to see what data has previously been reported. (5) Sift through all of the data, current and reported, and attempt to **DEDUCE A TENTATIVE HYPOTHESIS** and **WORKING MODEL** that reasonably fits all of the available information. (6) List further needed information, observations, and experiments that may refute or support your hypotheses. Seek **EXPERIMENTAL PROOF** and **ADDITIONAL OBSERVATIONS** and determine if the results fit or point a reformulation of the hypothesis.

The adventure titled "Silver Blaze," written by Dr. John H. Watson, provides many excellent examples of Sherlock Holmes' methods of scientific analysis.[2] There being too many illustrations to discuss thoroughly in the space allotted, and the fact that I have already elaborated upon them at length in previous communications, I will restrict my current focus to only two aspects that I have not focused on before: (1) how Mr. Holmes' knowledge of animal behavior and (2) the use of animals as experimental subjects significantly enhanced his ability to deduce the solution to the problem of the missing horse and the dead trainer:

ANIMAL BEHAVIOR

Sherlock Holmes was forced to became a student of animal behavior in a very dramatic and painful way. When Victor Trevor's dog attached himself to Mr. Holmes' ankle, the latter learned to study the behavior of canines very carefully before approaching them.[3] No doubt, from that time forward, he was alert to cues given to him by members of the canine species with which he came into contact.

This knowledge of animal behavior clearly helped Mr. Holmes when he investigated the interaction of Professor Presbury and Carlo the wolfhound.[4] His interest in the deportment of animals is clearly delineated in the statement he made to Dr. Watson in the introduction to this case. Among other statements, Mr. Holmes remarked, "A dog reflects the family life." Thus, it was surprising to Sherlock Holmes that the dog attacked his master. Seeking an alternative hypothesis, Mr. Holmes reasoned that the dog attacked Prof. Presbury because of his langur-like actions and scent. Behavioral evaluation of the professor indicated that the scholar had made a monkey of himself with the serum of languor.

Another example is the dog that did nothing in the daytime in "The Adventure of Shoscombe Old Place[5]." Although the Shoscombe spaniel recognized the carriage that his mistress used for her daily rides, her dog did not seem recognize her presence. This indicated that she was not in the carriage, and had been replaced by another individual.

In our story under discussion, this knowledge of animal behavior informed Sherlock Holmes that the person who sneaked into the barn and made off with Silver Blaze was a person that the dog knew very well. Hence, the classic conversation between Inspector Gregory and Sherlock Holmes, to whit:

"Is there any point to which you would wish to draw my attention?"

"To the curious incident of the dog in the night-time."

"The dog did nothing in the night-time."

"That was the curious incident," remarked Sherlock Holmes.

Can there be any doubt that the solution to Silver Blaze was greatly assisted by Sherlock Holmes' appreciation of how animals act?

ANIMAL EXPERIMENTATION

Now let us turn our attention to how Mr. Holmes' knowledge of the experimental use of animals in research and teaching also facilitated the clearing up of this mystery. Let's first start with establishing that Sherlock Holmes was exposed to such procedures. Sherlock Holmes had an excellent scientific education. He matriculated at one or both of England's major universities, the exact one depending on whose theories you accept and where the authors were educated. [3,6] Then, Mr. Holmes went on to do post-graduate training at St. Bart's laboratory associated with the University College of London. [7] There can be no doubt that Sherlock Holmes was educated in the use of animals in research during his stay at that institution. In the curriculum for the Winter Session for 1894 is listed the following courses that would include the use of laboratory animals: General Course of Physiology, General Course of Practical Physiology, Advanced Course of Practical Physiology, and Laboratory, and Special Instruction for "persons who are desirous of conducting original investigations in Physiology or Histology ...[8] " One might ask, "Were animals used in experimentation and teaching of medical students in England in the 1890s?" The answer I received in response to my e-mailed query was, "Regarding your question, animals were certainly used in research and in the teaching of physiology and medicine in the UK, and the practice was widespread from the 1870s onward. [9]" This is supported by a text titled *Antivivisection and Medical Science in Victorian Society*. [10] According to figure 19 therein, as far back as 1887 there were approximately 250 vivesections in physiology for research and training purposes in England.

Further, Mr. Holmes showed no compunction in the use of animals to determine whether sugar pills contained a deadly dose of poison. [7] Recall how he fed "the poor little devil of a terrier" the second of two pills to find that it contained a deadly poison? Also, Mr. Holmes experimented with the body of a dead pig hanging from the ceiling to see if he could drive a harpoon through it. [11] In addition, Mr. Holmes realized that the lame dog at the Ferguson residence was an experimental prelude to the attempted poisoning, by South American bird arrow, of the infant that so riled Mr. Ferguson's older son.[12] Thus, there is a surfeit of examples regarding Mr. Holmes' experience with the experimental use of animals.

Let us now return to the matter of "Silver Blaze." When Mr. Holmes learned of three lame sheep in Colonel Ross's paddock, he deduced that they were used by Mr. Straker to practice for his dastardly attempt to cripple Silver Blaze. [2]

Thus, there can be no doubt of the value of Mr. Holmes' training and experience, with both animal behavior and animal experimentation, enhanced to his ability to resolve the events that took place in Silver Blaze's horse-mapping and the death of Mr. Straker.

[1] Heifetz, C. L. 1997. Staying Focused. *Communication* (a publication of the Pleasant Places of Florida), No. 173 New Series, Volume 1, Issue 5, pages 3-4; Heifetz, C.L. 1998. The Scientific Detective Solves the Sign of Four. *The Wigmore Street Post Office*, Issue Number 11, Spring 1998, p 3-9; Heifetz, C.L. 1998. A Study in Scarlet Yields to the Methods of Sherlock Holmes, Scientist. *The Wigmore Street Post Office*, Issue Number 12, Summer 1998, p 18-21,24; Heifetz, C. L. Sherlock Holmes Crosses a Thor Bridge to Scientific Inspiration. *Holmes & Watson* Report, Vol.3, No. 4, September 1999, p 13-5; Heifetz, C. L. A "Second Stain" Saves the Day. *Holmes & Watson* Report, Vol.3, No. 6, January 2000, p 36-9; Heifetz, C. L. Keep Digging until You Find it, *Holmes & Watson* Report, 2002, in press.

[2] Doyle, A. C. "Silver Blaze" In: *The Complete Sherlock Holmes* by Arthur Conan Doyle, with a preface by Christopher Morley, Doubleday and Company, Garden City, New York, single volume, 1988, p335-350.

[3] Doyle, A. C. "The "Gloria Scott" In: *The Complete Sherlock Holmes* by Arthur Conan Doyle, with a preface by Christopher Morley, Doubleday and Company, Garden City, New York, single volume, 1988, p373-385.

[4] Doyle, A. C. "The Adventure of the Creeping Man" In: *The Complete Sherlock Holmes* by Arthur Conan Doyle, with a preface by Christopher Morley, Doubleday and Company, Garden City, New York, single volume, 1988, p1070-1083.

[5] Doyle, A. C. "The Adventure of Shoscombe Old Place" In: *The Complete Sherlock Holmes* by Arthur Conan Doyle, with a preface by Christopher Morley, Doubleday and Company, Garden City, New York, single volume, 1988, p1102-1112.

[6] Doyle, A. C. "The Musgrave Ritual" In: *The Complete Sherlock Holmes* by Arthur Conan Doyle, with a preface by Christopher Morley, Doubleday and Company, Garden City, New York, single volume, 1988, p386-397.

[7] Doyle, A. C. *Study in Scarlet* In: *The Complete Sherlock Holmes* by Arthur Conan Doyle, with a preface by Christopher Morley, Doubleday and Company, Garden City, New York, single volume, 1988, p15-86.

[8] "Courses of Instruction in the College . I. Winter Session from 1st of October to 27th of March." Photocopied 1894 schedule kindly sent through the courtesy of Keith Austin, Assistant Archivist, University of London Library..

[9] Personal communication via e-mail from Barbara Davies, Communications Director, RDS: Understanding Animal Research in Medicine.

[10] French, Richard D. 1975 Antivivisection and Medical Science in Victorian Society. Princton University Press, 425 pages.

[11] Doyle, A. C. "The Adventure of Black Peter" In: *The Complete Sherlock Holmes* by Arthur Conan Doyle, with a preface by Christopher Morley, Doubleday and Company, Garden City, New York, single volume, 1988, p558-572.

[12] Doyle, A. C. "The Adventure of Sussex Vampire" In: *The Complete Sherlock Holmes* by Arthur Conan Doyle, with a preface by Christopher Morley, Doubleday and Company, Garden City, New York, single volume, 1988, p1033-1044.

A "Second Stain" Saves The Day

Holmes & Watson Report, Vol.3, No. 6, January 2000, p 36-9; Practice *Notes*, June 2006, p 19-20

Scientific research is a laborious and convoluted process. Several impediments must be overcome prior to a successful conclusion. Thus, there are many similarities to the investigations of Mr. Sherlock Holmes. It would appear to the uninitiated reader of a scientific paper that everything was very straightforward: Introduction, materials and methods, results, discussion, conclusion - one, two, three - no sweat, everything lined up and done. As anyone who has worked in this area knows, there's always a stopping point - a block -- that needs to be circumvented before completion. Let's say, for illustration, that you are a young researcher working on your doctoral dissertation. Now, all that you need to do is to insert a human gene into *E. coli* by conventional means, have the activity show up in the bacterial culture supernate, isolate from it the active enzyme in pure form by gel chromatography, recover it in solution, and characterize it by standard means. Everything looks fine: The liquid from the *E. coli* cultivation has acquired the ability to perform the biochemical activity of the human enzyme, an aqueous solution of the semi-purified protein crystals demonstrates a very high enzymatic potency, the unstained slab of electrophoresis gel yields a very active extract, and the gel shows a narrow but concentrated colored band of pure protein at exactly the right distance from the electrode. What can go wrong? Well, what if the material extracted from the exact location of the stained band refuses to perform the expected activity in several replicated experiments under a variety of conditions? There goes the old Ph.D. unless you can somehow figure out what to do.

After a few beers at the local bar and three pipefuls of tobacco, you go visit good old Dr. Weisenheimer for advice. Not your own professor, Dr. Grant Swinger, who got the funding for your studies, but the neat old guy who has been there forever, has published hundreds of papers, still works in the lab with his own hands, and knows everything.

"Well lad, have you looked for a second substance in the gel?" he queries. "Maybe there's a cofactor," he continues, "like what happened to me in '76, or was it '77?"

"That's it!" you shout, and off you go to the lab to try several reagents to find an additional protein or carbohydrate in a nearby area of the gel that is required for the enzymatic activity. And there it is! Eureka! Another colored band several centimeters away. Combining the cuts from the two areas yields the desired effect in several experiments! You will get your Ph.D. this year after all! You will have a life! What a paper this will make, and a career of elucidating the interactions of these two biochemical agents WEI_1 and WEI_2. Yes, the "second stain" saved the day, as it did for Sherlock Holmes in *The Adventure of the Second Stain*[1].

Note that in this case, Sherlock Holmes was also stumped until a second stain appeared. Initially, Sherlock Holmes followed all of the procedures that I outlined as the "method of scientists[2]." He considered at all of the evidence regarding the missing provocative letter from the hot-headed foreign potentate. Having previously read and mastered all of the available **KNOWLEDGE** on the subject, and based on the statements provided by the Premier, Lord Bellinger, Mr. Holmes deduced exactly who penned this unfortunate letter. Similar to a research scientist who has delved deeply into the subject of his/her investigations, Mr. Holmes' depth of knowledge enabled him to select the most likely candidates for the theft of the letter: Oberstein, La Rothiere, and Eduardo Lucas. Also, Mr. Holmes deduced that the letter had to have been taken between 7:30 and 11:30 in the evening since both the unfortunate Trelwany Hope and his wife were together in the room containing the locked despatch box bearing the letter after 11:30 p.m. Additionally,

Mr. Holmes surmised that the earlier hour was more likely, and that Mr. Lucas was the likeliest culprit as the only one of the three possible suspects living nearby. Mr. Holmes was very diligent to **OBSERVE** everything no matter how unrelated it might have appeared at the time. For example, his suspicion against Mr. Lucas was further aroused by his murder that was reported in the paper, as the most likely reason that the letter had not yet surfaced in enemy hands. The unexpected visit by Lady Hilda Trelawney Hope, the wife of the unfortunate European Secretary, informed Mr. Holmes that she was somehow connected to the loss of the document. In the ensuing conversation with Dr. Watson, Mr. Holmes clearly stated the **PROBLEM** in its simplest form. He then went out to gather all of the **DATA** that he could find on the subject. However, in this case, it was to no avail. Here matters stood as they did with our hypothetical biochemistry graduate student. Suspicion and surmise led only to a very **TENTATIVE HYPOTHESIS** and **WORKING MODEL** that reasonably fit all of the available information. But, more information was needed to continue the case and to find the missing letter.

Three days passed without any further progress. A break was needed. Then it came. As happened in our illustrative research study, the "second stain" saved the day in a very dramatic fashion. Mr. Holmes was able to use this information to conclude his researches. To accomplish this goal, he made **ADDITIONAL OBSERVATIONS** and sought **EXPERIMENTAL PROOF** to determine if the results fit or pointed to a reformulation of his hypothesis. The fact that the stain on the rug was not in the same place as the stain on the floor, in the murdered Mr. Lucas's home, demonstrated that someone had recently moved it. After using guile to get Inspector Lestrade to leave the room, Mr. Holmes was able to locate the slot in the floor where the letter had most likely been placed and recently removed. By showing the picture of Lady Hilda to the constable, Mr.

Holmes confirmed his hypothesis that it had been she who had retrieved the item. These data confirmed Mr. Holmes' hypothesis that the wife of the Right Honourable Trelawney Hope was deeply involved in the theft of the item being sought.

The rest is history. Using the theories that he had formed, Sherlock Holmes was able to get Lady Hilda to cough up the letter in time for him to secrete it into the despatch box. Then, in his usual dramatic fashion, he sprung his find on the unsuspecting European Secretary without anyone realizing the extent to which his wife was involved in the theft. Again, we have another case neatly solved by the Sherlock Holmes and his application of the "method of scientists."

[1] Doyle, A. C. "Adventure of the Second Stain" In: *The Complete Sherlock Holmes* by Arthur Conan Doyle, with a preface by Christopher Morley, Doubleday and Company, Garden City, New York, single volume, 1988, p650.

[2] Heifetz, C. L. 1997. Staying Focused. *Communication* (a publication of the Pleasant Places of Florida), No. 173 New Series, Volume 1, Issue 5, pages 3-4; Heifetz, C.L. 1998. The Scientific Detective Solves the Sign of Four. *The Wigmore Street Post Office*, Issue Number 11, Spring 1998, p 3-9; Heifetz, C.L. 1998. A Study in Scarlet Yields to the Methods of Sherlock Holmes, Scientist. *The Wigmore Street Post Office*, Issue Number 12, Summer 1998, p 18-21,24; Heifetz, C. L. Sherlock Holmes Scientist Solves A Case of Identity. *The Wigmore Street Post Office*, in press; Heifetz, C. L. Sherlock Holmes Crosses a Thor Bridge to Scientific Inspiration. *Holmes & Watson* Report, Vol.3, No. 4, September 1999, p 13-5.

Sherlock Holmes Scientist Solves A Case of Identity

Published in *The Hounds Collection* Vol. 8, April 2003, p 13-15; *Communication* (a publication of the Pleasant Places of Florida), No. 280, Volume 12, No. 2, pages 1-4, 2008.

In today's Sherlockian science lesson, we will focus on Miss Mary Sutherland and Sherlock Holmes' use of the method of scientists to "find" her missing fiancé. In this adventure, which Dr. Watson has so nicely shared with us under the title of "A Case of Identity,"[1] we will learn how scientists often use great skill in the design of their experiments, how important it is for them to understand how their philosophical apparatus work, and the experience and background required to derive meaningful results from the output of their studies. During this discourse, I will also refer to concepts that I have discussed at length on prior occasions.[2,3,4]

Most of us are very well acquainted with eminent researchers - i.e. Hawking, Einstein, Moriarty - who made great scientific leaps by the power of their minds using, as their only equipment, a computer, chalk board, or ink, pens, and foolscap. However, these notables had to depend on the efforts of equally brilliant experimentalists to validate the results of their hypotheses. Most scientists, including chemists such as Sherlock Holmes, are not content to give someone else the privilege of proving their pet theories. They would rather derive their own experimental proof than let someone else's possible lack of expertise cast doubt on their dazzling theories. Intrinsic to this process are the skills required to design and perform the appropriate experiments and to skillfully decipher the output of their manipulations. I have often been amazed at the skilled interpretation that experienced scientists make in their oral presentations. Virologists deriving great meaning from shadowy scanning electron micrographs have always impressed me immensely.

What is even more impressive is the fact that other virologists seem to see the same thing, whereas, to me, the photomicrographs appear like random chaotic images. On the other hand, give me the results obtained with a new antibiotic in antibacterial chemotherapeutic studies in mouse infection models, and I can probably provide you with a fairly good idea of the likelihood of clinical success against that microbe in man.

You might ask: What has this to do with Mr. Sherlock Holmes and Miss Mary Sutherland? After all, the only use of scientific equipment mentioned in this account are the tools that Sherlock Holmes used to identify the salt that he was working on as the bisulphate of baryta. Yes, but consider the fact that Sherlock Holmes' clients themselves are part of the material upon which Sherlock Holmes works. The Master uses people in the same manner that bacteriological researchers would apply culture media. Just as a trained microbiologist is easily able to differentiate coliform bacteria from enteric bacilli by their pigmentation and colonial morphology on the agar medium formulated by Holmes contemporary Alfred Theodore MacConkey, the scientific detective is able to ascertain vast amounts of information by determining how his subjects respond to his verbal manipulations. Thus, it was not mere curiosity that caused Sherlock Holmes to first ask Mary Sutherland: "Do you not find that with your short sight it is a little trying to do so much typewriting?" And later, "Why did you come away to consult me in such a hurry?" Her astonished response to both of his skillfully designed queries provided Sherlock Holmes with some excellent clues regarding the ease with which Miss Sutherland could be mentally manipulated. This was a critical aspect of her personality that led Sherlock Holmes toward the appropriate tentative hypothesis that he later subjected to further investigation. How very differently Mr. Holmes' mind would have been directed had he found Miss Sutherland to be more mentally acute and less impressionable. And why did Dr. Watson bother to insert this seemingly irrelevant material about Sherlock Holmes' chemical investigations? My opinion is that the clever doctor wanted to draw our minds to the realization that there were many parallels between the methods that a trained chemist would use to identify an unknown chemical, and those needed by a scientific detective to identify an unknown person.

Now, let us examine the rest of this case to demonstrate those aspects of Sherlock Holmes' methodology that are derived from his training as a chemist and medical researcher. We start with Mr. Holmes' first observation of Miss Sutherland. By noting her "oscillation upon the pavement," he had already decided that she came to consult him concerning an *"affair de coeur."* When she entered the room, Mr. Holmes gave Miss Sutherland his well-known once over, demonstrating those powers of observation that are critical to a serious research scientist. As he later explained to Dr. Watson, he had observed a double line on plush cuffs of both of her sleeves, an indication of long hours spent using a typing machine. Marks on the bridge of her nose signaled that she wore pince nez and was therefore shortsighted. Her hurry to rush out to consult Mr. Holmes was evidenced by her wearing unmatched boots half buttoned, and by the hurry shown in writing a note, having dipped the pen too deeply into the ink well, making a fresh stain on her finger and glove. These led to the above-discussed questions that supplied Mr. Holmes with a great deal of information about Miss Sutherland's obvious gullibility.

Knowing the character of his client, Sherlock Holmes was able to see the ways in which her wicked stepfather, Mr. Windibank, was able to convince the very impressionable, near-sighted, and lonely woman that he was also another person, her erstwhile fiancé, Mr. Hosmer Angel. How many times has someone attempted to disguise their identity by typing or printing (remember "The Adventure of the Red Circle") their communications? How often have people changed their identities by wearing a mustache, bushy whiskers, and tinted glasses and speaking in a whisper? Coupling these observations with the knowledge that Mary Sutherland let her parents use her large income while she resided in her house, that her stepfather did not want her to meet other people or attend the gasfitter's ball, that Mr. Windibank and Mr. Angel were never seen together, and that the descriptions of these gentlemen had many similarities, Mr. Holmes reached a tentative hypothesis that he would later subject to experimental validation. His hypothesis was that Messrs. Windibank and Angel were indeed the very same person.

Everything was now in place for the experimental test of his hypothesis. Sherlock Holmes confirmed, with Mr. Windibank's employers, that the printed description of Mr. Hosmer Angel, without the obfuscating glasses, mustache, and whiskers, fit Mr. Windibank himself. Then Mr. Holmes made an appointment with Mr. Windibank to discuss his stepdaughter's case with him. The typewritten reply, as Mr. Holmes had hypothesized, was analyzed by Mr. Holmes who skillfully demonstrated that it was done on the very typewriter that Mr. Angel had used to correspond with Miss Sutherland. And finally, to prove his theory beyond doubt, Mr. Holmes browbeat a confession from Mr. Windibank when he was confronted with the evidence.

Thus, a case that was opaque even to such an intelligent person as John H. Watson, a recipient of the highly prized Doctor of Medicine Degree from London Medical, was made clear by the scientific detective, Mr. Sherlock Holmes, who applied the very same principles that have led to such modern wonders as the genetic code, miracle drugs, and Velcro.

[1] Doyle, A. C. "A Case of Identity" In: *The Complete Sherlock Holmes* by Arthur Conan Doyle, with a preface by Christopher Morley, Doubleday and Company, Garden City, New York, single volume, 1988.

[2] Heifetz, C. L. "Staying Focused," *Communication* (a publication of the Pleasant Places of Florida), No. 173 New Series, Volume 1, Issue 5, pages 3-4.

[3] Heifetz, C.L. 1998. The Scientific Detective Solves the Sign of Four. *The Wigmore Street Post Office*, Issue Number 11, Spring 1998, p 3-9.

[4] Heifetz, C.L. 1998. A Study in Scarlet Yields to the Methods of Sherlock Holmes, Scientist *The Wigmore Street Post Office*, Issue Number 12, Summer 1998, p 18-21,24

Keep Digging Until You Find It

Published in *Holmes & Watson Report*,6 (3):27-31, (July) 2002 and the Friends of Dr John H. Watson *The Formulary*, No. 25 Sept. 2009, pages 12-14 and Sept. 2012, pages 17-20.

In a series of essays regarding Sherlock Holmes' application of the methods used by research scientists to perform his function as a private consulting detective, I have focused on situations and circumstances appropriate to researchers whose labor is restricted to the pleasant environs of air-conditioned laboratories[1]. However, as we are well aware, many major scientific advances are made by investigators who very infrequently sit comfortably in chairs while peering through a microscope or viewing the patterns of lines on a slab of gel from an electrophoresis run. No, they tromp the earth in practical walking shoes, wearing jeans or khaki shorts, while carrying shovels, sand pails, screens, and/or pick axes as they explore nature looking for scientific evidence to support their theories. Sherlock Holmes also fits this mold. How often have we encountered him crawling in the mud looking for candles, matches, or cigarette butts, or digging through cinders in a fireplace?

Does this mean that such researchers do not use the method of scientists in a similar manner as their laboratory-bound colleagues? No, indeed. One can't just go digging helter-skelter anywhere, or search every cave in the world at random. They have to first know where to look. How else could four generations of Leakeys continue to unearth new evidence regarding the development of the human species, or archeologists discover additional undisturbed burial sites? As with all research scientists, they must follow the rules that I set forward previously: (1) Clearly state the **PROBLEM** in its simplest form. (2) Gather all of the **DATA** that you can find on the subject. (3) Be very diligent to **OBSERVE** everything no matter how unrelated it may appear at the time. (4) Read and master all of the available **KNOWLEDGE** on the subject to see what data has previously been reported. (5) Sift through all of the data, current and reported, and attempt to **DEDUCE A TENTATIVE HYPOTHESIS** and **WORKING MODEL** that reasonably fits all of the available information. (6) List further needed information, observations, and experiments that may refute or support your hypotheses. Seek **EXPERIMENTAL PROOF** and **ADDITIONAL OBSERVATIONS** and determine if the results fit or point a reformulation of the hypothesis. (7) With all data in hand, **PUBLISH** your observations, results, hypotheses, and conclusions in an appropriate format for others to read, challenge, and confirm.

Even though they have all of the available material in hand, scientific explorers must practice great diligence and patience in their quest for evidence. They may need to open many tombs, dig many holes in the earth, or scale many cliffs before they are finally successful. These requirements also pertain to scientific detectives such as Mr. Sherlock Holmes.

Acclaim and notoriety do not go to the scientists who fail in this quest, even if they try and try many times. No, it goes to the one who finally succeeds in locating the object being sought. Even if the prize eludes the initial investigator in five attempts, it is the one who succeeds in the sixth attempt who gets the fame and fortune associated with the accomplishment. Sometimes it is merely a matter of luck. For example, suppose a rare cache of golden Egyptian relics is in only one of six tombs. Using skill and acumen, an investigator may find and open five without finding what was sought. Statistically, this is an unlikely but possible occurrence. Thus, many scientists keep their explorations secret to avoid another from getting into their territory. This is done to prevent other investigators who come late into the field, from following the strategy already laid out to achieve the desired result for themselves. Perhaps we can see, in part, this mode of thought in Sherlock Holmes' reticence to reveal the details of his deductions until all of the facts are in hand and the solution has been clearly delineated.

Perhaps no case in the Canon serves as a more appropriate example of these principles than "The Adventure of the Six Napoleons." Take the situation of the unlucky Beppo. He very ably succeeded in finding the first five statues of Napoleon. Unfortunately for him, his capture prevented him from ferreting out the true location of the black Pearl of the Borgias that he had secreted therein the year before. But, not suspecting that an equally diligent searcher was following in his tracks, he left a trail of shards behind him for Sherlock Holmes to follow as Hansel and Gretel followed the stones laid down in their trek through the forest. Thus, on the sixth and final attempt, Sherlock Holmes found the item that poor Beppo so dearly sought -- the black pearl.

Adding up one piece of evidence after another until reaching a hypothesis, Sherlock Holmes was undeterred by minor side issues, such a bloody murder. After observing the remains left by several seemingly, to Lestrade at least, random attempts on the part of the unlucky villain of this story, Holmes was able to resolve the problem with a scientific evaluation of the data available to him. He opened the sixth cave, as it were, and uncovered the treasure therein.

Let us explore this process one bust at a time:

Bust 1: The first breaking of the Napoleonic statue appeared to be an isolated event. A nut walks into Morse Hudson's shop, seemingly becomes infuriated by the statue of Napoleon, and breaks it into pieces. "Queer madness," says Lestrade. "That's no business of mine," replies Mr. Holmes.

Bust 2 & 3: However, the report that burglaries were used to obtain and destroy two identical statues in two separate locations -- Dr. Barnicott's surgery and his residence -- get Mr. Holmes' attention. A pattern was starting to form. In three occasions, the identical statue was the victim. The fact that Morse Hudson's shop and the doctor's residence were filled with other Napoleonic representations revealed that this was more specific more than a hatred of Napoleon.

Bust 4: The events leading to the discovery of broken bust number four obfuscated the search for the hidden treasure. The killing of an unknown Italian, by Beppo, in self-defense we later find, got the full attention of Inspector Lestrade. Unlike Sherlock Holmes, Lestrade failed to note the possible relationship between that bloody event and the quest for the pearl. Lestrade, to investigate the "murder," went to great lengths to determine the identity of the corpse and the identity of the man in the picture that was in the possession of the felled individual.

Sherlock Holmes followed the trail of the Napoleonic busts. The fourth broken bust was found in the garden of an empty house down the street. A conversation with the owner of the bust, the journalist Mr. Harker, revealed its purveyor, Harding Brothers. Unable to obtain any information from that source due to Mr. Harding's absence from his shop, Mr. Holmes revisited Morse Hudson to locate the manufacturer, which was Gelder and. Co. A visit to Gelder and Co. revealed the date that Beppo ran through the shop fleeing from the police. Then, finally able to interview Mr. Harding, Sherlock Holmes was able to identify the purchasers of the final two busts. As we shall see, this information led to the capture of the unfortunate Beppo and the resolution of the mystery.

Bust 5: The events detailed in Dr. Watson's account document the trap that Sherlock Holmes laid leading to the arrest of the unlucky Beppo. Lured into the home of Mr. Josiah Brown, Beppo was captured after he came out of the window and broke the bust that he had removed from the residence. As with the previous four, this bust also contained nothing noteworthy.

Bust 6: The final bust arrived in the hands of Mr. Sandeford of Reading. He was enticed to visit Mr. Holmes' Baker Street quarters by a communication offering 10 pounds sterling for the bust of Napoleon that he had purchased from Harding Brothers. After the departure of Mr. Sandeford, Sherlock Holmes performed one of those theatrical stunts for which he is renowned. Using his hunting crop, Mr. Holmes broke the item into several fragments to reveal the Black Pearl of the Borgias that Beppo had secreted therein a years ago to hide it from the police. As had been determined by Mr. Holmes, Beppo's "visit" was consistent with the date in which the pearl was stolen.

"Follow the money," has become a favorite phrase in recent years. That is just what Sherlock Holmes did to solve the "Adventure of the Six Napoleons." In the process, he discerned the events leading to the death of the man eventually identified as the Mafioso Pietro Venucci, from Naples. He revealed that this death resulted from Venucci's unsuccessful attack on our friend, Beppo. Thus, by stringing together all of the information at his disposal, Sherlock Holmes was able to form a scientifically based hypothesis of the events leading to the destruction of the six Napoleons featured in this account. The experimental proof of his hypothesis came with the final denouement, the destruction of the sixth bust and finding the Pearl of the Borgias located inside.

[1] Heifetz, C. L. 1997. Staying Focused. *Communication* (a publication of the Pleasant Places of Florida), No. 173 New Series, Volume 1, Issue 5, pages 3-4; Heifetz, C.L. 1998. The Scientific Detective Solves the Sign of Four. *The*

Wigmore Street Post Office, Issue Number 11, Spring 1998, p 3-9; Heifetz, C.L. 1998. A Study in Scarlet Yields to the Methods of Sherlock Holmes, Scientist. *The Wigmore Street Post Office*, Issue Number 12, Summer 1998, p 18-21,24; Heifetz, C. L. Sherlock Holmes Crosses a Thor Bridge to Scientific Inspiration. *Holmes & Watson* Report, Vol.3, No. 4, September 1999, p 13-5; Heifetz, C. L. A "Second Stain" Saves the Day. *Holmes & Watson* Report, Vol.3, No. 6, January 2000, p 36-9.

[2] Doyle, A. C. "The Adventure of the Six Napoleons" In: *The Complete Sherlock Holmes* by Arthur Conan Doyle, with a preface by Christopher Morley, Doubleday and Company, Garden City, New York, single volume, 1988, p582.

Tunnel Detection in Victorian London

Presented at the Pleasant Places of Florida 27th Fall
Gathering, November 1, 2002; Published
in *Communication* #227 New Series Vol. 6, Issue 9,
November/December 2002 p2-4, Pleasant Places of
Florida; Published in *Holmes & Watson Report*, 6 (6): 13-
16, (January) 2003.

In the 24th century, if science-fiction literature and television programs are useful predictors of future progress, our descendants will be able to use remote sensing devices to scan distant planets. They will be able to detect new life forms, nutrients, energy sources, and just about anything else they are looking for.

Even today, a wide variety of subsurface features and objects can be detected using Surface Geophysics.@[1] For example, the category identified as Evaluation of Soil and Rock Properties and Man-Made Structures@ includes mapping of abandoned mines, tunnels, etc.@ To achieve these objectives, many technical processes have been utilized: Ground Penetrating Radar, Frequency Domain Electromagnetics, Time Domain Electromagnetics, Very Low Frequency, Resistivity, Spontaneous Potential, Seismic Refraction, Seismic Reflection, Magnetic, Metal Detector, Gravity, Thermal, and Radiometric.

A noted Sherlockian geologist suggests that geoseismology and geomagnetic processes would be the best methods to locate tunnels.[2] Geoseismology involves generating sound waves that reflect back from underground strata. Geomagnetic work involves using fluctuations in the earth's magnetic field to help figure out what's deep underground.@ The details of these methods will not be pursued further. They are both beyond the scope of this thesis and the technical expertise of the author. Suffice it to say that tunnels are very easily found using the technical skills currently at our disposal in the hands of people who know how to apply them.

But what has all of this to do with Sherlock Holmes? The answer to this rhetorical question jumps clearly to the mind of the experienced Sherlockian. In August 1891, readers of *The Strand* magazine were thrilled to learn that Sherlock Holmes had thwarted a daring robbery of 30,000 napoleons in French gold from the Coburg Branch of the City and Suburban Bank.[3] To accomplish this feat, Mr. Holmes needed to detect the presence of a tunnel running from the rear end of the cellar of Mr. Jabez Wilson's pawn shop to the vaults of the bank on the street behind the shop. Lacking the technological assists that are quite available today, just how did he accomplish this?

The answer, of course, resides in the fact that Mr. Holmes was a trained research scientist. As I have pointed out previously, he uses the method of scientists to guide his facility for observation, deduction, and hypothesis building and testing.[4] The only scientific instrument at his disposal was a stout walking stick able to withstand being "thumped vigorously upon the pavement."

Let us summarize the various pieces of information that led Mr. Holmes to his scientifically valid conclusion that a tunnel was being dug from the back of the pawn shop cellar to the bank vault. The first inkling came in his interview with Mr. Wilson. Mr. Holmes easily saw through the ruse of the "Red-Headed League." He realized that this scenario was merely a clever a means of removing Mr. Wilson from his place of business for long periods of time to accommodate a crime therein. The fact that this event followed shortly after the hire of a bright young man, Vincent Spalding, for a much lower salary than the going rate, convinced Mr. Holmes that this was the man who had plans to use the premises in Mr. Wilson's absence. Mr. Wilson's investigations, after being notified that "The Red-Headed League is dissolved," supplied the information that it was a bogus group that no one had ever heard of. Mr. Wilson's description of this young man, especially the "white splash of acid upon his forehead," and the fact that "his ears were pierced for earrings" signaled that a major criminal event was being planned by the "fourth smartest man in London" and the third most daring, John Clay. Spaulding's apparent penchant for photography, and the fact the he was forever "diving down into the cellar like a rabbit into its hole to develop his pictures" convinced Mr. Holmes that a subterranean crime was about to ensue.

One more clue was all that was required for Mr. Holmes to deduce that a tunnel was involved. Upon visiting Mr. Wilson's place of occupation, Mr. Holmes observed that the knees of Mr. Spaulding's trousers were dirty, indicating that he had been digging. Thus, he was likely to be excavating for a tunnel. Since Jabez Wilson had never mentioned buried treasure and had not himself been digging for it, Mr. Holmes was convinced that his tunnel hypothesis was correct. The recent closure of the Red-Headed League indicated that the crime was going to be committed very soon. After that weekend, no one cared if Jabez Wilson returned to his shop during the day or not.

But where did the tunnel lead? Did it lead forward or towards the back? Using his only scientific device, Sherlock Holmes used his stick to pound the pavement looking for signs of hollowness to locate the cellar, the starting point for the dig. Seeing that the cellar was not forward of the shop, Holmes led Watson around the corner to the street immediately behind the pawn shop, the prosperous business district behind Saxe-Coburg Square. There it was! The only logical target for all of the effort put forth by the criminals was directly in line with the rear of the pawn shop -- the Coburg Branch of the City and Suburban Bank. Somewhere in the underground recesses of that financial institution was a fortune worthy of the planning, cost, and immense effort put forth by the thieves.

The scene was set for the test of hypothesis -- to whit, a pair of daring and intelligent criminals were burrowing under the earth, from the pawn shop cellar to the underground recesses under the bank to obtain vast riches. It is to this location that Sherlock Holmes, Dr. Watson, Bank Director Mr. Merryweather, and Mr. Jones of Scotland Yard wound their way down and around to their final destination. It was at this location that Mr. Merryweather both provided the final link in the logical deduction that brought them to this site and almost ruined Mr. Holmes' plan of attack. "Nor from below," said Mr. Merryweather, striking his stick upon the flag stones that lined the floor. 'Why dear me, it sounds quite hollow!' he remarked, looking up in surprise."

We are all familiar with the exciting events of that evening as the *partie carreé* waited silently in the dark. The emergence of John Clay through a hole in the ground into the bank's vault, provided strong support for Mr. Holmes' hypothesis. Again, Mr. Holmes had utilized the "method of scientists" to neatly solve a criminal case.

[1] Surface Geophysics by Technos Inc (Internet address: http://www.technos-inc.com/Surface.html)

[2] Finding Caves & Tunnels, personal e-mail communication with Peter E. Blau, Oct. 12, 2002.

[3] Doyle, A. C. The Red-Headed League@ In: *The Complete Sherlock Holmes* by Arthur Conan Doyle, with a preface by Christopher Morley, Doubleday and Company, Garden City, New York, single volume, 1988, p176.[4] Heifetz, C. L. 1997. Staying Focused. *Communication* (a publication of the Pleasant Places of Florida), No. 173 New Series, Volume 1, Issue 5, pages 3-4; Heifetz, C.L. 1998. The Scientific Detective Solves the Sign of Four. *The Wigmore Street Post Office*, Issue Number 11, Spring 1998, p 3-9; Heifetz, C.L. 1998. A Study in Scarlet Yields to the Methods of Sherlock Holmes, Scientist. *The Wigmore Street Post Office*, Issue Number 12, Summer 1998, p 18-21,24; Heifetz, C. L.

Sherlock Holmes Crosses a Thor Bridge to Scientific Inspiration. *Holmes & Watson* Report, Vol.3, No. 4, September 1999, p 13-5; Heifetz, C. L. A A Second Stain@ Saves the Day. *Holmes & Watson* Report, Vol.3, No. 6, January 2000, p 36-9; Heifetz, C. L. Keep Digging until You Find it. *Holmes & Watson Report* Vol. 6, No. 3, July 2002, p 27-31.

A Victorian Christmas Classic

Published in the *Suncoast News* (Wednesday, November 29, 1995, page 20-21; and Communication #188 of the Pleasant Places of Florida, New Series Vol. 1 Issue 10, page 1; Practice Notes, The Friends of Dr. John H. Watson, Dec. 2009, pages 3 - 4.

It is December 27. The excitement of Christmas has now faded into the languorous days that fill the interim preceding the New Year. The tree is resplendent in the living room in the far corner diagonally opposite the crackling fire place. The train set is now unattended except for the miniature figures that populate the surrounding village. All of the discarded wrapping paper has been cleared away and the contents neatly stowed in the proper toy chests. A gentle snow outside the window can be barely perceived through the lacy handiwork left by Jack Frost during the night, and sleigh bells are faintly heard over the sound coming from the family room. There, several figures can be seen cuddled on the floor leaning against the over-stuffed sofa. The largest figure is that of Grandpa, his neatly cut white hair and beard set off on top by the deerstalker cap perched gently on his head, and the new red and green turtleneck sweater, bearing leather patches on the elbows. Under his left and right arms rest, respectively, the twin nine-year-old grandchildren Tommy and Tammy. On Grandpa's lap, quietly sleeping, is the baby, and at his feet in placid and comfortable repose is the family spaniel, Topper. All eyes are focused on the giant television screen in front of them as they watch together, in the annual renewal of their family custom, the marvelous Christmas classic unfolds before their eyes.

Let us now shift the scene to Grandma's warm, enormous kitchen, filled with the delicious, fragrant odors of turkey hash simmering for dinner. Sitting around the large oval table that has been passed down through several generations are the two teenaged grandchildren -- Bobby and Bonnie, who have joined Grandma, Mom, and Dad at a late breakfast. The conversation has drifted to a discussion of the same well-remembered tale and the impact that it has had on their lives over the years. How an attempt to reunite Mr. Baker with his abandoned goose and hat led, via a goose's crop, to the discovery of the criminal who stole the remarkable and singular blue gem.

Yes, if you are a fan of the exploits of Mr. Sherlock Holmes and his companions, you very quickly perceived the subject of this essay. All of the characters in this sketch were doing what Sherlockians have done since 1934, that date of the founding of "The Baker Street Irregulars." They were all renewing their acquaintanceship with *The Adventure of the Blue Carbuncle*. As originally suggested by Christopher Morley himself, the founding father of the BSI, this is a perfect way to observe the spirit of the Christmas season. We tell and retell the kind acts of the commissionaire Peterson who first rescued Henry Baker from the Tottenham Court Road loungers and then his desire, via the assistance of Mr. Sherlock Holmes, to locate the rightful owner of the goose and hat which were abandoned during the skirmish. This parable is then climaxed by the spirit of forgiveness displayed by Mr. Holmes when he allowed the novice thief John Ryder to "go forth and sin no more."

Can there be any better way to mark holidays and special occasions than by passing on the lore of the Canon to our heirs and offspring? This is a Sherlockian imperative paralleling the words of an even more ancient canonical tradition "And thou shalt teach them diligently unto thy children." This, and other narratives are readily available in bookstores everywhere, generally at a nominal cost. I invite you to join us in our efforts to keep green the memory of the individual whom the good Dr. Watson proclaimed to be, "the best and wisest man whom I have ever known," Mr. Sherlock Holmes.

Baker Street Browsings

Published in *Communication* (#184 New Series Vol. 2,
Issue 6 July/August 1998 p 6-7)
Pleasant Places of Florida

The morning of Wednesday, July 8, 1998, was cold and damp - at least by Florida standards. However, just the joy of being on Baker Street, the place where Sherlock Holmes and Dr. Watson and other characters that populate the Canon trod many years ago, was enough to overcome the mild discomfort that I felt.

My first stop was the Abbey National Bank, which now occupies the address 221 Baker Street. Although I was not able to penetrate to the "b" level, where Mr. Holmes' personal secretary still resides and answers his correspondence, I was able to pick up a few goodies at the information desk: a post card with a color picture of Mr. Sherlock Holmes and a beautifully illustrated brochure that discusses several topics -- Holmes the Man, The Letters (to Sherlock Holmes), Sir Arthur Conan Doyle, and the relationship between the Bank and Sherlockians worldwide.

The Sherlock Holmes Museum was delightful, and in my opinion well worth the 5 pound entry fee. Free handouts included autographed Sherlock Holmes business cards and a small illustrated brochure describing the Museum and giving some background material concerning the former inhabitants at that address, which they also claim as 221b Baker Street. The Museum Gift Shop contains a plethora of marvelous items, and "she who must be obeyed" allowed me to select a few for purchase. At the connected Mrs. Hudson's Restaurant, I was able to scrounge an illustrated bill of fare.

The next stop was the Sherlock Holmes Memorabilia Company directly across the street from the Museum. Unlike the "tsotskis" in the Museum, the items for sale at the Memorabilia Company were more serious and included many magazines and books, including some of which are collector's items. The other articles were quite different from those found across the street.

The most disappointing locale was the Sherlock Holmes Hotel, where I was permitted to purchase a photograph of Sherlock Holmes. I saw no displays and there were no freebees.

For the more completest Sherlockians, I recommend a visit to "The Wallace Collection." Therein, one may view a fair sampling of the works of two artists mentioned in the Canon: Jean-Baptiste Greuze (Moriarty's favorite) and Emile-Jean-Horace Vernet (Sherlock Holmes great uncle). Although the full-scale works of art are beyond my budget, I was able to purchase four postcards for each artist's work.

Birthday of Louis Pasteur Celebrated

Posted December 27, 1996, to the Hounds of the Internet

On December 27 we celebrate the birthday of Louis Pasteur who lived from 1822-1895. During those years he set the stage for many advances in the study of microbiology and infectious diseases. How does this impact the Canon? In the narratives that are the subject of these discussions are contained many reference to infectious diseases. Most noteworthy, which shall be our story to be studied on that date, is *The Adventure of the Dying Detective*. You will recall that in this case Holmes pretended to be dying from a rare tropical disease, possibly "the black formosa corruption" or "tapanuli fever." By virtue of Dr. Watson's intervention, Mr. Holmes is able to do a "gotcha" on Culverton Smith, a Sumatra planter and expert on this illness. Mr. Smith was the individual who thought that he had tricked Sherlock Holmes into contracting this dread and incurable illness by sending him a box booby-trapped with an injection device. According to Baring-Gould, Mr. Hugh L'Tang's researches have identified this disease as a condition known as tsutsugamushi fever or scrub typhus. Effective antibiotic therapies for this rickettsial infection has been available for roughly 50 years. Thus, this disease is not incurable today; however, in the golden era of the Victorian age, it was associated with a high degree of morbidity and mortality.

No doubt, the life of The Literary Agent had a great impact on Mr. Holmes' and Dr. Watson's interest in this subject. First of all, Arthur Conan Doyle received his Doctorate of Medicine with a thesis concerning the bacterial infection, syphilis. His wife "Touie" died of tuberculosis after a lingering illness. Further, in May, 1892, a letter from Dr. Joseph Bell suggested a story idea for a "bacteriological criminal." In addition, it has often been suggested that Dr.

Watson's first(?) wife, Mary, also died of tuberculosis. This was a century of great advances in the knowledge of infectious disease and microbiology in general: Jacob Lister led the way to aseptic surgery; Pasteur developed vaccines for anthrax and rabies; Koch worked out the pathogenesis of tuberculosis; and a discussion between Mr. Sherlock Holmes and Professor Paul Ehrlich in Montpellier in 1894 led to the latter's discovery of arsphenamine, the first antibacterial drug.

Also, 1899 was the year that the American Society for Microbiology (once known as the Society of American Bacteriologists), the largest single biological society in the U.S., was founded.

The Canon abounds with bacteriological references. Dr. Watson had been afflicted with enteric fever during his recuperation from a gunshot wound in *A Study in Scarlet*. Jonathan Small had been "racked with ague" during his imprisonment in the Andaman convict barracks in *The Sign of Four*. In *The Stock Broker's Clerk*, Holmes deduced that Watson had been "unwell lately" with a summer cold. Consumption (tuberculosis) is mentioned in three accounts: *The Final Problem, The Adventure of the Missing Third Quarter, and The Hound of the Baskervilles*. Other infectious diseases in the Canon are as follows: diphtheria, *The "Gloria Scott"*; erysipelas, *The Adventure of the Illustrious Client*; suspected leprosy, *The Adventure of the Blanched Soldier*; suspected spinal meningitis, *The Adventure of the Sussex Vampire*; pneumonia, *The Adventure of the Three Garridebs*; rheumatic fever, *The Adventure of the Lion's Mane*; tetanus, *The Sign of Four*; and yellow fever, *The Yellow Face*.

Dr. Watson's Adventure of The Deadly Medusa

Being a Reprint of the Reminiscences of John H. Watson, MD,
Professor of Mental Disorders at University of London

Published in the Friends of Dr John H. Watson *Practice Notes*, Dec. 2008, pages 17-23 & *Baker Street West 1*, 15:1, Summer 2009, 27-37..

Never in my life had I ever anticipated the mysterious events that were to bring me out of a state of fugue and back into the world of joy. For I was terribly distressed. My nerves had been shattered by the deaths of my two closest friends - Mr. Sherlock Holmes, at the Reichenbach Falls in 1891, and the untimely demise of my beloved wife, Mary, not long after.

Fearing that I might fall back on the two vices, too much Beaune and excessive betting on horses, that almost destroyed my being when I first returned from my military duties in 1881, I sought the comfort and advice of my friend Dr. Percy Trevelyan, the well-known alienist, for whom Sherlock Holmes and I had performed a small service. Not only did Trevelyan's council bring me back to my senses, but it prodded me to renew my studies of mental disorders, the subject of my doctoral dissertation in 1878. This led me to our research collaboration resulting in my appointment to the faculty of the University of London Medical School. However, I found it difficult to maintain my own practice while devoting time to Trevelyan's researches. Consequently, I returned to my initial vocation -- full-time family practice while using my psychological skills to augment my ability.

Even so, I could barely keep up with the patient load. Apparently, the glamour of my long as my partnership with Sherlock Holmes drew to my door droves of patients with mysterious illnesses that defied diagnoses by other physicians. It got to the point that I found it necessary to bring in a brilliant rising young physician who agreed to half-wages for the experience, Dr. Verner, as an assistant. However, even the stimulation supplied by my busy practice could not completely lift the gloom that accompanied all of my waking thoughts and even my dreams.

But I digress from writing this narrative which, if I were permitted to publish it, would signal a remarkable advancement in medical science as well as proving of immense interest to the general reader. However, for reasons that will become obvious, this account must forever be buried, along with all of my other private reminiscences, locked safely away in my tin dispatch-box at Cox and Co.

It had been an exceedingly hectic day. The torrents of rain that forced people into close contact with one another exacerbated the incidence of influenza just as the season was reaching its apex. The day found both my partner and I driving willy-nilly throughout London dealing with the sick while my nurse set patients in queue in the waiting room for our sporadic return. Thus, it was quite late in the evening when my assistant returned to his own quarters and I was alone in a silent house with only my buttons for company. After a well-deserved taste of the fruits of my gasogene and Tantalus, I settled in for a deep but troubled sleep to repair my aching shoulder and leg for another busy day.

Or, so I thought. Sometime well after midnight, I was awakened by a loud pounding on the door and my buttons' piping voice shrieking: "Monsieur Djembe's sons are here! Their father is dying of influenza! They say you must come quickly!"

Ordinarily, I would have sent the boy to summon Dr. Verner, my assistant, to handle the case After all, that's what assistants are for. But in this instance, I leaped out of bed, lit a candle, and opened the door with great dispatch. There, in the hallway, I saw the two beautiful round faces of my good friend's sons, their eyes and teeth gleaming white in contrast to their ebony complexions, and terror in their expressions. In perfect English, consistent with their obviously excellent educational accomplishments, they blurted in unison: "Come quickly! Papa is gravely ill! He is dying!"

Instantly, I instructed my buttons to run to the nearest stall and find an all-night cab as I quickly donned my clothes and rain garments and caught up my medical bag and stethoscope. With the boys in tow, I ran down the street to the closest cab stand, where the driver had already prepared his horse and brougham for our instant departure.

As we wended our way through the silent and vacant streets of London, I recalled my great debt to the Haitian drummer, M. Djembe. There is nothing that I wouldn't do to assist this great friend. Someday, when all of the principals have passed out of public prominence, I will be able to describe the means by which he saved the lives of Mr. Holmes and me from a gang of thugs loitering outside of his place of occupation. Let it be sufficient to state that the current chief magistrate would not enjoy it very much if I cast aspersions on the lack of safety of London streets in a busy district in broad daylight. There would also be questions regarding the fact that M. Djembe was very well armed and well-trained in the use of several weapons.

We rode for only a short time to a location that contained the modest villas usually populated by owners of small shops, not of poor itinerant musicians. As the sun began peeping up into the London skyline, I could see candle lights begin twinkling on in the neighboring windows as the businessmen breakfasted before going early to their shops. However, in M. Djembe's window, the bright glistening of multiple gas lights suggested that the occupant was of a higher order of society than the other inhabitants of his street. This further aroused my suspicions, but I held my queries in check so that I could focus on matters at hand, possibly of life or death.

As we departed the brougham, I noted that a huge, grey-bearded black man, in matching black frock coat, vest, and trousers was blocking an open door of the house. He yelled at the boys in French. [I will paraphrase their conversation in English because my faded memory of French grammar has made it impossible for me to accurately reproduce what was said, but the essence follows.]

The man bellowed in a well-trained, deep basso, "Pierre and Leon, stupid boys, where have you been, and who is this stranger with you?"

"He is Papa's friend," they replied in unison," He is an English doctor whom we asked to look in at father. He is the famous Dr. Watson."

The man lowered the timbre of his voice to a menacing grumble and stated grimly, "I, Dr. Laval, a respected Haitian physician, am your father's trusted medical practitioner. Certainly, he would never permit a foreigner to care for him while I am at his side."

The boy on the left, later identified to me as Pierre, earnestly responded, "Father has been gravely ill for three days. You have treated him with your chants and extracts to no avail. We hoped that perhaps English medicine might be more effective against an English disease."

"You may be right," the big man answered in a somewhat modulated tone. "Who can anticipate what strange plagues might accompany the terrible climate of this downcast and rainy country, far from the beautiful sunshine of our native land."

As the huge man stepped aside to let us pass, the boys each took me by the hand and gently escorted me through the open doorway into the room in which M. Djembe reposed. Although the curtain was drawn, I could plainly see signs of distress on my friend's visage. He looked very unlike the energetic musician that I remembered from earlier times, with a clean-shaven face and a gigantic smile of welcome. His face was now covered in stubble and he was shaking with fever and chills. A coverlet was pulled up to his neck as if to ward off the cold.

Assuming that he had contracted the wide-spread influenza, I quickly checked for expected physical signs and symptoms while asking the children to fill in where necessary from their recollections of the previous days.

As I anticipated, my examination revealed that M. Djembe had an elevated temperature, fever and chills, fatigue and malaise, cough, chest discomfort, and myalgia. However, in response to my queries, I ascertained that he lacked several typical signs of influenza, such as headache, sore throat, rhinorrhea, all of which led me to ascertain a different etiology for M. Djembe's malady. Further, the joint presence of shortness of breath and his denial of severe nausea and vomiting prompted me to consider that the causal agent was a respiratory bacterium. But what could it be? Further, what could I do?

I doubted that it was within my power to ameliorate the disease, but perhaps in the hands of an expert, something could be accomplished. I was aware that outstanding bacteriological research was opening new vistas into our understanding of bacterial infections, and research with vaccines was beginning to promise eventual cures. With this in mind, and a last gasp at assisting my client, I instructed the boys to send a commissionaire to deliver an urgent note to my former dresser, and current friend and colleague, and now noted researcher in infectious disease, Dr. Stamford, requesting him to bring around the appropriate equipment and gelatine tubes, so that we could diagnose the cause of my patient's agony.

Stamford soon arrived in full medical regalia. He was now a tall, well filled out man with an air of prosperity in a black frock coat, grey trousers, and matching vest, newly shined boots, and stylish top hat. Several metal disks of distinction adorned his Albert chain. He now had a long, black beard protruding below his pug Irish nose and round, pale face. Following him was a retinue of similarly, but less richly dressed mustachioed helpers, whose several containers revealed, when opened, tubes of culture media, round dishes, slides, and other laboratory paraphernalia There was even a modern high powered microscope.

He set right to work, ordering his three assistants to perform the necessary taking of blood and respiratory samples, preparing cultures and slides for microscopic examination. Then we set to an examination of M. Djembe's body, something that I had just begun after summoning my friend into service. For the most part, M. Djembe appeared thin and malnourished, a typical sign of serious disease. There were no other clinically significant manifestations on his body. However, we noted a very strange set of unexplainable lesions on both hands and arms as if someone had sliced away parts of the skin and allowed them to heal. Was this the result some primitive religious ceremony used by Dr. Laval in an attempt to ameliorate his patient's condition? If so, more effective means were required. However, could even modern English medical practice resolve this malady?

I turned to the two boys who were watching, wide eyed, our every step. "Boys," I said, "Please summon Dr. Laval so that I could find out if he had treated his patient in some manner to produce these injuries."

I could hear them trampling throughout the house piping Dr. Laval's name, but there was no response. "Dr. Laval is no longer here," they cried, "And all of his belongings are gone from his rooms."

I was concerned by this turn of events, but I focused on the matter at hand. I turned to the lads and asked, "Do you know what these sores are caused by?"

"Yes, doctor.," they again responded in unison.

Then, it was Leon's turn to add more information. "These are where papa gets the black skin sores. They are carried by the spirits of the drums that he makes and that he plays. When the sores appear, Dr. Laval cuts them off with a heated knife and puts medicine on the sores."

"What does your doctor do with the skin that he removes?" I queried.

"He puts them in a jar in his medicine case for further use," responded Pierre. "Come, I will show you."

Both Stamford and I followed the boys to a dimly lit chamber smelling of medicinal plants and noxious distillations. In the corner was a glass medicine jar filled with dried, shriveled pieces of human epidermis covered with black spots. We took the jar to Stamford's temporary work room where he very carefully removed one of the pieces with a forceps and instructed one of his young assistants to prepare cultures and slides.

"I will take samples to my laboratory for further examination. Return here at noon tomorrow. I think that I know what to do to ameliorate this situation, but am not willing to speculate until I have performed more procedures," stated my colleague." At that time, your patient may either be dead or on the way to recovery. With this statement, he began to remind me of my late friend and housemate, Mr. Sherlock Holmes. This must be the way of scientists, I thought, and did not even attempt to pry any further

With that, I arranged for a nurse to watch over my client and take care of his children while I returned home for a hearty breakfast and a nap before my rounds the remainder of the day. I could barely wait for noon the following day. The entire time, I turned over in my mind the strange events of the previous night and following dawn. First I concentrated on my client's mysterious lesions. In the back of my mind, trying to come out but blocked by the ravages of age, were the glimmerings of a solution to the mysterious disease. How was a respiratory infection possibly associated with the black lesions that were excised by the now missing

Dr. Laval? Further, where had he gone and why had he left? And was he somehow involved in this situation?

Then there were the accommodations of M. Djembe. How came an itinerant musician to such a well-decorated home? I recalled the generous supply of expensive gas lights and central heating. Further, on reflection, I recalled that my client's room of entry, no doubt a library, was well stocked with books in French and English, with a smattering of Greek and Latin. The walls were well-decorated with tasteful works of art, and there were silver containers scattered on the beautiful wooden tables. He clearly was a very well-educated and cultured man of higher position. He was not just a common musician. Further, he could afford a private doctor on the premises, and his boys were obviously well-educated and cared for.

After a restless night, I was awakened at 7 a.m. by my buttons, who announced that a very large man was waiting to accompany me to my patient's chambers. To my surprise, there was an enormous bulk of a man blocking the morning sun. Through my bleary, half-awake eyes, I recognized that it was Mr. Mycroft Holmes himself awaiting me. I was astonished that the gentleman, so important to affairs of state, should offer to escort me in his official carriage.

Mr. Holmes looked at me with a twinkle in his eyes and said "Good morning Dr. Watson. I see from your expression that you are surprised to see me 'off of my usual tracks,' as brother Sherlock often said. There is fresh coffee, courtesy of Her Majesty's government, to awaken your full mental powers. Sip this wondrous beverage as we discuss the strange events leading to my confronting you this fine day."

As we rumbled through the now busy street of our crowded metropolis, I quizzed Mr. Holmes as to his mission. "How could you be involved in the health of an itinerant drummer and drum maker?" I expostulated in surprise. "How is this an affair of state?"

He replied very evenly, as is typical of a trained diplomat, "It might surprise you to learn that the gentleman you knew as Mr. Djembe is an imposter. Djembe is the type of drum often used by Haitians. He is really an extremely accomplished man, a scholar of note and man of means, who was a member of the recently deposed democratic government of Haiti. Were you wondering how a brougham was at your beck and call in the hours after midnight. We arranged your transportation and suggested that the boys contact you as both an excellent doctor and a man to be trusted with state secrets. My agents who are guarding the villa informed me by telephone, that Dr. Stamford may have good news for you."

I could barely restrain myself as we turned the corner to my patient's villa, the morning sun now revealing a lovely garden and clean, well-kept appearance. I leaped out of the grand four-wheeler, through the door, and into the chamber where I had previously left my client. To my surprise, the man lying in the bed was smiling, shaven, freshly dressed, and apparently on the way to complete recovery. His sleeves were rolled up and Stamford's assistants were carefully plunging a clear, red tinged liquid into his veins. The boys were sitting on the floor at the foot of the bed watching the proceeding with curiosity and brightly smiling faces.

"Stamford," I asked, "What have you done? Have you performed a miracle?"

"No miracle," he replied, "Merely an application of modern medical theory to a real situation. He motioned me to the desk where he was seated, and arose so that I could replace him. "First, look at these cultures and the microscopic slides," he continued. "They are from the patient's throat and blood."

At his request I examined the surface colonies on the culture plate with his powerful hand lens. There I saw the medusa-like images that brought recognition to my mind. Then, I examined the methylene blue stained slides under the high power microscope. The huge rod-shaped formations, lined up as strands of pearls, completed the picture.

"It all falls together now!" I yelled. Black skin lesions from a handler of animal skins coupled with rod-shaped bacilli. Anthrax, it's anthrax! But how in blazes did you effect a cure."

"As you have seen," replied Stamford, as if addressing a lecture hall full of students, "your friend has had numerous encounters with the cutaneous form of this illness without succumbing to its clinical manifestations. They did not develop into a penetrating skin lesion resulting in sepsis. He obviously had developed a degree of immunity by virtue of frequent contact with the microbe."

"How came he to the form that we encountered, obviously a respiratory infection, one not associated with a spread from his dermis?" I asked.

"That has yet to be defined, but I would like to at least clear up the method of therapy that appears to be effective."

"Proceed," I countered.

"Well, you recall the work of Koch, Pasteur, and other scientists who demonstrated that the sera from immunized animals were able to counter this infection. I have been working in my laboratory on this passive immune therapy using sera from immunized rabbits to prevent lethal infections in mice. I thought, why not try this in humans? Thus, I pooled all of the sera from the immunized rabbits, rushed it to our patient, and have been administering it intravenously throughout the night. Fortunately, the therapy has produced no deleterious effects to prevent our continuation overnight."

"What a paper this would make for the *British Medical Journal*!" I exclaimed.

"Unfortunately, I have been instructed by the huge official that I saw with you, the one that the soldiers called "M," that this was a government matter and must forever be kept secret."

With that, Mr. Mycroft Holmes surrounded my left arm in his massive hands and gently pulled me out of the room into the library. I noticed that the many volumes had been relocated to cartons and that the furniture was being removed to a lorry bearing no identification.

He then stated "Dr. Watson, thank you for your service to the British government. As a result of your actions, your client known to you as Mr. Djembe is safe from the current dictatorial regime in his native country. He will be relocated to another locale where, under the protection of Her Majesty's government, he will have an illustrious career as a professor of French literature, under a false name and credentials indicating French birth."

"What of Dr. Laval?" I queried. "Has he been located?"

"Yes indeed," replied Mr. Holmes, "He is also under the protection of Her Majesty's government. However, his accommodations may not be quite as elegant. Posing as a loyal friend to your client for many years, Dr. Laval was a trusted accomplice of the cutthroat regime that has wanted to eliminate any persons affiliated with the democratic government. That, sadly, is the reason that your client's wife is not present. She unfortunately fell prey to these ruthless minions before a rescue could be effected. But," he continued, "we have another quandary. Just how did your friend acquire a respiratory anthrax infection? We were unable to obtain such information from Laval, himself, although we are certain that he is the culprit in this action. As Dr. Stamford indicated, and I overheard, the skin infections could not have proceeded to a respiratory disorder. It appears that the two events are unrelated. Although my experience with agricultural matters informs me that respiratory anthrax has been associated with agricultural workers who shear infected sheep and inhale large quantities of infected airborne filaments. I feel that we cannot rule our human intervention as a possible cause. More detailed investigation is required. This is a task that I would have given my brother, had he been available. I hope that you learned his lessons well and would apply them to this situation, so that we could be forearmed to prevent such happenings in the future."

"I would be most happy to endeavor to solve this conundrum," I countered, and thought to myself, "What would Sherlock do?"

He would likely search the premises to determine if there were any clues that could cast some light on this situation. With this in mind, I sought the assistance of Pierre and Leon to help me search the house. After all, these boys had probably, in their youthful inquisitiveness, explored every nook and cranny therein. Suspecting the mysterious Dr. Laval, I took the children by the hand and followed them to Dr. Laval's well-decorated quarters. Every wall was covered with brightly colored wall-paper showing scenes of tropical splendor and white sandy beaches with beautiful white-sailed ships at dock. There were three rooms: a large room with an immense bed suitable for his immense size, a modest-sized sitting room with a pair of comfortable chairs and an electric lamp and well-stocked book cases, and the laboratory that I had already mentioned. What struck me the most was that nothing private or personal remained. There were no pictures on the wall, no letters or personal papers, or credentials. The apartment had been cleansed of all materials that would shed any light on Dr. Laval's activities for the last few months. There was no doubt in my mind that he had planned his escape very well in advance.

I looked at the boys, and shaking my head, stated: "I don't think that we will ever find anything incriminating in the doctor's rooms."

"To the contrary," responded Pierre, "There is his secret room where he keeps some very unusual objects. We had found them in our explorations about the house."

My mood brightened as I replied: "Well, my little detectives, I am very impressed. Let's take a look at this secret chamber."

With that, both boys took my hands and led me into the bedroom. With effort, they clambered up to the bed that was standing high off the floor. Then, with both using all of their strength in unison, they pulled the massive headboard away from the wall to reveal a door leading to a room whose floor was level to the mattress. They climbed in, retrieved a candle, and beckoned me to light it since they were forbidden to carry matches. After I followed them into the chamber, the light of the taper revealed a space large enough to accommodate the height of a tall man, and approximately two yards in width.

"Be very careful," I warned. "Don't touch anything with your bare hands."

On the far corner of this room was a large leather case that the doctor had probably left in his haste to escape. Alternatively, he might have suspected that he would be apprehended and did not want to have to explain the nature of the bag's contents. I could barely restrain my curiosity, but took great care to request the boys to retrieve my gloves so that I could protect my hands from the potentially deadly contents.

I carried the luggage back to the front room where I deposited it on a sheet on the floor before opening it. Surrounded by Mycroft Holmes, two burly government agents in plain clothes, Stamford, and the now partially recovered Mr. Djembe, I began to sort through its strange assortment of contents. The first thing that caught my eye was a medium sized bellows with a rubber hose attached.

"That is the instrument that Dr. Laval used to treat my father's colds and to prevent pneumonia," piped Leon, who was standing back where he was placed out of range for his protection. Stepping forward, he pointed to a glass ball with a tube at both ends and a hole on top capped with a cork.

"That is where he placed the medicine to treat papa's throat. He did this very often, usually after he removed the black spots on his hands and arm."

I was not surprised, therefore, to also uncover a jar with pieces of black-tinged dried skin, a mortar and pestle, a pair of fine scissors, and a jar labeled 'Glycerin.'

"Eureka!" we expostulated together, "That's how it was done."

"I have no doubt," stated my friend Stamford, "that bacteriological cultures of these implements will grow very large spore-forming bacilli that, when injected in mice, produce the symptoms of anthrax."

"We have him," Mycroft Holmes said in a dignified tone. "He is no doubt a murderer who must answer for his crimes. However, this account will never appear in a court of law. Her Majesty's government has a more fitting punishment for men such as these."

Stamford interjected "What a wonderful article this would make for *Lancet* or the *British Medical Journal* -- an experimental means to produce anthrax for experimental studies in animals."

Showing signs of regret, an emotion rarely seen on his face, Mycroft Holmes stated, "I'm very sorry doctors. This case will now be considered a state secret, and must not be revealed until the 21st century."

Although I was disappointed that I could not publish this adventure in *Strand Magazine*, I was buoyed by the experience and my part in it. My ennui had completely lifted, and I was now able to face the future with verve and a square jaw.

References:
"Notice to Readers: Considerations for Distinguishing Influenza-Like Illness from Inhalation Anthrax in *MMWR*

Weekly, November 9, 2001, 50 (44): 984-6. (Http://www.cdc.gov/mmwr/preview/mmwrhtml/mm5044a 5.htm)"

Schwartz, Morton M. Chap. 33 Aerobic Spore-Forming Bacilli in *Microbiology Fourth Edition,* J. B. Lippincott Company (Philadelphia), 1990, pp 625-631

Chap. 75 Anthrax in *Topley and Wilson's Principles of Bacteriology and Immunity,* Vol. 2, Williams and Wilkins Company (Baltimore), 1961, pp 2079-2094..

Anthrax on African Drums in World Wide Drums, Monday 14 July, 2008. Http://www.wwdrums.com/anthrax-on-african-drums-faq-a-17.html

Dr. Watson's Coal Tar Solution

Being a Reprint of the Reminiscences of John H. Watson, MD,
Professor of Mental Disorders at University of London

Published in the Friends of Dr John H. Watson *Practice Notes*, July. 2010, pages 20-28

Herewith is documented a strange mystery whose description will never see the light of day for several reasons: The identities of the murder victims were never revealed to me, nor were the perpetrators of these actions. Certainly, no mystery tale can be published without these elements. What I have ascertained is the method by which these multiple murders were accomplished, and that is the major subject of this unpublishable account. Perhaps even more relevant is the fact that I have been warned that I would serve many years as a "guest" of the British government, under less than pleasant circumstances, if this story were ever revealed to the public.

Why then do I take the trouble to dip my pen in ink to record these events? Why, because I am a completest. As with other obsessive compulsive individuals, I feel obligated to completely describe all of my activities in my personal reminiscences. Unlike my now deceased colleague Mr. Sherlock Holmes, I am incapable of leaving things undone. In addition, the solution as to the cause of the homicides was, if I may say so, ingenious and a tribute to my skills as a medical detective.

It all began very quietly. It had been a very busy day and I was fatigued. My patient calls were tightly fitted in between my presentations at Bart's, and I didn't sit down to dine until late in the evening. I had just finished a cold supper in my private quarters on the top floor of my medical offices and was enjoying a post prandial snifter of brandy. I sat dozing over the latest issue of the *British Medical Journal* even though the article interested me greatly, since it concerned the utility of prefrontal lobotomy vs. electric shock therapy for severely insane individuals. However, sleep eventually overtook me.

Whilst so engaged, I thought that I dreamt that I heard a low voice gently calling to me in a slightly foreign accent: "Dr. Watson, please wake up. We need your expert services."

After this plea was repeated several times, I opened my eyes, and as I slowly lifted my head I saw before me the figure of a short, well-muscled man in a modern short jacket, dark grey and well-tailored. There was no vest nor adornments except for the obvious outline of a revolver in his right hand pocket and the handle of a large knife protruding from his waist. Looking at his face, I realized that it was a man whom I had not encountered in many years. It was the man that I had come to know as Mr. Melas, the Greek Interpreter.

I looked upon him in amazement and pinched myself to see if this were a real event or part of an alcoholic dream. I was reluctantly convinced that it was indeed true and that he had passed several barriers to my personal suite. I exclaimed: "Mr. Melas, is that really you standing before me! The front and rear doors are locked shut, my buttons is asleep in the room at the entry, and my female servant is just below the front door in her quarters near the kitchen. How could you possibly have gained access to my personal rooms on the upper floor?"

The short but well-built, clean-shaven man smiled and answered: "First of all, Melas is not really my name, but you may refer to me with that appellation if it suits you, since my nation of origin is Greece. Secondly, if you wish to secure your personal lodgings from agents of the British secret service, you must repair the extremely useful footholds in the rear of your building and replace the window locks with more modern devices."

"However," he continued, "Mr. Mycroft Holmes has asked me to summon you to assist Her Majesty's government in a very special secret mission. Please dress quickly and leave by the rear entrance, so that the servants are not aware of your exit. Follow the mews on the left of your garden to the next street, where I will await you with a four wheeler. We cannot be seen together, so I will exit by the means in which I made my entry into your suite and meet you in the cab."

With that, he quickly disappeared out the window, fastening it firmly behind him. I followed his directions, dressing warmly to ward off the cold, and more feeling rather than seeing my way, I followed the snorting of the two horses and I eventually joined Mr. Melas several minutes later in his four-wheeled contrivance.

"Where are we going?" I asked, "and what is my part in this mission?"

"All will be revealed in due course," he replied.

Although I tried to determine the route of our journey, I soon gave up since it was obviously intended that I not be able to trace the location of our destination. We rattled slowly through a dark circuitous route. The driver carefully avoided contact with foot traffic, avoiding the West End, where the crowds swarmed the streets as they left the theaters to find their late night entertainment or hire a cab for their ride home. Also, we did not come within hailing distance of the East Side where gentlemen of the evening crowded the byways seeking female companionship. Briefly, we left London entirely, traveling through the dark night on dirt roads, and then finally re-entered on cobblestone street coming up an unlit drive to a very large building with a carriage entrance.

Once inside, the driver slammed shut the doors and I could make out the sound of a chain being affixed to the door and a bar lowered to guarantee our privacy. Glimpses of my surroundings, partially revealed by the sweep of Mr. Melas's powerful bull's eye lantern, augmented by my sense of smell, revealed a well-equipped barn with stores of straw and feed for the horses, and an elegant hansom next to our vehicle. There were also three elegantly decorated stalls with two more beautiful horses.

Guided by Mr. Melas, I slowly walked along the side wall until we came to an oak door that opened into a cavernous brightly gas-lit room. I immediately noticed that there was a sharp chill in the air and the faint smell of sulfuric acid underlined by that familiar odor of decomposing flesh. I was pervaded with feelings of dread. Was I being led into a horror tale by Edgar Allen Poe? Was I still asleep in the throes of a nightmare or a psychological breakdown?

After all, what did I really know about the motivations of Mr. Melas? Was he really what he claimed to be, an agent of the British government? Perhaps I was an additional victim in the plot of the adventure that I published as "The Greek Interpreter" and Mr. Melas needed to put me out of the way.

I turned to Mr. Melas and quizzically asked, "What have you gotten me into? I don't understand why you summoned me to this dreadful place."

He quietly responded, "All of your queries will soon be answered, and you will then acknowledge that you can provide a great service to the government of Her Majesty."

Then came relief. I saw, coming from the deep recesses of this immense facility, what appeared to be an enormous penguin lumbering in my direction. As he came closer, I realized that it was the massive bulk of Mr. Mycroft Holmes in his usually dark, serious attire. Now, I thought, it will finally be revealed why I was dragged out of my comfortable quarters in the middle of the night to this mysterious location.

Mr. Holmes finally finished his long, slow laborious trek to my side. His attempt at a welcome smile, producing cavernous dimples in his fleshy face, and his cordial hand shake relieved my mind. I thought, "With Mr. Holmes in command, everything will be under control."

He greeted me with, "Good of you to come, Dr. Watson. Thank you very much for your courteous response to our request. It is sad that my brother was unable to join you in this venture since it has certain attributes that would please him very much. I am in hopes that you collaboration has provided you with the skills that this task necessitates "

"I'm always happy to be of service to our country, Mr. Holmes. What is it that you require of me?"

He led me to the center of the room, where I learned the source of the odor of decomposing human flesh. There I encountered five sheet-covered giant blocks of ice serving as tables. Upon each was the figure of a man's nude body, their faces obscured in towels.

To my questioning look, Mr. Holmes supplied the following information: "You are now in a special room in an experimental ice-manufacturing plant in London run by Messrs. Siddeley and Mackay. The sulfurous odor is that of sulfuric ether used to freeze the water running through the pipes. You cannot be told our location. Suffice it to say that for permitting the scientists to run an unregistered secret operation, they have permitted us access to their facility. This room is the rented property of the British government, as is the covered stable, horses, carriages, and all other appurtenances. What transpires herein is a government secret which can never be revealed. Even the owners of this facility have no idea of our activities, and they are well paid to keep it so. What you see before you are the bodies of five of our very special espionage agents. They all died of mysterious circumstance within hours of each other. My job, and that of Mr. Melas and my other agents, is to find out how anyone knew who they were, who killed them, and why."

Turning to Messrs. Holmes and Melas, I stated, "I'm a doctor, not a detective. What is my part in this?"

"Very simply, my good doctor, we need you to determine the cause of death of five men in the service of Her Majesty's government. This is such a secure operation that even the medical examiners of Scotland Yard cannot be involved. We know that you can be trusted to keep this activity a secret. I have had my brother's sworn guarantee of this. You will find a complete set of tools on hand for you to examine the bodies."

"Very well. However, before I begin I will need to advise my associate that I will be unavailable for my medical duties for quite some time," I mentioned with some trepidation. "I fear that I leave some very ill people without medical attention."

"Fear not, doctor," replied Mr. Melas, who now stood beside Mr. Holmes, "My agents have so informed Dr. Verner who will spread the word to your nurse, buttons, and other retinue as needed. Dr. Verner has, by now, called for the services of your research partner, Percy Trevelyan."

Looking at the end of the tables, I noted a beautiful set of surgical appliances. There was even a microscope and a high-powered hand lens. The huge electric lights, the largest that I have ever seen or could conceive of, illuminated the bodies sufficiently for my needs.

"Very well," I stated, "but I will first need to know if there are any descriptions of the symptoms surrounding their demise."

Mr. Holmes replied, "As you would expect, there were few witnesses to the deaths of these men. We quickly secreted them away before there were any physicians in attendance. However, each of the few bystanders stated that the men appeared highly agitated and then complained of pain in their chests. Their hearts seemed to slow to a stop. The insides of their mouths appeared to have been eaten away by some caustic substance. Those are all of the clinical signs that I can relate to you. Oh yes, there is a black stain on their teeth and lips. "

I then performed a perfunctory examination of each body -- a Lascar, a tanned man of obviously middle-eastern heritage, and three long-time native inhabitants of the British Isles with dark body hair. There were no evidences of trauma -- no bullet or knife wounds or marks of a blunt force damage. Also, there was no sign of choking or suffocation. The men appeared to be very strongly built and quite capable of defending themselves. Yet, there were no signs that they had attempted to do so.

I then turned to Mr. Holmes and Mr. Melas, who had returned to his side after a brief mission outside of the room, and told them, "Your clinical description is not much to go on, but in light of the fact that there are no evidences of traumatic causes of death, I would consider poisoning with a caustic agent such as phenol the most likely cause. However, I must ask you to reveal their faces so that I may see their lesions for myself."

After a slight hesitation, as if considering all of the ramifications of my identifying the victims, Mr. Holmes reluctantly nodded his assent.

Sometimes events produce unexpected consequences. Such was the case in this instance. When it was intimated that I could not be trusted to view the visages of the murder victims, I was irked and put off. After all, my former colleague and friend, Mr. Sherlock Holmes, had always trusted me to keep secret the details of his investigations. However, in this case I was grateful. As I peeled the coverings off of the men's faces, I noted a strong odor that reminded me of that foul smelling medicinal used treat disorders of the skin -- *Liquor Carbonis Detergens* or, in English, Coal Tar Solution.

Armed with this knowledge, I prepared to dissect the first body.

I was distressed at the thought of the vastness of the job ahead. Thankfully, Mr. Holmes interrupted my efforts. "Just one minute," he said. "I have provided some assistants to help leaven your efforts. I realize that at this late hour it would be unconscionable of me to expect you to perform this massive effort yourself."

"Hey Nate, it's our, professor Dr. Watson! What is he doing here?" a young male voice cried out.

It was one of one of my young medical students, Anthony Clifford, talking to his fellow student Nathan Abrams. You could have knocked me over with a feather as I saw these young men, resplendent in long white laboratory coats accompanying Mr. Melas in my direction. Mr. Abrams was a very tall red-headed man. Due to his ethnicity and crimson hair, he was often referred to by his classmates as King David. The short, powerful Clifford with blond hair was called the Viking Warrior.

"Let me explain their involvement," stated Mycroft Holmes. "These two gentlemen are attending medical school under a scholarship from Her Majesty's government. We have long felt the need to have our own physicians for events such as this. Show them what needs to be done and they will finish the job while you enjoy a well-deserved rest. Dictate your findings to Mr. Melas, and he will keep very careful notes. He is an excellent secretary."

Thus, as the two assistants witnessed my work. I carefully dissected the first subject while professorially lecturing my students as I often did in the psychology classes that I taught. Looking for the expected substance, I was rewarded for my efforts. Lining the man's intestines was a black, sticky amorphous material that could only have been coal tar. I collected scrapings from the body and reviewed them microscopically and with the hand lens. With the exception of cells one would anticipate finding in the body cavity associated with each of the organs examined, there was no particulate matter. However, all of the samples revealed an amorphous material identical to each sample. The urine also reeked of coal tar. Thus I collected samples from each kidney into the clean glass bottles that were provided.

Anticipating that my new colleagues would obtain the same results, I turned to my audience and stated, "I have no other option than to consider that these deaths were caused by poisoning with a coal tar product. Further, the victims ingested the material willingly, since there is no evidence that would indicate that they were forced to do so. Thus, in whatever form it took, what they ingested was devoid of the malodorous properties of coal tar."

Mr. Holmes asked, "How could that be? Are you aware of an odor-free preparation?"

"I am not," I replied, "but I think I know where I might get some answer to that question. I must visit W. V. Wright and Company, a leading manufacturer of coal tar solution and soap. I'm certain that they would attempt to produce a more tolerable product to gain an advantage over their competition. They are located on Southwark Street, S.E, removed from 11 Old Fish Street. They would not be open at this late hour, but I could visit them in the morning with, if you agree, my samples. As a practicing physician who occasionally uses products such as theirs, they might be willing to accommodate me."

Mr. Melas looked askance at this suggestion, but Mr. Holmes said, "Splendid, I will send Mr. Melas with you to protect the materials. We will make a cab available in the morning for any of your needs as you continue this activity. Now, I suggest that you rest for the evening. The grateful government can provide you with a refreshing bath, some snacks, and a liquid refreshment from Her Majesty's own cellars. After a well-deserved good night's sleep and a hearty breakfast, you will hopefully be able to complete your mission. Don't worry about completing the work and cleaning up; your students and other assistants will take good care of the materials. They will complete the physical aspects of your efforts, pack your samples in ice to preserve their integrity, and wipe down all of the surfaces and the equipment."

"Mr. Holmes, thank you for your kind hospitality. I'm certain that I will sleep very well tonight provided that I can calm myself after this adventurous activity. However, I have one additional request. Did anyone scour the victims' abodes to see if there were any clues providing a common thread?" I asked.

"Yes," retorted Mr. Melas. "Each had a supply of six bottles of stout, and each had two partially consumed bottles. There were no other points in common."

"Excellent, now we may be getting somewhere. Please bring all of the bottles with you on our visit to W. V. Wright's establishment."

The stresses of the preceding night must have had a great effect on my physical and mental resources. It was late in the following morning that I awakened in a very comfortable bed in a well-decorated room with the latest wall paper festooned with large red roses. I noted that viewed through the top of the window, the sun was well up in the sky. All of my needs were nicely taken care of by the toilet articles arrayed on a lovely bow-legged oak end table: a bowl of hot water, a fresh bar of soap and a towel, a fresh change of well-fitting clothes, a shaving mug and shaving soap, a new razor, a hair brush, toothbrush, and bottles of nice smelling hair tonic and shaving lotion.

After my morning ablutions, attracted by the odor of freshly grilled bacon, I joined Mr. Melas at a table laden with a full English breakfast replete with eggs, toast, butter, bitter orange marmalade, kippers, beans, and a huge pot of excellent American coffee. While enjoying our repast, Mr. Melas and I excitedly reviewed his notes of the previous evening's activities.

As I expected, all of the subjects had the same amorphous black material in their organs and the same odor in their urine. I smoked a pipeful of Ships and Mr. Melas enjoyed a Turkish blend as we continued to discuss the data, accompanied by many cups of coffee. Surfeited with this splendid repast, I finally roused from my languor and was ready to face the day's activities.

Mr. Melas regarded me and stated, "I see that you are ready to continue our investigations, Dr. Watson. I have a cab at our disposal containing all of the samples that we collected last night as well as the purported bottles of stout that we obtained from the victim's residences. As to the notes, they are the property of the government, and I must retain them for the Crown as well as the bits of evidence. Since it is during the day, it would not be inappropriate for us to be seen together. However, until we arrive in Central London, I will need to shutter the windows of the cab to keep last night's location from you."

"Very well," I replied. "I suggest that we first go to the offices of W. V. Wright and Company as they are experts in coal tar. Maybe they can shed some light on the existence of odor-free and tasteless coal tar."

Try as I might to define our path from the feel of the road and the smells and sounds of the surroundings, I was unable to perceive the direction of our journey. Apparently, the efforts of the preceding evening extending into the early morning hours had taxed my resources to the point that my last memories of our trip were the continuous beats of the horses' hooves and the gentle swaying of the well-sprung coach.

My next awareness was that of the voice of Mr. Melas stating that we had arrived at the manufacturing facility of W. V. Wright and Company. He turned to me and stated he had announced my arrival and that we were being awaited in the quality control laboratory of the large manufacturing facility. As we negotiated a long labyrinth of hallways, we finally emerged in a well-equipped chemical laboratory that was at least the equal of the one at Bart's itself. There were several young men in long white laboratory coats laboring over retorts, beakers, balances, and test tubes, as they ascertained the purity and quality of their products.

We were approached by a tall middle-aged man in a well-tailored vested suit of the latest cut, bearing on his thick gold chain the emblems of several prestigious scientific societies. His long face was decorated with a well-cut Van Dyke beard. His whole attitude was that of command, a man clearly at the peak of his profession. He approached me with a well-manicured extended white hand and, in a classical German accent, said: "Welcome to our laboratories, Dr. Watson. Let me introduce myself. I am Dr. Martin Von Helsing, director of Research, Development, and Quality Control for this corporation. Perhaps you recall my cousin, the King of Bohemia. I am pleased at last to make your acquaintance and to thank you for your efforts on his behalf, although I do not always support his style of life. I have been following your exploits in *The Strand* as well as in German language publications for several years, and regret that you have lost your good friend Mr. Sherlock Holmes. You have my sympathies. Now, as to your needs. I understand that you would like us to analyze some materials for you. Several samples have been provided by Mr. Melas and his colleagues for our attention, which we are happy to evaluate at no cost to you. In addition, we will deliver a *gratis* supply our product for our use and recommendation. I will now turn you over to our director of quality control who will personally provide laboratory analyses. He is just arriving." At this, gave he us a courteous bow, stiffly turned, and left.

We were then approached by a sandy-haired man of medium height in his mid-thirties. Unlike his superior, he was more modestly garbed, and a long white laboratory coat obfuscated his attire except for his white shirt and Oxford neck tie. He came in my direction with an effusive smile on his well-shaven reddish freckled face and gave me a firm handshake saying, "I am pleased to meet you. My name is Mr. John Smith. I, too, am a fan of your stories, although I am not certain as to their entire veracity. However, that is neither here nor there, since I enjoy them very much and also miss their absence. I have looked at all of the biologically-derived samples and they appear visually to bear a strong resemblance to coal tar."

He continued, "I can make a presumptive diagnosis of coal tar poisoning."

As he worked with his equipment, he provided an ongoing commentary: "I will mix one milliliter of urine with one-tenth milliliter of 20% ferric chloride. See the purple color? This is indicative of phenol, a major component of coal tar. Let me try one more sample of urine. Yes, there it is, the same purple color. See the reference sample of phenol and note that it provides the same reaction. In my opinion, the chemical tests and the tarry odor can point to no other conclusion. There is coal tar in the urine. Now let us turn our attention to the black material on the swabs. I will select two. I now take up the material in alcohol and test them in a similar fashion. Note again the purple color. Now, let us test the bottles of stout that you suspect."

He carefully opened one at an arm's length from his nose, apparently to avoid inhaling any toxic fumes. He then poured some of the contents in a flask and added the 20% ferric chloride with a very deep purple color resulting.

."I cannot understand why there is no odor of coal tar emanating from the bottle. The concentration of phenol is obviously very high. If you like, I can perform a quantitative analysis. Further, I can run the rest of the samples, but in all likelihood, they would test the same. There is another test that we need to run to confirm our observations."

With that, he picked up from the floor and placed on the laboratory bench a small square cage containing two squealing white mice and opened it. Holding one mouse in his hand, the experienced scientist took up about 2 milliliters of the purported stout in a Pasteur pipette and administered it *per os*. The animal convulsively thrashed in his hands. Mr. Smith tenderly put his two middle fingers on the mouse's thorax and stated, "The poor fellow's heart is beating very slowly and will stop soon. Dr. Watson, would you like to confirm this observation?"

As he held the mouse out to me in a supine position, I felt for a heartbeat and found it highly diminished.

Holding out the second mouse, he invited me to feel the heart. To my touch, its heart was beating furiously in its chest. Then, after Mr. Smith administered contents from another sample of stout, I felt the thrashing and the heart slowing in its chest with my practiced hands.

"I believe that we have confirmed the diagnosis, Dr. Watson. Would you like further testing?" queried the scientist.

Stepping forward, Mr. Melas replied, "Thank you very, Mr. Smith. You have been of great service. If you every need a recommendation, please contact me. I cannot provide you with my address or position, and my name is not officially recorded as such. However, a note directed to me at the Diogenes Club will reach me. We will now relieve you of all of the samples, the test material, and the deceased mice for further analysis now that we know we are on the right track. One question, though."

"Please ask it and I will attempt to provide an answer."

Continued Mr. Melas, "Are you aware of an odorless and tasteless preparation of coal tar?

"No," replied Mr. Smith. "We have been attempting to diminish the odor of our product to gain better patient acceptance without any success. You may want to communicate further queries to the source of our coal tar, The Gas Light and Coke Company. Their works are located on East Ham Levels to the East of London. The chairman is the well-known Samuel Adams Beck. As you no doubt are aware, coal tar is derived during the manufacture of coal gas."

Our retinue left the laboratory and wended our way back to the cab. While we awaited the arrival of Mr. Melas' helpers bringing forth the packed materials, I asked Mr. Melas, "Should we now proceed to the Gas Light and Coke Company?"

"No, Dr. Watson," he answered, "We have taken up enough of your time and energy on this project. We will contact Mr. Beck from higher levels of our government. After all, they owe their existence to Her Majesty for permitting them to operate such a large all-pervading and profitable enterprise. Perhaps they will understand that their government would like to provide an odor-free medicinal to our brave soldiers."

With that, we continued our journey to my home and office, while chatting about Mr. Melas' presumed hometown on the Aegean Sea. During our drive, I learned that my two excellent students would be transferred to another government operation where they could continue their medical education at another institution without fear of running into me. On the way, we made a mysterious stop at the French Embassy. Mycroft Holmes was outside and he greeted me effusively. Before we left, two armed guards under his supervision transported the materials therein. As we left, I overhead one of the guards call out to the other over the sounds of the street, "Did he say to deliver the stuff to a Mr. Sigerson in Montpelier?"

So I returned home to the hubbub of my busy life, refreshed in the knowledge that I had provided an important service to Her Majesty's government, received a very fine new suit of clothes, and an expectation of receiving a generous supply of *Liquor Carbonis Detergens*. I never did find out if odor-free coal had ever been developed.

.

(Note added later: It was not until several years later, at the return of Sherlock Holmes, that the significance of this conversation registered in my mind. Sherlock Holmes and I never discussed the nature of his researches with coal tar, but I am certain that I know.)

References:

Doyle, A. C. "The Greek Interpreter" In: *The Complete Sherlock Holmes* by Arthur Conan Doyle, with a preface by Christopher Morley, Doubleday and Company, Garden City, New York, single volume, 1988, p435-446.

ARTIFICIAL   ICE
http://www.usgennet.org/usa/ny/county/allegany/Ice%20Ha rvesting%20&%20History/5Artificial%20Ice.htm

Coal-tar Poisoning: Introduction in *The Merck Veterinary Manual*,
http://www.merckvetmanual.com/mvm/index.jsp?cfile=htm /bc/210600.htm

Coal Tar (Crude) Misc.: AHFS Detailed Monograph
http://www.medscape.com/druginfo/monograph?cid=med& drugid=5045&drugname=Coal+Tar+(Crude)+Misc&monot ype=monograph&print=1

Liquor Carbonis Detergens in *Medical Times Gazette Advertiser*, August, 31, 1867, page 248.

Dr. Watson's Adventure of the Deadly Medusa, *Being a Reprint of the Reminiscences of John H. Watson, MD, Professor of Mental Disorders at University of London, Friends of Dr John H. Watson Practice Notes*, Dec. 2008, pages 17-23.

Gas Light and Coke Company in Wikipedia, the free encyclopedia.
http://en.wikepedia.org/wiki/Gas_Light_andCoke_Compan y

Examining the Chronology of The Adventure of Wisteria Lodge

Based on a presentation at the 20th fall gathering of the Pleasant Places of Florida, Saturday, November 18, 1995, Ybor City Brewery, Tampa Florida

No opening statement has puzzled the Sherlockian world more than the first lines of "The Adventure of Wisteria Lodge." In Dr. Watson's own words, we read: "I find it recorded in my notebook that it was a bleak and windy day towards the end of *March in the year 1892* (my emphasis)."(1) How can this possibly be? It is utterly preposterous! Everyone in the civilized world knows full well that this is right smack in the middle of THE GREAT HIATUS! It is virtually holy writ that Mr. Sherlock Holmes disappeared towards the end of the Spring of the year 1891 and was thought to be dead, due to an encounter with Professor Moriarty at the falls of Reichenbach, and did not resurface until the beginning of April 1894. (2,3) To believe otherwise would be considered heresy.

Apparently, I am not alone in this belief. I regard "The Oxford Sherlock Holmes" as representing the very highest level of pure Doylean scholarship, not easily lured into the "make believe" world that so entrances Sherlockians and Holmesians. Yet, this dating was so outrageous that even the chief editor of this otherwise staid and conservative series of books was impelled to change the date in the narrative itself to 1895, with the following explanatory note: "1895: erroneously '1892' in all texts." (4) Holmes's disappearance after Professor Moriarty's death is given in the appropriate stories ('The Final Problem' (Memoirs), 'The Empty House' (Return) as from Apr. 1891 to Apr. 1894)."

Many other highly regarded researchers have struggled to determine the chronology of this adventure. As shown in the appended table, there is a vast difference of opinion amongst these scholars.(5) With the exception of my recent observations, which I will further develop in later sections of this treatise, dates for this narrative have ranged from March 1890 through 1902. An examination of all of these would be beyond the scope of this writing, and would be essentially irrelevant anyway, as we shall see. However, it may be instructive to understand the types of arguments that have been utilized by earlier chronologists.

For example, "The Oxford Sherlock Holmes" contends that its date of 1895 is appropriate based on one fact, and one fact alone.(4) In the account of "The Norwood Builder," which took place several months after Sherlock Holmes' return, mention was made of "The case of the papers of ex-president Murillo" and one of the main actors in the drama under current discussion is, coincidentally, a deposed Latin American despot known a Don Murillo, the Tiger of San Pedro. This hypothesis must be regarded as very tenuous indeed. There is no real evidence that ex-president Murillo is identical to Don Murillo, the Tiger of San Pedro. In fact, the excellent analysis of Latin American Rulers, presented very recently by David McCallister, demonstrated that no such ruler as Don Murillo ever existed in Latin America, and no actual rulers who could possibly have fit his description were deposed or fled in the appropriate time frame.(6)

Another eminent scholar, William S. Baring-Gould, claimed a date of Monday, March 24, to Saturday, March 29, 1890 for this adventure. (7) He used weather reports as the main source of evidence to justify his contentions. A careful review of weather reports searching for a year, before the disappearance of Sherlock Holmes, in which in the year 1890 there was a "bleak and windy day towards the end of March." That seems to be as reasonable a hypothesis as any. However, if Dr. Watson was mistaken about the date, what assurance do we have that he was not in error regarding the month or weather or anything else? No, that will not do!

Finally, T. S. Blakeney based his broad dating of this adventure, either in 1896 or between 1898-1902, on several seemingly legitimate arguments: (1) It must be later than 1890 since mention is made of "The Red-Headed League" (he confidently placed that tale on Saturday, October 11, 1890), (2) it could not be 1895 because there were already to many cases to fit it in, (3) it could not have been between 1891 and 1894 due to the absence of Sherlock Holmes during the Hiatus), and (4) it could not be 1897 due to the fact that in March of that year, Sherlock Holmes was sick in Cornwall. (8) However, Baring-Gould contends "The Red-Headed League" took place in 1887, which would support an earlier date such as the one that I will suggest below.(5)

Lacking agreement among all of the many astute chronologists to provide us with a consistent argument for dating "The Adventure of Wisteria Lodge," we must strike out on our own to find the true answer to this very important puzzle. Let us begin with questioning Dr. Watson's opening statement, which is clear as a bell. What are we to believe? There are several possible options to explore. Was the Great Hiatus itself only a mere subterfuge that Dr. Watson finally set straight when he reported "The Adventure of Wisteria Lodge" in 1908? Or, did Dr. Watson merely make a mistake in the date when he wrote this story, as" was claimed by Michael Hardwick? (9) Or, was he lying about the actual date of this adventure to hide something else that went on at the time? Or, finally, did Sir Arthur Conan Doyle screw up when he arranged for publication this account. (4) As a scientist, I am not qualified to seek such answers by attempting to define Dr. Watson's motivations, and must instead freshly, and with an open mind, and strict compliance with the "scientific method" review the evidence in the narrative itself. Only a careful reading of the adventure, with a fresh mind wiped clean of all prior perceptions will allow the answer to percolate through.

After reading and rereading the narrative, avoiding all reference to annotations, I was struck by an obvious clue to the solution of this mystery. Dr. Watson had used the word grotesque on five separate occasions in the introduction of the narrative. For someone with his literary depth and extensive vocabulary, Dr. Watson must have had a very good reason for repeating this one word so many times. On Page 869-70 in the "Doubleday" edition, appear the following statements:

1. "I suppose, Watson, that I must look upon you as a man of letters," said he. "How do you define the word grotesque?"
2. "If you cast your mind back.......you will recognize how often the grotesque has deepened into the criminal."
3. "That was grotesque enough in the outset...."
4. "Or again, there was that most grotesque affair of the five orange pips...."
5. "Have just had most grotesque experience. May I consult you?"
                    "Scott Eccles,
                    "Post Office, Charing Cross."

The word grotesque is repeated two more times at the summation of the narrative, and in the very same sentence, so that we are reminded of the five-fold replication at the opening of the story. On Page 887-888 in the "Doubleday" edition we read: "It is grotesque, Watson," Holmes added, as he slowly fastened his notebook, "but, as I have had occasion to remark, there is but one step from the grotesque to the horrible."

Can anyone believe that Dr. Watson did not intend for us to understand that there was something very significant about his use of the same word over and over in this story? No, he is telling us something. It is up to us to squeeze out its meaning.

Another point of evidence is the issue that Dr. Watson makes of time in this case. By subterfuge, Mr. Scott Eccles is made to believe that he was awakened at one a.m. to supply an alibi for the activities of Mr. Garcia. Clearly, the use of this device calls out to us, urging us to explore the temporal anomalies found in this chronicle.

Thus, a hypothesis emerges. The date of this account is hidden from view, and must be deduced from the data provided for us in this story. After all, the given date of this case is not very likely. And, just in case we missed that not so subtle hint, another point is made regarding the illusory nature of time. Now, having decided that the year must be deduced from the other clues, let us turn our attention to the word grotesque, which, as I indicated, occurs five times at the beginning of the story. What event of a grotesque nature occurred five times during the late 19th century? The activities of Jack the Ripper, the best known serial killer of his age, spring to mind. The year was 1888, and five prostitutes were killed in a most grotesque manner, and their bodies were then mutilated in a most grotesque way.(10) Thus, it seems to me that 1888 must be the year that the events described in The Adventure of Wisteria Lodge actually took place. Whether there is any relationship between this case and the Jack the Ripper slayings is a unknown at this time, and remains a matter for further investigation. However, I do believe that they did take place during the same time period.

SUMMATION:
1. In the most puzzling sentence in Sherlockian literature: Dr. Watson clearly wrote: "I find it recorded in my notebook that it was a bleak and windy day towards the end of March in the year 1892."
2. During that time, Mr. Sherlock Holmes, thought to have perished in the Reichenbach Falls, was traveling the world,

as Sigerson, during the three-year hiatus from April 1891 through April 1894.

3. Much importance is given to the difference between the time that Mr. Scott Eccles went to bed and the time that he was convinced that he went to bed. This is a major but subtle clue regarding the importance of the timing of this adventure to the author. It is up to us to squeeze out its meaning.

4. The word grotesque is used five times at the very beginning of the narrative. Grotesque is reiterated twice in the conclusion to remind us of its central importance in dating this adventure.

5. The most grotesque series of events involving the number five in the nineteenth century were the serial murders perpetrated by the killer known as "Jack the Ripper."

6. These slayings all occurred in 1888.

7. Thus, through the use sound deductive reasoning and the application of the scientific method, we must support the hypothesis that The Adventure of Wisteria Lodge had to have taken place in 1888.

References:

(1) Doyle, A. C. "The Adventure of Wisteria Lodge" in The Complete Sherlock Holmes, Dorset Press, Garden City, New York, 1988, pp 869-88.

(2) Ibid. "The Final Problem," pp 469-80.

(3) Ibid. "The Adventure of the Empty House," pp 483-96.

(4) Doyle, A. C. His Last Bow in The Oxford Sherlock Holmes, Edited by Edwards, O.D., Oxford University Press, New York, 1993, p 174.

(5) Weller, W. Elementary Holmes, Sherlock Publications, Hampshire, 1994, pp 56-73.

(6) McCallister, D. R. The Face of the Tiger A Rogue's Gallery of Latin American Rulers, Presented at the 20th Gathering of the Pleasant Places of Florida, Tampa, Florida, November 18, 1995.

(7) Doyle, A. C. "The Adventure of Wisteria Lodge" In The Annotated Sherlock Holmes edited by Baring-Gould, W. S. Volume II, Clarkson S. Potter, New York, 1967, p238.
(8) Blakeney, T. S. Sherlock Holmes: Fact or Fiction? Otto Penzler Books, New York, 1993, pp 100-1.
(9) Hardwick, M. The Complete Guide to Sherlock Holmes. St. Martin's Press, New York, 1986, p 156.
(10) Redmond, C. A Sherlock Holmes Handbook. Simon & Pierre, Toronto, Canada, p 142.

EXAMINING THE CHRONOLOGY OF THE ADVENTURE OF WISTERIA LODGEM

Chronologist	Date
John H. Watson	End of March, 1892
William S. Baring-Gould	Monday, March 24, 1890
H. W. Bell	Late March, 1895
T. S. Blakeney	1896 or 1898-1902
Gavin Brend	March, 1894
Jay Finley Christ	Monday, March 21, 1892
D. Martin Dakin	Late March, 1894
Henry T. Folsom	Late March, 1890
John Hall	End of March, 1895
Ernest B. Zeisler	Monday, March 24, 1902
"Oxford Sherlock Holmes"	1892
Carl L. Heifetz	1888

Good Luck Irene

Prepared for
SHERLOCK'S SUNSHINE STATE BIRTHDAY
CELEBRATION V OF THE PLEASANT PLACES OF
FLORIDA
(January 19, 2002; Jessie's Seafood House; Dunedin,
Florida)

(Pronounced I-REEN and sung to the tune of "Good Night,
Irene)

Good luck I-ree-ee-een,
You thought you would be queen,
But the king's dalliance,
was not true romance,
and he wanted you out of the scene.

Good luck I-ree-ee-een,
Your photo can't be seen.
You on the king's lap,
Would cause such a flap,
And threaten the Bohemian regime.

Good luck I-ree-ee-een,
Your ex lover king got real mean.
He hired a louse,
To ransack your house,
But your picture remained unseen.

Good luck I-ree-ee-een,
Ormstien hired a detective most lean,
For 300 in gold
And 700 pounds rolled,
He thought the case quite keen.

Good luck I-ree-ee-een,
Your wedding was not
quite serene.
Sherlock, on the contrary,
Disguised as an equerry,
Solved a problem that was
not foreseen.

Good luck I-ree-ee-een,
With Sherlock Holmes on
the scene.
Disguised as a minister,
With plans quite sinister,
The photo's location did glean.

Good luck I-ree-ee-een,
With your intelligence most keen,
You thwarted the plot,
And abandoned the spot.
And left a solo print at the scene.

Unexpected Guests At The
Sunshine State Sherlockian Scion Symposium I
Or Guess Who's Coming to Dinner

Published via Hounds of the Internet E-Mail May 9, 1996; *The Formidable Scrap-Book of Baker Street*, 1997, Classic Specialities Books, Cincinnati; and *The Accursed Jezail Bullet*, the official publication of The Salon Pistols of Gainesville Florida (Issue 4, January, 1997).

The day was progressing as usual. My postprandial pipe was drawing freely, having been properly filled with Ships tobacco and well tamped. My customary overstuffed chair in the British veterans' home was soft and cosy. Facing the western picture window with its beautiful view of the surrounding park, I was whiling away my much too free time by reminiscing about past adventures, reviewing yet again the contents of the tin dispatch case sitting open upon my lap. The late April day was warm and bright. My eyes had grown tired. I had just completed my perusal of the latest issues of *Lancet*, the *British Medical Journal*, and other medical journals, as attested to by the jumble of soft-cover publications laying in a pile at my feet. Bleary eyed from my reading and feeling the drowsiness that follows a large mid-day meal, I drifted off into the afternoon slumber that has been my habit for many years.

I was awakened several hours later by the faint perception of aged feet shuffling slowly towards my station. Who the devil could it be bothering me during my nap time? I was about to express my outraged indignation for this egregious assault upon my routine when I realized that I had heard that familiar sound many times before. As I slowly and painfully opened my eyes towards the now bright sun streaming in through the window, I barely saw framed in the haze what appeared to be the figure of a Nonconformist clergyman.

He finally spoke: "Watson, old friend, aren't you even going to offer me some wine or a cigar?"

"Holmes! Is it you?" I queried, with great surprise, since it was not his normal day to visit. "What brings you here all the way from Surrey on a day on which you normally stay at home?"

"Get packed," he replied. "The game's afoot. We are going to visit the Pleasant Places of Florida."

"Holmes, now I know that it really is you." I countered. "You know that my allergies prevent me from leaving the confines of my air-conditioned domicile, and my chronic arthritis keeps me bound to this chair."

"My dear Watson," said Holmes, seating himself in the adjoining chair and lighting his ever present briar, "Do not worry. In Florida, the flora that exacerbate your chronic respiratory difficulties will be absent from the air and the nice, warm climate of a beautiful day in May in the Sunshine State will do wonders for your rheumatic condition. Besides, I would not think of returning to the location of one of my very early cases, one which has never been documented by your pen, without my good friend and companion at my side."

"But Holmes, why now? You have not been to Florida in many years. What is the special occasion?"

"Watson, as you know, I have a secretary who works at the bank located at 221 Baker Street, in London. He receives and forwards many letters to me every day. Many weeks ago he sent me a very intriguing communication from a group calling itself the "Pleasant Places of Florida." They are inviting both of us to a very special event. I hesitated a long time, but I could not resist the urge to attend."

"But Holmes, it must be an extremely important occasion that strikes your fancy so. In your later years, you have become as set in your ways as your elder brother Mycroft."

"Watson, this event is the Sunshine State Sherlockian Symposium I. It is in the Florida Suncoast, not far from the location of the adventure to which I alluded earlier. Whilst enjoying the company of our admirers, we can also journey to the beach community that now bears my surname."

"That sounds very interesting. However, why are you dressed as a Nonconformist clergyman?"

"I am traveling incognito, Watson. I do not want to get tired out by reciting the events of past cases, and be forced to fend off demands for narratives regarding unpublished adventures for which the world is still not ready."

"But Holmes, I have read in the *Communication* that they already have a Nonconformist clergyman. If you go in that guise, everyone will mistake you for Ben Wood."

"What is wrong with that? It might be fun to play that role until he arrives. Let them try to figure out who the real Ben Wood is."

"No, Holmes that will not be appropriate. I know Ben Wood. Ben Wood is a friend of mine. And Holmes, you are no Ben Wood. You will need another disguise."

"All right Watson, how about this: I will go as Bob Burr."

"But Holmes, won't everyone recognize that you are not Bob Burr? He is a very famous follower of yours. He publishes one of the best known periodicals that extols your name: *Plugs and Dottles*."

"That is not possible, friend Watson. No one outside of Peoria, Illinois has ever seen him. He never goes anywhere. That will be the perfect disguise."

"What should I go as, Holmes?"

"Go as Nigel Bruce. No one seeing you looking like that would ever think that you are the real Dr. Watson. Now let us review again the details that I see in the communiqué before me."

Sherlock Holmes withdrew a small note written in a neat, even hand, on very expensive lime green paper, bearing the watermark "PP of F" in the upper left hand corner. He unfolded it lovingly with great care and spread it out on his lap for us both to read the contents, which are duplicated below:

25 September 1996
Palm Harbor, Florida

Dear Mr. Holmes,

The Pleasant Places of Florida wishes to invite you and Dr. Watson to join us for a fun filled weekend in which we will honor your name and that of our esteemed leader Dr. Benton Wood, BSI. This weekend event, Sunshine State Sherlockian Symposium I, will take place in the elegant Dolphin Resort in St. Pete Beach, Florida, 2-4 May, 1997. Further information will be forthcoming. For further details, please apply to:

Carl L. Heifetz
"Representative both with the Servants and with the tradespeople"
Pleasant Places of Florida Scion of the Baker Street Irregulars

"Watson," Holmes concluded as he rose to leave, "I will notify you further of the plans that I have made for this journey. I will send you a telegram or an E-mail message when all arrangements have been made. This sounds like it will be a splendid weekend."

"Yes, Holmes, I am very much looking forward to it. I think that Sherlockians all over the world should experience both this event and, as you would put it, the charming climate of Florida."

In Defense of the Greek Interpreter

Posted on The Hounds of the Internet

My dear fellow Hounds,

I have been following, with a great deal of interest, the discussion regarding the inconsistencies in "The Greek Interpreter."

First of all, you must understand that this is an entirely concocted tale designed to hide the true facts surrounding the secret espionage activities of Mr. Sherlock Holmes and his mysterious brother Mycroft. Although I have many secret materials at my disposal, I am unable to reveal them since they were entrusted to me by a descendant of the good Dr. Watson. As a gentleman, I must guard them very carefully lest they fall into evil hands. Thus, I must be content to limit my discussion to those materials that are generally known to the world due to the courtesy of Sir Arthur Conan Doyle, MD, noted author and literary agent, and the biographer of this series of reports that we now revere as the Canon, John H. Watson, MD.

Let us first turn our attention to the chain of events that led to the surfacing of this fictional story. Several months after the events in question, there appeared an item in a newspaper in Buda-Pesth concerning "how two Englishmen who had been traveling with a woman had met with a tragic end. They had been stabbed, it seems, and the Hungarian police were of opinion that they had quarreled and had inflicted mortal injuries upon each other. Although seemingly unrelated to any activities in Great Britain, those in the diplomatic and espionage inner circles began to compare notes and to put two and two together. The party out of power, seeing an opportunity to expose secret illegal government machinations on foreign soil, threatened an investigation into possible assassinations by government agencies. People were beginning to find secret memoranda. Leaks to the press were revealed. A Mr. Milverton was threatening to blackmail the Prime Minister himself. Several Greek names appeared to be associated with the case, including a Mr. Melas and a Mr. Kratides. Mr. Mycroft Holmes, later known merely as "M," was perplexed. People must not find out the true identity of Mr. Melas, and his association with the British secret service as a valuable counter spy. Thus, a story was cooked up between the brothers Holmes, and the biographer was persuaded to issue, five years after the fact, the adventure that we have been discussing this week. The story needed to be consistent with the few facts that were known to those outside of the inner circle, on one hand, and interesting enough to be published, widely read, and believed, on the other.

Now let us investigate several pieces of information to help support these contentions. In the first place, there are several aspects of the story that do not make sense. If Mr. Melas was as much of a coward as depicted in the carriage scene, when he was first taken away to perform as an interpreter for the villains, how did he have the courage to hoodwink the dangerous criminals with his secret conversation with Mr. Kratides (not his real name of course), that very same evening? Further, why did Mycroft Holmes, a highly intelligent man, later set it up so that these criminals (really traitors to the Crown for a nation whose identity cannot be revealed) would feel obligated to kidnap and attempt to assassinate Mr. Melas, and why indeed did he allow himself to be a sitting duck? Why, because he wanted to get back into the house, spy on these traitors, attempt to free his compatriot Mr. Kratides, and get the goods on the scoundrels. Since Mr. Melas did not know where he had been taken previously, this was his only recourse to divine the location of the enemies' hideout and secret headquarters. It was unfortunate for Mr. Melas and more unfortunate for Mr. Kratides that the brothers Holmes arrived too late to follow his carriage, as had been the original intention. Since the traitors had made good their escape, the only way that they could be eliminated and the secrets that they carried with them retrieved was for the female agent, another Greek-born British patriot, to accompany them on their escape, and assist in their demise. Doesn't this true account make more sense than the fictional account that Dr. Watson was required, against his will but as a true patriot, to concoct to protect Her Majesty the Queen and Her loyal government?

Several other pieces of publicly available evidence support my claim that Mr. Sherlock Holmes was truly a secret agent for the British government for many years. These have been presented by several investigators, even those without the true facts at hand. For a summation, I invite you to read my account titled "Sherlock Holmes, Master of Espionage" that appeared on pages 21-8 in *The Whitechapel Gazette*, issue No. 4, Mid-1994. A review of publication dates reveals that "The Greek Interpreter" was the first in a series of accounts (published in September 1893) involving Mr. Sherlock Holmes as an agent of the British government. To further obfuscate the record, and to show that Mr. Holmes' involvement with the government was merely in his capacity as a detective, "The Naval Treaty" was published the very next month. It was not until December, 1904, when, in "The Adventure of the Empty House," it was obliquely admitted that Mr. Holmes had performed some diplomatic services for his government. Can there be any question that these were also really espionage missions? It even brings into question the identity of Prof. Moriarty and the true reason for his being killed. Was he really a criminal gang leader, or was he a foreign agent lured to his assassination by Mr. Sherlock Holmes, a baritsu-trained hit man? My lips are sealed on this subject, and it is not relevant to the discussion at hand. Then, as leaked reports concerning Mr. Holmes spy activities began to surface again in 1908, "The Adventure of the Bruce-Partington Plans" was published to again to confuse the perceptions of the enemies of the British state regarding Mr. Holmes' connection with the British secret service and his contact "M." Finally, the true story was revealed in 1917 with the publication of "His Last Bow." By that time, Mr. Sherlock Holmes and Mr. Mycroft Holmes had no further involvement with the espionage system, and there was no longer any need to hide their long term dangerous association with their government. Younger men and women had now picked up the gauntlet, and the old order could now retire to contemplate, in secret, the many services that they had rendered to protect their island from nefarious foes, and to keep bees.

So let us raise a glass of ouzo to the brave British agents Messrs. Kratides and Melas and Ms. Sophy Kratides for their brave, unselfish, and until now, unheralded actions on behalf of the British government in September of 1888.

I wish that I were able to circulate the secret records that support my true account of this incident, but I am sworn on my oath as a microbiologist not to reveal them. I know that my position will be challenged by Sherlockian scholars, but the truth will win regardless of the available evidence.

Moriarty, An Encounter of the First Kind
(or Smoke Gets in your Eyes)

Published in *Holmes & Watson Report*, 4 (6): 16-21,
(January) 2001, and *Pipe Smokers Ephemeris*, Winter –
Spring 2004, 83-4.

Over my many years of acquaintanceship with the great detective Sherlock Holmes, I have mentioned the name of Professor Moriarty on only a very few occasions. In fact, there has been much discussion as to whether he really existed at all, but was merely a plot to hide the fact that Mr. Holmes went on a series of secret missions for the British government that required him to be presumed dead for several years. How could Moriarty be real when I appear not to remember, from story to story, when I had first heard of him. Well, the truth be told, there really was a Professor Moriarty, and the account that I am about to narrate in this brief reminiscence will detail the exact events that led to his discovery without defining the time frame, which I must continue to obfuscate for reasons that I will never be able to clarify.

It all began one bright and warm Tuesday afternoon as I returned home to Baker Street from my business in the City. Armed with my recent race course winnings from my favourite bookmaker, I jauntily climbed the stairs leading to our shared rooms, intending to invite my companion to help celebrate this rare event by inviting him to dine with me at my club. However, I was stopped in my tracks by olfactory signs that Mr. Holmes had several visitors. Taking slower and more dignified steps, to avoid alarming his guests, I began my deliberation using the deductive logic that Sherlock Holmes had taught me, to determine that this indeed must be the case. In the atmosphere were the aromas of several fine pipe tobaccos. There was the sweet smell of a highly spiced, imported blend that bespoke a taste for

Oriental delights, likely as a result of long-time residence in the Indian colony. Then, there was the odour of a dry Dutch blend similar to those that were only available at the most expensive purveyors of tobacco. Also, my nose detected the rich blending of fine Connecticut and Virginia leafs -- surely the sign of an American. And finally, there was that very rare pure, single leaf Turkish whose possession bespoke great sophistication and wealth. Most significant by its absence was the disgraceful aroma of Holmes' acrid shag. This indeed signaled that the visitors were so exalted that Mr. Holmes even went to the great lengths to forgo his blend of pipe tobacco in their honour. The likely gaiety of the occasion was evidenced by the sound of tinkling glass emanating through the door as I approached the first floor portal leading to our sitting room.

"Come in, my dear Watson," shouted Holmes in his shrill, tenor voice as I gazed in astonishment at the empty scene. Only Sherlock Holmes himself was in evidence, as he sat bent over his low power microscope, a new pipe resting in the corner of his mouth. "You are just the man I need for a very important assignment. Bring your pipes over here!"

Hardly knowing what to make of this discrepancy between my logical deductions and the scene that had actually unfolded before my eyes, I merely shrugged my shoulders in disbelief, nodded in the affirmative, and mumbled, "Anything to be of assistance. What would like me to do?"

"Merely sit down next to me and enjoy this fresh tobacco that I have purchased at Mortimer's, the tobacconist that you may recall from our adventure involving the pawn broker with red hair. But please, when you are done, very carefully extract the plug and dottle and place them onto this glass slide for my review."

"But Holmes," I retorted, "You usually purchase your pipe tobacco at Bradley's emporium. Why did you go so far out of your way to Mortimer's? Are you on another case in that locale? And why are there so many different odours of pipe tobacco wafting through the air of our quarters."

"You have many questions, friend Watson, but I suggest that you save your breath for the long experiment ahead. We have many tobaccos to explore," retorted my friend. "Let's merely state that the identity of the proper tobacco and its owner will lead us to the solution of a very challenging case. Whilst you are enjoying your first of many pipefuls of smoke, consider these notes that were found on the bodies of three men who died of mysterious circumstances," he continued as he handed me three slips, each the fly leaf of a small pamphlet or book, bearing this legend:

Upon the Distinction between the Ashes of the Various Tobaccos
by Sherlock Holmes, Esq.
Private Consulting Detective

"What can this mean, Holmes?" I queried as I exhaled the very nice tobacco that I had been offered.

"It signifies that someone has gone to great lengths to attract my attention," replied Holmes. "Each flyleaf is from an individual copy of my monograph identifying a hundred and forty forms of cigar, cigarette, and pipe tobacco. Some unknown individual has purchased 15 copies of this monograph. Although I am flattered by this attention to my work, I am concerned that he has gone to great lengths to attract my notice. I am afraid that several more people will be needlessly slaughtered unless I can deduce the identity of the agent of their death and the perpetrator of this foul deed."

"How does smoking innumerable pipefuls of tobacco help in this effort?" I asked as I cleaned the remnants of my first pipeful onto the previously proffered glass slide.

"Would it help to know that each corpse was also decorated with the plug and dottle of the same identical blend? However, I regret to say that this tobacco is unique. It is one that I have never encountered before. I believe that it was left as a clue by some cold-blooded murderer, who uses the death of innocent people as a game to test my skills. Should I determine the source of this identity and tobacco, I may be then able to determine the name of the purchaser, obtaining further evidence to track this villain and eliminate him as a threat to society. Now no more questions. Here's your next tobacco, smoke away quickly and in silence whilst I examine each of our last products to see if either is the same as those found on the victims. No luck. Keep smoking away. We only have 20 more samples to try."

Whilst filling and lighting my pipe, and carefully taking the first puffs of the newly acquired tobacco, I glanced over towards Mr. Holmes to discover that there were scores of glass slides surrounding him, each with its finished product of tobacco consumption. How long had he been at this experiment? Surely, even for an addict such as Sherlock Holmes, this would represent a major affront to his upper respiratory apparatus. Stimulated by his display of self-sacrifice and discipline, I more quickly responded to the task ahead, all thoughts of celebration now vanished from my mind as I, with single purpose, set myself to the task ahead.

Finally, at the conclusion of our researches, Mr. Holmes glanced over at me with a defeated look upon his long thin face. He said, with an unusual muted tone to his voice, "We have failed miserably. There is no tobacco in the world that produces a plug and dottle identical with those left upon the corpses. Since this has already been a one-hundred pipe problem I think that I will turn to the contents of the Tantalus and gasogene to help my further thought processes."

Filling a beaker with the clear amber Scotch whisky that he preferred, Mr. Holmes lay upon the floor, his feet elevated upon the divan. As he slowly sipped at the liquid refreshment, I noted a subtle change in his features. His countenance, which I had well learned to read from our long relationship, was beginning to show signs of resolution of the crisis. Then, startling me, he quickly leapt up from his position of cogitation to his full length shouting, "How stupid I am! Truly, smoke gets in my eyes! I truly have descended to the depths of the official police! Without thinking matters through, I have docketed vast numbers of useless pieces of information, save those which may help me update my monograph. Come Watson. For the resolution of this exercise, we will need to consult an expert in pharmacognosy, a fully qualified member of the apothecary profession."

With that, Mr. Holmes dragged me off of the arm chair with one quick motion whilst, simultaneously, with a well-practiced motion, wrapping the evidence in paper and stuffing it into the pocket of his trousers. Running down Baker Street, Mr. Holmes, in his haste, shoved everyone in his path leaving me to apologize in his wake. Then, bursting into the chemists shop, we nearly frightened Mr. Pendlebury to death until he recognized his old acquaintance Sherlock Holmes as the source of tumult.

"Well, Mr. Holmes," he said, quickly returning to his normal calm professional manner, as if providing advice on the best cure for a minor ailment, "How can I help you? It must be a serious matter."

"Mr. Pendlebury, I am sorry to have startled you and to take you away from your manufacture of belladonna extract, which my nose informs me is the substance in your metal cylinder. However, I need your expertise in identifying the material folded in this paper."

"Ah yes, I can tell by the odor that it is an unusual plant drug that I have been requested to obtain by a university professor who said that he needed it for his research. Since he showed me his credentials, I didn't feel the need to be concerned that it would be inappropriately applied. Was I wrong in my assertion?"

"I'm afraid so, Mr. Pendlebury. Does that fact that it appears to have been smoked in a pipe concern you?"

"Yes, Mr. Holmes. As I look at the remains through my microscope, I note that it has been mixed with tobacco to make it burn more easily. I have no information on the effects derived from inhaling smoke from this substance, but 'Weed of Silent Death,' as it is called in its native Western African environs, is highly toxic when administered slowly via the oral route. This is indeed a novel method of inflicting a rapid death with an undetectable source. Someday, a chemist will use these experiences with poisons to write mystery novels."

"Pray tell, Mr. Pendlebury, who was the purchaser of this product?"

"Let me look in my book. Yes. It was Professor Moriarty. Surely, as a professor, he has the right to purchase such an item to pursue scientific research, doesn't he?"

"Yes, if that is his true goal," retorted Mr. Holmes. "Please give the Professor a message from me. Tell him that I have passed his test. Inform him that I am serving notice that I have divined his nefarious means of murder and that I will do all that I can to thwart any of his future plans. He has thrown down a personal challenge. No matter how many years it may take, I will see him suffer the consequences of his dastardly deeds."

It was thus that Sherlock Holmes first learned of the wicked Professor, the man whom I spoke of in some of my writings concerning the career of the great detective. The man that we hoodwinked the public into believing had killed Sherlock Holmes at Reichenbach Falls.

I must also note that at the conclusion of this case, Mr. Holmes, appetite returned, and he was very happy to join me at our now late celebration of my good fortune.

Regarding the True Aetiology of the Skin-Lightening Syndrome in "The Adventure of the Blanched Soldier"

Presented at the Pleasant Places of Florida Fall Gathering November 1, 1997; Published in *The Holmes & Watson Report*, 1 (7): 42-8, (March) 1998; and *The Formulary* (The Journal of the Friends of Dr. Watson) No. 15, December 2003, p 11-15.

From Wednesday, January 7 through Monday, January 12, in the year 1903, Mr. Sherlock Holmes investigated the mysterious malady that seems to have afflicted Mr. Godfrey Emsworth, and which is the subject of this essay.(1) Since Mr. James M. Dodd, Mr. Holmes' client and the former army comrade-in-arms of the afflicted man, had not had any communications from his friend for six months, he visited the home of Mr. Emsworth to find him to be hiding on the estate but mysteriously changed in physical appearance. Through a series of observations and scientific deductions, prior to and during the visit of Messrs. Holmes and Dodd to the Emsworth habitation, Mr. Holmes reached the tentative hypothesis that Mr. Emsworth may have contracted leprosy in South Africa, and was hiding this disastrous news from everyone except his family, trusted servants, and personal physician. It was this latter gentleman, a Mr. Kent, the primary care physician, who diagnosed the condition as leprosy without calling in an expensive consultant to confirm his findings. Deprived of the services of John H. Watson, M.D., who usually filled the role of physician-advisor to the detective but who had deserted him for a wife, Mr. Holmes was required to call in a favor and ask the noted dermatologist and tropical medicine specialist Sir James Saunders to provide a long-needed second opinion in this matter. The diagnosis of "pseudo-leprosy" or ichthyosis was gratefully received by all in attendance at the denouement of this adventure.

As is often the case in the field of medical literature, some controversy has arisen regarding the true aetiology of the skin condition that afflicted Mr. Godfrey Emsworth. Was it really leprosy as Mr. Kent had initially diagnosed it? Was it really "pseudo-leprosy" or ichthyosis, as stated by the expert Sir James Saunders? Was it something else again, as discussed in more recent medical literature? (2,3) It is unfortunate that Dr. Watson had not the opportunity to present this account to us. I am certain that the clarity of his medical observations would have obviated all of the obscurity associated with this narrative by a scientifically brilliant though medically inexpert detective. Thus, we must make do with the evidence that is available to us through the less than medically expert descriptions provided by Mr. Sherlock Holmes' account to explore the several possible alternative diagnoses. (1)

Medical diagnoses are generally based on considerations of patient history, presenting symptoms, and the results of laboratory tests, and on occasion, surgical intervention. In this case, neither laboratory analyses nor diagnostic surgical procedures were performed. Thus, we are forced to rely exclusively on the patient's case history and symptomology, and the diagnostic skills and personal experience of the physician.

Mr. Godfrey Emsworth had seen military action in South Africa during the Boer War. (1) According to his comrade, Mr. James M. Dodd, "They took the rough and smooth together for a year of hard fighting. Then he was hit with a bullet from an elephant gun in the action near Diamond Hill outside Pretoria. I got one letter from the hospital in Cape Town and one from Southampton. Since then not a word -- not one word, Mr. Holmes for six months and more, and he my closest pal."

Then, we continue with Mr. Emsworth's own account that after he was wounded, he spent the night collapsed in a leper's bed in the Leper Hospital, and during this time that he was in a weakened condition, he had a brief but close encounter with one of the infected inhabitants of the facility.

Let us first examine the foregoing, while the clues are fresh in our minds, before discussing the clinical signs. For approximately one year, Mr. Emsworth was subjected to the exigencies of warfare. There must have been many occasions during which he was malnourished, poorly protected from the environment, and lacking in proper hygiene. All of these influences may have reduced his resistance to infection. However, there is no evidence that anything was amiss for the six-month interval between his being wounded and the time that he arrived in Southampton, prior to returning home. Then, for some reason, probably the rapid visibility of horrendous symptoms, he dropped out of sight, thinking that he was a victim of leprosy, and afraid of the terrible social consequences associated with this misunderstood affliction. Thus, whatever disease revealed itself did so very quickly and completely during the time Mr. Emsworth was disembarking from Southampton or just as he arrived home. It was not a long-standing disease that can be traced back to childhood nor one that would take a long time for symptoms to reveal themselves.

Now let us turn our attention to the signs and symptoms. (1) It should be noted that Mr. Dodd's visit, which resulted in his observations of Mr. Emsworth, were made some weeks after the last communique, thus more than six months after the events that ended the military career of Mr. Emsworth. Consequently, the symptoms described by Mr. Dodd, Mr. Holmes, and Sir James are not those of the initial stages of the disease. As viewed in the window, illuminated by lamplight, Mr. Dodd provided the following description: "He was deadly pale -- never have I seen a man so white." And further: "...that ghastly face glimmering as white as cheese in the darkness." And again: "His face was -- how shall I describe it? -- it was of a fish-belly whiteness. It was bleached." In response to Sherlock Holmes' query, it appeared that the face was not "equally pale all over." Then, we have Mr. Holmes' own written description: "One could see that he indeed had been a handsome man with clear-cut features sunburned by an African sun, but mottled in patches over this darker surface were curious whitish patches which had bleached his skin." Finally, the words of the great dermatologist/tropical disease expert Sir James Saunders: "A well-marked-case of pseudo-leprosy or ichthyosis, a scale-like affection of the skin, unsightly, obstinate, but possibly curable, and certainly non-infective."

There we have it. First, the disease had a rapid progress from the time it was not evident until the time that it manifested itself with significantly marked symptoms. Secondly, the lesions on the face were patchy, very white, and scaly. And thirdly, an eminent dermatologist/tropical disease specialist had ruled out leprosy.

The subject under discussion has not been completely ignored by medical scholars. (2,3) Dr. Herman Beerman, in several landmark papers, discussed several diseases that appeared to him, based on his extensive experience as a dermatologist, as the agent responsible for Mr. Emsworth's discomfort. (3) He concluded that the disease was more likely the affliction vitiligo or the fungal infection tinea versicolor, a ubiquitous disease produced by *Pityrosporon orbiculare* (formerly*Malassezia furfur*), rather than ichthyosis. He said: "Unless Godfrey Emsworth had had scaling skin lesions since infancy he certainly did not have ichthyosis." In considering vitiligo he stated: "...what is the differential diagnosis of scaly, hypopigmented facial patches occurring in adulthood during wartime or post-war conditions? Vitiligo is one diagnosis." **However, there were no evidences of preexisting conditions such as hyperthyroidism, hypoadrenalism, or Addison's disease, and "furthermore, vitiligo is not scaly." On the other hand, "Tinea versicolor is found in "equal frequency in temperate and tropical zones, and one which an unbathed soldier might easily have contracted." I can state from personal experience, subsequent to short-time exposure to my sister's cat, that tinea versicolor develops rapidly after contact producing significant clinical manifestations.**

With these few facts and hypotheses in mind, let us now turn our attention to each of the possible aetiologies of Mr. Emsworth's disease: leprosy, ichthyosis, vitiligo, tinea versicolor, and to add a new entry, xeroderma.

The fact that the family physician Mr. Kent misdiagnosed the affliction as leprosy should come as no surprise for several reasons (4,5), although according to some, "early clinical indications of skin lesions and muscular and neurologic deficiency are usually significantly diagnostic in patients from endemic areas."(6) Even today, there are many cases in which a wide variety of illnesses have been attributed to leprosy, especially to the inexperienced observer. According to Mr. Keith Skillicorn, in his experience a review of other sources there are at least 30 diseases that may be wrongly attributed to the leprosy bacillus. (4) He states that "there are four Cardinal Signs of leprosy, at least two of which must be seen in a patient before we can safely diagnose that person as having leprosy: (1) Hypopigmented, localized skin patches, (2) Anaesthesia or sensory deficit, particularly of touch and temperature, (3) Thickened nerves, particularly peripheral nerves, (4) Non-cultivatable, acid-fast bacilli present in skin lesions and/or nasal mucosa. In addition, leprosy produces anhidrosis or absence of or deficiency of sweating of the skin, is not highly contagious requiring continuous close contact for transmission, and has an unusually long -- 6 months to 30 years -- incubation period to manifest itself; only about 5% of contacts acquire the disease, and it rarely appears as hairless hypopigmented patches until later stages of the disease. (5,6) Although Sir James Saunders did not appear have used the services of a laboratory, he was no doubt sufficiently experienced to make the diagnosis on clinical grounds and the brief history of exposure and short time to onset.

Let us now turn our attention to Sir James's diagnosis was "pseudo-leprosy or ichthyosis." According to Beerman, Sir James' use of the term pseudo-leprosy or ichthyosis was not a definitive diagnosis, but that "it is more likely that the specialist was more sure of what the condition wasn't than what it was. In other words, he used these terms with the primary intention of reassuring young Emsworth that he did not have the disease he so feared." (3) Ichthyosis is an inherited "disease characterized by excessive accumulation of scale on the skin surface."(5) Further, the age of onset is from birth to early childhood. As Dr. Beerman said: "Unless Godfrey Emsworth had had scaling skin lesions since infancy he certainly did not have ichthyosis." (3) A similarly appearing disease, xeroderma, might be implicated. However, this affliction "usually occurs on the lower legs of middle-aged or older patients most often in cold weather and in patients who bathe frequently."(5) This also does not match the pattern of history, patient age, and disease site that were described previously for the patient.

Vitiligo is another condition that merits our attention. After all, several statements in the narrative refer to a very white or pale facial appearance- "white as cheese" and fish-belly whiteness." (1) Who can forget the remarkable transformation that this disease has made on the facial appearance of a Mr. Michael Jackson, a singer of some fame? This disease is often misinterpreted as leprosy by inexperienced practitioners, and a recent poignant account by a dermatologist stresses the importance of differentiating these two disorders which can have very profound social consequences in certain societies. (7) There is no loss of sensation in vitiligo as there is in leprosy, and no loss of sweating so that the patch is not warmer as in leprosy. (4) As pointed out by Dr. Balin, the lesions develop slowly over time, not precipitously as described in our story. (7) In addition, the lesions are subject to sunburn. (5) and thus could not have been so prominent in the lamp light. Also, there is no evidence that Godfrey Emsworth suffered from any of the preexisting associated conditions: hypothyroidism, hypoadrenalism, pernicious anemia, or Addison's disease, "And, furthermore, vitiligo is not scaly."(3)

That leaves us with Dr. Beerman's favorite diagnosis -- the fungal infection tinea versicolor, an ubiquitous disease produced by *Pityrosporon orbiculare* (formerly named *Malassezia furfur*). **Unlike vitiligo, "Tinea versicolor is found in equal frequency in temperate and tropical zones, and one which an unbathed soldier might easily have contracted." I can state from personal experience, subsequent to short time exposure to my sister's cat, that tinea versicolor develops rapidly after contact producing significant clinical manifestations.** Any microbiologist can very easily ascertain the evidence for tinea versicolor "by finding groups of yeast and short plump hyphae on microscopic examination of scrapings from the lesions."(5) The lesions have been described as "tan, brown, or white, very slightly scaling, which tend to coalesce, are seen on the chest, neck, and abdomen and occasionally on the face. (5) However, although the descriptions of the clinical signs encountered in this story under discussion may somewhat match those listed above, this disease is relatively widespread and should be easily recognized by a competent physician, even one who is not an expert in dermatology and tropical medicine. On the other hand, tinea versicolor is a disease that may be confused with leprosy. Differentiation is accomplished by microscopic examination of skin scrapings and noting that there is no loss of sensation at the site (4). It is almost certain that this clearly recognizable disorder would be named as such by the dermatologist Sir James Saunders, rather than using the term "pseudo-leprosy." However, this is mere speculation, and we cannot definitively rule out tinea versicolor on these grounds.

In conclusion, we have analyzed the paltry available data for the aetiology of the condition that afflicted Mr. Godfrey Emsworth, as recounted to us by Mr. Sherlock Holmes in his narrative "The Adventure of the Blanched Soldier." (1) Although I have reviewed clues in an attempt to define which of several conditions might fit the few pieces of information available to us, and the discussions of a highly qualified expert (3), we can draw no final conclusions, except the very felicitous conclusion that it is not leprosy. Perhaps the main message to come out of this adventure is the unfortunate fact that, as pointed out by Mr. Skillicorn and Drs. Balin, even in today's sophisticated medical climate many diseases are still misidentified as leprosy, (4,7) resulting in horrendous psychological and social consequences to the innocent victim of this medical error.

1.   Doyle AC. 1988. The Adventure of the Blanched Soldier In: Baring-Gould WS, Ed. *The Annotated Sherlock Holmes*. Clarkson N. Potter, New York, Vol. II, pp 707-21.
2.   Rodin AE and Key JD. 1984. *Medical Casebook of Doctor Arthur Conan Doyle*. Robert E. Krieger, Malabar, FL, pp 224-5.
3.   Beerman H. A few remarks about the Blanched Soldier. 1973. *Baker Street Journal* 23:148-155.
Smith EB and Beerman H. 1977. Sherlock Holmes and Dermatology. Int J Dermatol 16:433-8.

Beerman H. 1978. Sherlock Holmes and medical history. Trans Stud Coll Physicians Phila 45:243-8.

4. Skillicorn K. 1997. Misdiagnosis. Personal communication. Mr. Skillicorn is the retired Director of Health Services (Leprosy and Tuberculosis) with the HEED organization in Bangladesh. He has 31 years of experience in leprosy control.

5. Berkow R, Ed. In Chief. 1987. *The Merck Manual of Diagnosis and Therapy*, 15th ed. Merck Sharp & Dohme Research Laboratories, Rahway, NJ, pp 127-131, 2271-2, 2299-300, 2294-5.

6. Anonymous. 1987. Infections Chap. 3 In: *Professional Guide to Diseases*. Springhouse, Springhouse, PA, pp 191-3.

Anonymous. 1987. Skin Disorders Chap. 21 In: *Professional Guide to Diseases*. Springhouse, Springhouse, PA, pp 1220-2..

7. Balin AK and Balin LP. 1997. The Life of the Skin. Bantam, New York, pp 100-13.

Sherlock Holmes and the Adventure of the Pearls of Death

Published in *The Hounds Collection* Volume II, First Edition, April 1997

The squishing and splashing sounds, that were interwoven with the rhythmic rattling of the wheels of Dr. Watson's hansom cab, were the only remnants of the torrential rain and gale force winds that had deluged London for the past week. The storm had been replaced by a clear bright, moon-filled evening and a chill breeze. The cold wind and clear sky presaged the coming of the winter season. Dr. Watson regretted his lack of foresight as he sat shivering, protected only by his professional attire. The changing climatic conditions and the strenuous efforts required to quell the raging influenza epidemic had conspired to exacerbate both of his war wounds. His shoulder and leg throbbed with pain. Now, bone tired and aching, he was destined for a lonely evening devoid even of the comfort of his wife's company.

As he endured the long ride back to his apartments, nestled above his now prosperous practice, Dr. Watson's mind reflected back to the recent past events. He lay back, resigned to his fate, and shrugged his shoulders with acceptance of his sorry plight. His young, manly, and handsome mustachioed face, ever mobile and expressive of his emotions, responded to the thoughts that flowed at the edge of his consciousness. Sorrow and despair for those whom he had been unable to heal and had died despite his best efforts, were followed by anger and frustration at the limits placed upon him by the lack of therapeutic measures available to thwart this dread disease.

Then, a gentle smile flowed over his features as he remembered the kindly face of his lovely wife Mary and their parting conversation as he left the Lower Camberwell domicile of Mrs. Cecil Forrester. He could still see the drawing room door closing behind Mrs. Forrester as she, in robe and slippered feet, weakly retired for the evening. Then, they were alone together at last. His wife Mary, after rising on her toes and gently kissing him on their special spot just below his right eye, and using her private pet name said: "My dear James. How thoughtful and accommodating of you to allow me to tend to my former employer in her time of need, with both her and her husband dreadfully ill. They have been the only parents I have known since the death of my poor father, and they have always treated me as a beloved member of their family."

To which Dr. Watson smiled and replied: "I would not want it to be otherwise, my sweet angel of mercy. Although I will miss you terribly, I expect to share many a day with you, and that knowledge of our continued companionship will keep me happy until you return home to my side."

Finished with his reverie of recently past events, Dr. Watson permitted his mind to drift back to earlier memories. He recalled with glory and pain his military adventures in the service of the Queen, his subsequent return to England, and his momentous first meeting with his friend and erstwhile colleague Sherlock Holmes. He smiled as he contemplated the many interesting discussions that they have had, usually in the afternoon after tea, concerning the changes in weather patterns associated with the tilt of the earth, various athletic competitions, literature, music, and philosophy. Sitting upright with a new look of resolve upon his face, he leaned out of the window of his cab, and shouted to the driver: "Belay the previous instructions, cabbie. Take me to 221 Baker Street!" A visit to Mr. Sherlock Holmes would be just the ticket. A comfortable fire, a nip or more of the contents of the spirit case and the gasogene, a fine cigar from the coal-scuttle, and an interesting dialogue with his old friend and companion, followed by a good night's sleep in his old bedroom, was just the medicine he required to restore his spirits, and allay his dread of spending yet another lonely night with none but the servants for company. His pleasure was doubled as he spotted the light glowing in the facade of the well-remembered cozy Baker Street quarters. "Good!" he thought, "Holmes is both at home and still awake."

As Dr. Watson labored up the 17 steps, which seemed like miles to his bone-weary and pained body, a high-pitched voice rang out, "Watson, my old companion, I would know that tread anywhere! You are just in time to join me in a celebration as I reach the climax of another difficult and challenging case. There is something I must show you while we await a response to my message. Then we must be off on a long carriage ride."

These were the last words that Dr. Watson expected to hear or wanted to hear. But, how characteristic it was of his old friend Sherlock Holmes. It had been thus from their first meeting at St. Bart's, and had never changed. Gone were the dreams of pleasant, cozy surroundings and relaxing conversation. The meditative, philosophical Holmes that Watson had envisioned was replaced by Holmes the sleuth, the blood hound, the pursuer of evil. "What have I gotten myself into now?" queried Watson to himself. Realizing that it was now too late to turn back, he continued his slow progress to Holmes' abode.

Then he saw Sherlock Holmes. The tall, lank figure of the man was bending almost in half to accommodate the height of the table that supported the device through which he was now looking. His lean, hawk nosed, angular facial features were somewhat softened by the beaming smile that lightened his usually dour, clean shaved countenance. "Come see my new high powered microscope!" shouted Holmes, looking at the strange black instrument as a child would gaze at a new toy at Christmas. "It is the same as that utilized by the famous German physician, Herr Professor Dr. Robert Koch, to study the life

143

cycle of the tubercle bacillus. Certainly you have heard of his great discoveries!" blurted Holmes. "It can magnify images several hundredfold larger than they really are! There are, as yet, very few in England, although they have become popular in Germany. Look through this top lens and very, very slowly focus by turning this large cylinder. But, whatever you do, do not touch the slide with your fingers! It may be a deadly error. Tell me, what do you see?"

As Watson slowly, and timidly followed Holmes' instructions, a very strange sight resolved itself out of the mist. Before his eyes was revealed the image of tangled, sinuous threads. Glistening in the center of the threads were evenly spaced opalescent, shining, ovals. The appearance was that of a treasure box filled with strings of identical, lovely pearls. "Holmes, what is this? This is a beautiful, priceless sight that nature has prepared for us, is it not?"

"I am afraid, my poetic friend, that this object that you so admire is the mechanism for a diabolic, murderous scheme by a highly intelligent criminal. However, we must travel far to the other side of London, should we wish to learn the identity of this brilliant villain," said Holmes, very concernedly, "Or additional subsequent murders may result. Before we leave, however, you must also look at the same slide in a standard high power objective, one that you are more conversant with."

Watson's practiced eye gazed at the more familiar microscopic field and he quickly announced, "Holmes, that is the bacillus of anthrax. There can be no mistaking it. But what has this to do with your current case? Certainly there is no mystery to be attached to this affliction that is somewhat prominent in butchers, wool sorters, and others who handle potentially infected animal products. It is very easy to diagnose from a patient history and clinical grounds."

"Watson, let us continue our observations further with more scientific evidence. Look in the low powered microscope, it is also very illustrative."

Quickly focusing this device to which he was most accustomed, as a result of his medical training, Dr. Watson saw a mass of some brownish vegetative fibers in which were embedded a few strands of hair. "Is that tobacco?" he asked, "and animal hairs? What a very strange combination of items."

Retorted Holmes: "I see that your mind has been opened to unlikely possibilities as a result of our shared adventures. Yes, you are correct. Not only are the hair and tobacco part of the threads that tie together the available evidence in this case, but the material on the slide that you have previously viewed as well. In association with your suspicions voiced in a recent conversation that we had, these findings form a link to the discovery of the murderer of Lord Herbert McFallow, and possibly others. Now, I see that you are weary. Since we have time before a response takes us to our early morning vigil, I suggest that you rest yourself in front of the fire, and enjoy one of the cigars that I had imported from Tampa, Florida, in the United States. Here is a glass of whisky and soda to accompany your relaxation while we chat about this matter."

After drawing deeply on the cigar, and taking a long drink of the warming beverage, Watson finally continued their conversation: "Holmes, how is that possible? What did I say that led you to this line of reasoning?"

"My dear fellow, it was you who suspected that the death of Lord Herbert may not have been the result of the ongoing influenza epidemic. You stated that, although the respiratory symptoms that preceded his death appeared to be similar to those encountered with influenza, there were signs of toxic manifestations not found in that disease. Also, in your judgement, and from your personal experience with the current epidemic, there were subtle nuances that led you to call me into the case. You yourself stated that the signs of shock and the rapid onset of lethality ruled out influenza in your mind. You suspected foul play, poisoning."

"Yes, Holmes, it was due to my recent experiences and my hearkening to the teachings of my professor of surgery at Edinburgh, Dr. Joseph Bell, whom you appear to emulate in many respects."

To which Holmes replied: "Of all living men, his teachings provide the best examples of logical deduction. But, we digress. Do you recall my examination of your patient?"

"Yes, Holmes, you crawled all around the body on your hands and knees looking at everything carefully with your hand lens. Then, you looked all around his mouth with a small mirror after taking a whiff of his breath to detect the presence of poison, and then you looked into his nose."

"Yes," replied Holmes, who then asked, while exhaling fumes from his recently lighted pipe, "Did I do anything that you have never seen me do before?"

"Why Holmes, now that I think of it, you took a scraping from his nose. I never saw you do that before."

"That is quite true, Watson. You must take your clues where you find them. I am always puzzled why you do not ask why, when I do something different. A curious scientist would have wanted to look and see just what was in Lord Herbert's nose that aroused my inquisitiveness."

"But Holmes, there were no cutaneous lesions to point to anthrax, and the history of the illness would tend to rule out men of the character of Lord Herbert, who has never been accused of doing any physical labor in his life. What is the relationship between your demonstrations and the death of that noble gentleman?"

"That is the deviousness of the whole incident," replied Holmes. "Someone with your forthright and gentlemanly character would have a difficult time connecting these events. But, I both suffer from and am assisted by an advanced case of cynicism where every action is suspect, no matter how unconnected and innocent they may seem. Also, to my advantage, I trust no one, except of course you and my brother, Mycroft."

"Are you proposing that the tobacco was a means of transporting the bacillus of anthrax to Lord Herbert, and the animal hair was the source of the microbe? What a terrible yet ingenious plot," continued Watson. "Only a very evil scientist could have devised this scheme."

"Yes," responded Sherlock Holmes, while lighting another pipeful of tobacco, "You are probably correct in your hypothesis. We will need some further evidence, however, to confirm our theory."

Before Dr. Watson could reply, a sound of young feet rapidly padding up the stairs heralded the appearance of a very dirty, very smelly, and very scruffy young street Arab. Holmes said quickly to Watson, "Ah, one of my worthy associates has a message for me. Our wait is over. We must now hurry." Turning to the lad, he continued: "I trust that a conveyance awaits us to take us to the end of our search."

A positive nod from the street urchin brought a shilling coin into his hands and he sped off, rapidly followed by Sherlock Holmes with Dr. Watson being pulled along as he attempted to don the large baggy coat tossed to him by his companion.

"Where are we off to?" asked Watson.

"I do not know," shouted Holmes over the loud clatter of wheels and the hoof beats of the two galloping steeds that rapidly pulled their four-wheeler through the empty, cold streets of London. "Our lad will guide the driver, but I suspect the final destination will be in a slaughterhouse or tanners, possibly on Aldgate Street or Harrow-Alley."

Now wide awake, all pain and drowsiness removed by the adrenaline coursing through his circulation, Dr. Watson still shivered, but not with the cold, which was allayed by the warm clothing supplied by Sherlock Holmes from his vast supply of costume over-garments, but by the thrill of the chase. It was good to be back in the hunt with his friend! It was good to share another exciting adventure with Sherlock Holmes! "Holmes, I really missed our little excursions together. Thank you for enabling me to accompany you on yet another."

In response to that statement, Sherlock Holmes dug into the right hand pocket of his Ulster, retrieved several newspaper clippings and a telegram, and tossed them to Watson. "Regard these, friend Watson, while I plan our course of action as we note the area in which our journey takes us. I will need to have my wits about me, and devise an extemporaneous plan of attack, depending upon our surroundings."

"Just like Holmes to thrust information on me, rather than simply answering my straightforward questions." mused Dr. Watson. Continuing, he thought, "Holmes is always trying to get me to think like him. Doesn't he realize that he is of a rare breed?"

With great difficulty, due to the violent swaying and bouncing of their carriage, Dr. Watson was barely able to read the following item from the agony column of *The Times* for that morning:
To the Tobacconist: I require some more of your special snuff. Please deliver three bags full to the usual location. Little Bo Peep.

Preceding that date were several other private notices of the same sort. "What could it mean?" thought Watson, glancing at his inscrutable companion who was placidly peering straight ahead, his pipe firmly clenched between his teeth, his mind completely focused on the problem at hand. Watson knew that any attempts at conversation or questioning would be ignored when his friend presented that visage to the world, and resigned himself to a silent journey. Then Watson turned his attention to the telegram, which, surprisingly enough was from Germany:

"Mr. Holmes, description of symptoms, clinical signs, laboratory findings confirm your suspicions. Await further word." Most interested. R. Koch

The last, of course, he understood fully. It had to do with the identity of the microbe, an identity that he himself had confirmed minutes ago in the Baker Street sitting room. As Watson, still somewhat puzzled, mused about the full import of all that had occurred that night and into the early morning, the four-wheeler lurched to a sudden stop. "Quick, Watson, we must follow this lad to see where he leads us!" whispered Holmes, as he drew Watson forcefully from the conveyance to the ground. "We must make haste, we do not know when our prey will arrive. I am certain that he suspects nothing. I suggest that you be careful where you step, though. And do not remove your gloves for any reason. And wear this scarf around your nose and mouth for further protection."

As they watched, the boy was joined by an older one, clothed in gloves and scarf, who, as disreputable appearing as his companion, seemed to be in a command position. Rapidly, the street was filled by other similarly clad, silent boys, who seemed to flow endlessly from the shadows into the bright moonlight, that was just giving way to a pale dawn. Slipping out of the alley to their left, another furtive youngster quickly took Holmes' hand, and the trio proceeded into the darkness, around two corners and into the back door of an establishment smelling of dead animals and their feces.

"Be very quiet, Watson, we do not wish to apprehend our man here. We need to follow him to his delivery point to catch the criminals at the next higher level in this enterprise."

Joined by a second lad, the four furtively followed the dim lantern glow into the cavernous slaughterhouse. Turning another corner, the entourage spotted a door framed in bright light on the other side of the immense room. Extinguishing the lantern, Sherlock Holmes led his assembled patrol towards the source of light, like moths to a flame. As they slowly inched their way through the silently opened doorway into the blinding light pouring in from the window, they could perceive nothing of interest. Then, from behind, came the unmistakable dull thud of a rifle being cocked. Apparently startled by the sound, the figure of a man, with a long, sharp object clutched in one hand, rose up before them and was framed against the glare of the sun at the level of the eastern horizon.

"No! Don't fire!" shouted Holmes, "Hold your fire or all is lost!"

But his plea was useless. The roar of a powerful rifle reverberated in their ears as the human figure fell to the floor. The heavy treads of human feet heralded the entrance of a plainclothes detective and two burly constables into the room.

"You ruined everything;" shouted Holmes to the police. "Why did you shoot him? He would harm no one with his blade, and he could lead us to his superior."

"But Mr. Holmes," said the inspector, "We are not armed. It was not us who killed the man."

"I am very sorry that I accused you and your men Inspector; please forgive me," Holmes replied contritely.

"We all make mistakes, don't we Mr. Holmes, even famous consulting detectives?" concluded the policeman, with a sarcastic tone that one would use to a recalcitrant child, a slight smile on his face.

"Alas, then, we have been outsmarted," Holmes continued in a voice so quiet that only the nearby Watson could understand his words. "Leaving nothing to chance, the master criminal behind this enterprise arranged for his agent to be spied upon and eliminated to avoid capture. That was his insurance policy against betrayal. However, there is nothing we can do to remedy the situation, and I am certain that the killer has left the premises and will never be found. Watson, I note that you have rushed to provide medical assistance to our quarry. How does he fare?"

Watson glumly replied, "He is dead Holmes. We will get no further information from him."

The glow of the bright sunlight revealed an unusual scene. They were in the midst of a dirty slaughterhouse. On the floor lay a short, stout, unkempt, unshaven, blonde-haired man of about twenty years of age. Next to where the man was laying was the only living four-legged animal in attendance. It was a sick, scraggly sheep, partly shorn of its wool. Nearby, on the floor, were a pair of shears and a basket that contained the wool that was no longer attached to the body of the animal.

"Why, that man is Melbourne, the son of your tobacconist!" exclaimed Watson. "What the deuce is he doing here? What is he up to?"

Turning to Watson, Holmes very quietly said, "He or someone in his father's employ was the logical candidate as the assassin or his helper. But this account book that I found in the shop, among this man's things, now completes the picture. Let us continue this discussion after I have dismissed the official representatives of the law."

"Gentlemen," continued Holmes more loudly, addressing the policemen and then favoring Watson with a wink of his eye, "You may remove the body. I think that the case of the phantom wool-gatherer is solved. I suggest that you remove the body and file your report. Due to my false accusations regarding his demise, the least that I can do is allow you the privilege of taking full credit."

After the police had left, and the Irregulars were dismissed with their earnings, Watson turned to Holmes and in a conspiratorial voice remarked, "It will be interesting to see how the police and newspapers will report the crime of phantom wool-gathering that has not as yet been brought to their official attention."

"Yes, my friend, let us now turn to matters at hand," said Holmes, his eyes still twinkling with silent amusement from the joke that he had just perpetrated on the official police. "It appears that this young gentleman, once a medical student, but now fallen to a lower level, has collaborated in a series of murders. I am certain that the names in his book will not reveal to us the clients who used his services to carry out assignations behind the veil of the influenza epidemic. They are no doubt obfuscated by a secret code. But thank you for initiating this most interesting case. Your perceptive medical skills were essential in beginning the process of deducing the rest of the puzzle from the pieces that revealed themselves to my inquiry. That set into motion a series of events which eventually led to his unfortunate death. Let us now return to my lodgings where we can rest and resolve any outstanding issues."

Once again in the familiar surroundings of 221b Baker Street, Dr. Watson finally realized that all of the pain and fatigue that led him to seek quiet solace in these chambers had been eradicated by the exciting events that had ended less than an hour ago. He knew that he had earned a good night's sleep from his endeavors, but that his reward would not come until his mind was made easy by the discourse from Sherlock Holmes that was certain to follow the maddeningly prolonged routine now underway: the cleaning of the pipe, the filling of the pipe with tobacco, the lighting of the pipe, letting the fire go out, tamping it just so, and finally, carefully making certain that the entire surface was evenly lighted. Only then did Mr. Sherlock Holmes commence the discourse long awaited by his friend and former associate: "Well, my good friend and patient companion, I perceive that you have, for the most part, penetrated the solution to our little problem from the evidence that I have so far revealed to you and from what you have seen tonight. Are there any questions that you wish to ask me to assist you in its elucidation?"

"Yes, Holmes, what is it that you saw in Lord Herbert's nose that initiated your studies in this matter?" replied Dr. Watson. "What could it have been that led you from Lord Herbert's nose to a filthy slaughterhouse in the worst part of London? And what do the newspaper clippings and telegram have to do with it?"

"Well, would it help if I told you that there was a pustule in his nose?"

Dr. Watson looked up and nodded his head in affirmation. All was now clear. "Of course," he replied, "The hair-laden tobacco was the means of delivery of the bacillus. The animal hair that was mixed with the tobacco must have been from an infected sheep such as the one we encountered in tonight's excursion. The tobacco and hair were scraped from Lord Herbert's nose, and I assume that the same material was found in his snuff box."

"You are quite correct in you assessment. Now let me tie all of the facts together, with the information that you only had a chance to glance at, into a uniform narrative, and you tell me if you agree, or if I have overlooked any points that require further elucidation," Holmes said.

He then began a recitation in the style of a professor. "Let us start anew. That Lord Herbert died from a respiratory infection other than influenza, or possibly even poisoning, was a hypothesis derived from your clinical observations. For that, you have my gratitude for providing me with a case to drive away the ennui of the last few days, that were filled with constant rain and no crimes worthy of my attention. Even the activities of members the criminal class were curtailed by the horrendous weather. To continue my discourse -- an observation of the body revealed an unusual lesion in the nose. When I later looked at the nasal scrapings in my low-powered microscope, I saw the presence of inflammatory cells -- see, I did learn something from you -- and some tobacco and animal hair. My microscopic analyses of these items was simplified by the fact that I am preparing monographs on both topics. It was clearly a mixture of sheep's wool and a type and cut of tobacco only used in snuff. Not only that, but I could see, in my examination, that it was identical to that purveyed by my personal tobacconist, and few others. Is it clear so far, Watson?"

"Yes, absolutely, please continue, while I help myself to another excellent cigar," said the good Doctor, lighting the cigar and then puffing easily as he sat comfortably in the overstuffed chair, patiently awaiting the continuation of the scholarly exposition.

Sherlock Holmes went on: "The next thing that I did was sample Lord Herbert's snuff supply, and find the identical suspected product. A sampling of the products at the few stores revealed no contaminated snuff on their premises. The contaminated snuff was solely localized to Lord Herbert's abode. This meant that the material had to be placed at the victim's home by someone after the snuff had been especially prepared elsewhere for delivery. And, that it was done deliberately for the purpose of murder, not as a result of inadvertent contamination at the manufacturer's."

After going through the pipe ritual again, the recitation continued thus: "What would tie together the snuff, sheep's wool, a pustulant lesion, and a respiratory infection? A perusal of the medical references at the British Museum seemed to point to wool-sorter's disease as the most logical solution. Certainly, if wool-sorters can be infected by inhaling the wool of diseased sheep as they process it, couldn't the same material, carefully and continuously placed in an individual's nose achieve the same end? And wouldn't the symptoms emulate those of influenza to all but the well-trained and experienced observer? What a diabolical plot!"

With that, Dr. Watson's face lit with appreciation of his friend's detective skills. He expostulated: "Holmes, your ability to tie these diverse aspects together is marvelous. Once you gave me the available information, I was able to see that Lord Herbert died of anthrax. But to know what to look for to discern that the wool-sorter's disease was conveyed to the site of infection by the continuous application of snuff laced with the wool of infected sheep is excellent! A marvelous deduction! My hat is off to you. I fully understand the microscopic pearl necklace and the German telegram. But, the Baker Street Irregulars and the mysterious newspaper clippings, what part did they play?"

"Watson, you know my methods. To confirm the identity of the infecting microbe, I contacted Herr Professor Dr. Robert Koch for information on cultivating and identifying the causative bacillus. The high-power microscope, purchased at his suggestion, revealed identical images from gelatin cultivations of the microbe from the nasal scraping, the snuff sample, hair from infected sheep, and finally, a specimen obtained from Dr. Koch himself. These are the deadly images of pearl necklaces that you so admired. One drop of a suspension containing them would kill a man in 24 hours. Also, the spores will remain infective in the snuff supply for many years due to the resistance of the spores to environmental conditions. Dr. Koch's telegram merely confirmed the validity of pursuing my observations, as did your microscopic analysis. But how do I find the individual personally responsible for this heinous crime, and how do I trap him into revealing his nefarious activities? I suspected, immediately, that the answer may lie within the establishment of only a very few tobacconists who purvey this particular blend of snuff, but I needed to perform one of my little experiments to test this tentative hypothesis. There was no other plan that I could pursue, since no suspect product was found at any of the locations. By the way, I seem to have purchased a large amount of snuff, would you like to have some for yourself? Anyway, hoping that standard means of communication were used to order the lethal snuff, I scoured every newspaper for the last several weeks leading to the death of Lord Herbert, and found in *The London Times* a series of notices from the 'Little Bo Peep' to the 'tobacconist.' I theorized that 'Little Bo Peep' was actually the person who arranged the murders, and that he was looking for lost sheep, in the form of 'special snuff.' In order to locate these individuals, I placed the advertisement that drew 'the tobacconist' out. I had members of my unofficial police force follow all of the members of these tobacconists' staffs and family everywhere. However, it did not take long to identify the individual tobacconist. My informants kept me posted throughout the day. My proprietor's son was followed to the closest newsstand where he avidly waited for the arrival of *The Times* every day. On the day in question, he quickly turned to the agony column, and rushed off as soon as he had read my advertisement. He hurried back to the shop, and made preparations to acquire more infected wool for his special snuff. The rest you know. Once his final destination was identified, we were summoned for the final resolution of the problem."

Watson looked up at his friend in admiration and asked, "When will we ascertain the identity of 'Little Bo Peep,' the one who is probably the actual murderer?"

"I am afraid that we have a long way to go on that score. The only available witness has been executed. All of the addresses in the special ledger were blinds -- a warehouse here, a pub there. Short of exhuming and examining the nasal cavities of all of the thousands of victims of the recent epidemic of influenza, no further steps are available to us. This bears the mark of the unknown master criminal who always stays beyond my reach. I acknowledge his intelligence and skills. Someday, he will come within my grasp, but until then, I will have to be satisfied with countering each and every one of his clever thrusts until he finally makes the one fatal error that will undo him."

"Holmes, I cannot wait to write this case up for our annals. It is remarkably singular and demonstrates your skills of deduction to the utmost."

"No, my dear friend and associate, we may never reveal this adventure to the public. Think how such a discovery, if it fell into the hands of a wicked foreign power, would provide a weapon for which we have no available defense. Let us keep this concept of a biological weapon to ourselves and leave it to others to conceive of it on their own. Also, it is essential that, just as the identity of the unseen hand behind these murders remains unknown to me, so must my intervention in his affairs remain hidden from his view. It is likely, however, that he will never use that *modus operandi* again."

Turning his head towards Dr. Watson, Mr. Sherlock Holmes saw that his comrade had finally drifted off into a long-awaited and well-deserved slumber. The events of the very long day had finally taken their course. Gently, Holmes lay a blanket across his now sleeping friend, and retired to his bedroom to undergo the depression that overcomes him after the completion of an interesting little problem such as the one that has just been concluded.

Sherlock Holmes and the Magic Bullet

Published in *The Whitechapel Gazette* (spring 1995 issue
no. 6), *The Hounds Collection* (Volume 1, first edition,
April, 1996); and *Baker Street West* 1 Vol. 11, No. 1,
Summer 2005, p 15, 21-7; *The Formulary* (The Journal for
the Friends of Dr. Watson), No. 28, March 2011 pp 20-5.

Darkness has finally fallen over the enclosed
courtyard cafe adjacent to the luxurious hotel. The cool
breezes, fed by the chilly Mediterranean Sea, have displaced
the high daytime temperature that is so unusual this early in
the summer. The flurry and hubbub of the busy mealtime
hours are no longer in evidence. In the distance can be heard
the faint clatter of dishes being washed, dried, and stacked
for the next day's activities, and the muted conversation of
the staff as they go about their final activities for the
evening. The low murmur of two young lovers -- a soldier
and his fiancee -- are the only other sounds. It is quite
dark. The only visible sources of light are provided by the
quarter moon trying to peep through the holes in the clouds
above, the faint electric bulbs that mark the perimeter of the
brick wall, and the candles illuminating the two occupied
tables -- one holding the couple in the center of the tree-lined
court yard and the other a dark-garbed figure surreptitiously
ensconced in the far corner.

If one were to allow his eyes to adjust to the dim light,
the figure would resolve into an upright gentleman, almost
military and Prussian in bearing. However, the match with
which he lights his Havana cigar reveals the bearded,
bespectacled face of a kindly, late middle-aged man in
repose. The gentleman is Paul Ehrlich. The year is
1910. The city is Montpellier, in the South of France.

It had been a tiring journey -- a seemingly endless
series of conferences and banquets to introduce his new
chemotherapeutic agent Salvarsan to the medical opinion

leaders of France. At each stop along the way he dealt with frustration and controversy. The endless arguments and nitpicking by his fellow physicians and researchers taxed his energy as he attempted to penetrate their long-held beliefs and convince them of the safety and superiority of his novel organic arsenical over the traditional inorganic bismuth and arsenic treatment of syphilis. Finally, at this last destination, he gratefully accepted the plaudits and support from the learned professors at this most ancient of medical facilities. They had the wisdom to accept, with open minds, the veracity of his data. Their intense interest in eliminating the therapeutic applications of such poisons as arsenic and bismuth stemmed from the experiences of a former staff member of theirs, Hans Sloane, who investigated the effects of arsenic over dosage on the famous actor Barton Booth, over two hundred years earlier.

Now the conference and banquet were over; the attendees had left in the morning to enjoy the companionship of their families and friends. Dr. Ehrlich can now enjoy, in solitary quietude, his final cigar and cognac before retiring. As the smoke of his exhalation rises to join the clouds above, Professor Ehrlich is able to now allow his thoughts to carry him back to the events of the day. He remembers again how he concluded his address with expressions of sincere gratitude to those who had made such a major impact on his efforts: Pasteur and Henle for laying the framework for the study of infectious diseases; his older cousin, Carl Weigert, who had introduced him to the organic dyes and their tissue-specificities and selective powers; his friend and mentor, Robert Koch, the discoverer of the etiology of tuberculosis who laid the foundation for many of the major developments in immunology; and to his good friend Hata for developing the critical test of cure -- the rabbit model of syphilis, and his mentor Kitasato, a former colleague. But one man had to remain nameless, the one man that he wished to laud above all others, the man who had such a major influence on him and encouraged him in his thinking to such an extent that the world of medical research would be forever changed as a result.

As Professor Ehrlich closes his eyes, allowing the gentle bite of his fragrant beverage to impart its pleasant feel and taste, his consciousness flows back to a time in 1893 when he first met the man whose wisdom and encouragement gave him the needed impetus to carry out his mission which culminated in the development of a synthetic chemical agent remarkably capable of safely curing millions of sufferers of the dread disease syphilis. The scene is as clearly seen tonight as it had been those many years ago on a warm noon day in early summer.

"Herr Professor, may I share your table for a late supper?" the tall man asked in perfect Hoch Deutsch, leavened with an unknown foreign accent. "I see that we are both in a hurry to get back to our researches, I to the chemical analyses of new coal tar derivatives and you to their medical application as dye substances. Perhaps, while we dine, you can tell me what new chemical breakthroughs are being made in Berlin."

"Of course you may share the table," replied the good doctor. "But how do you know so much about me, that I am from Berlin, that I am working on aniline dyes, and that I am in a hurry to return to my researches? Have you been spying on me?" he chuckled.

"No," retorted the former, as the tall, heavily bearded man seated himself and carefully arranged his napkin with long, acid stained fingers. "It is a habit of mine to define the occupation, character, habits, and geographic origin of people whom I see on the street, confront in business, or, in your case, have the honor to share a table with. It enhances the powers of observation and logical thought which are the hallmarks of a good scientist and immensely aid scientific enquiry."

Ehrlich continued his questioning with: "Would you please tell me, then, how you were able to know so much about me by using these powers of yours?"

"That is simple, once you have honed your powers by constant practice," replied the tall, bearded man. "I knew that you were a professor by the reverence shown to you by the students who follow your every step, as well as the shape of your beard, which announces both your status and your city of origin. Recognition of the latter is assisted by the gold emblem on your chain, inscribed from the most noted medical research institute in Berlin, the Charité, and the additional distinct emblem, only given as a very special award for meritorious service at the professorial level, granted by the medical faculty of Berlin University. That you are a physician is especially obvious, due to the unique coupling of the bear, the symbol of Berlin, and the caduceus, the symbol of medicine." After pausing, as if for effect, he took a bite of the bread that had finally arrived and a sip of the moderately priced table wine and continued with his recitation, as if lecturing a class of medical students: "The rapid movements of your head and eyes, as you attempt to locate a waiter in this clime that features a more *laissez faire* attitude towards service, is evidence enough of your desire to eat more quickly than is customary in the South of France. This is fortified by the fact that although you are very correctly dressed, as befits your station, your clothes and shoes are rather large, indicating that you object to spending any time in trying them on, or no doubt, any other activities that are not of major importance to you. Also, your hurry and recent laboratory activities are clearly announced by the many multicolored dye stains on your fingers that have resisted your perfunctory attempts at scrubbing them away, and the mud on your shoes that could only have been attained by taking a path through the new construction that is the shortest route between the university and the hotel."

When the stranger had completed his erudite discourse, Ehrlich, in a voice signifying delight and respect, exclaimed "That is an outstanding exhibition! What else do you know from our brief meeting?"

"Very little, only that you are originally from Silesia, are married, and of the Jewish faith. Nothing further comes to mind at the moment."

"I am deeply impressed by your skill, and I would like to ask your indulgence to see how I could attempt, in some small way, to emulate your methods." Encouraged by the smiling nod from his taller companion, Ehrlich continued, "When I first saw you this morning at breakfast, from a short distance, and did not know that I was to have the pleasure of your company, I did make some observations about you. It is a habit of mine. When I noted how tall, thin, and energetic you were, I immediately suspected that you were an American. Your height, facial shape, and luxurious hair and beard are quite reminiscent of the photographs of the former American president Abraham Lincoln. Then, after hearing you speak, I thought that you were Swiss. Your ease in quickly shifting between French and German was something that I thought only citizens of that multinational land could accomplish. However, it now becomes obvious to me that such is not the case. Although it is clearly not your native tongue, you speak perfect Hoch Deutsch. Even the most erudite Swiss cannot disguise the fact that his native tongue is Suisse Deutsch, a very distinct dialect, indeed. Also, yesterday, when I drew closer to you, I could tell that your French is perfect Parisian. This would not be uncommon to an ethnocentric French-speaking Swiss, or an upper-class Parisian, but it is marvelous to find such a confluence in another. I do see by the scars on your fingers that you do enjoy the science of organic chemistry, and the stain on your beard signifies that you are a frequent pipe smoker, although you have not demonstrated that habit in public. The fact that you hide this aspect of your life could reveal that you may be discretely avoiding other activities so as to obfuscate your true identity. Certainly, your clothes are quite new and yet not French in cut or style. Also, unlike other gentlemen of your obvious breeding and professional standing, you wear no signs or symbols of honor, service, or even luxury. Yet you have appended to your watch chain a disk bearing the likeness of Queen Victoria. Is that a British coin?" He paused and continued in a less certain tone: "I am afraid that I have reached the limit of my abilities in this direction. As a scientist, I have trained myself never to theorize beyond that which I can prove by repeated experiment or observation. Could you please tell me what is your nationality and with whom I have the pleasure of dining? It would appear that the staff at this facility has conspired to prolong our discussion. I doubt if we will ever be able to obtain anything else to eat besides bread and wine."

"I thoroughly agree with you in both respects. I appreciate both your burgeoning new-found skill in observation and deduction and your disinclination to reach a conclusion on the very little evidence of my persona that I have revealed to your senses. It is a capital mistake to theorize before you have all of the evidence. It biases the judgement. Please permit me to introduce myself," the taller man said. "Suffice it to say, at this moment, that my name is Mr. Sigerson, I am Norwegian, and before resuming my deductive activities, I went on a two-year pilgrimage of exploration. Perhaps you have read of my exploits in the newspaper."

"I am sorry that I do not usually follow the news as thoroughly as I should, so I have not read of you. I am a monomaniac, concentrating exclusively on my work. I believe that one must not fish in too many waters. That is the secret of my success. My name is Professor Paul Ehrlich, and I am currently continuing to research the specific staining affinities of coal tar dyes and am initiating studies in immunology at the Institute for Infectious Diseases in Berlin with Professor Robert Koch."

Ehrlich's table companion looked keenly into his eyes, obviously relishing the turn that their conversation had taken, and said: "I cannot agree more with your observation regarding selective intake of information. In fact, I believe that a man's brain is originally like a little empty attic, and you have to stock it with such furniture as you choose. A fool takes in all the lumber of every sort that he comes across, so that the knowledge which might be useful to him gets crowded out, or at best is jumbled up with a lot of other things, so that he has a difficulty in laying his hands upon it. Now the skillful workman is very careful indeed as to what he takes into his brain-attic. He will have nothing but the tools which may help him in doing his work, but of these he has a large assortment, and all in the most perfect order. It is a mistake to think that little room has elastic walls and can distend to any extent. Depend upon it there comes a time when for every addition of knowledge you forget something that you knew before. It is of the highest importance, therefore, not to have useless facts elbowing out the useful ones."

Ehrlich replied:" This has been a most illuminating conversation. Although I had originally been in a rush to return to my researches, there comes a time when discussion and reflection on the problem may provide more progress than any individual experiment. If you can spare the time, I would greatly appreciate your giving me your thought on a subject that has been foremost in my mind for many years."

"Yes, of course," he retorted. "I am certain that your researches must have the highest degree of significance, if someone of your obvious scholarly attainment considers them of such overwhelming import that he is willing to sacrifice even part of his noon time meal for them. However, I may have a visitor and I may need to leave your company very quickly. I hope that you will understand."

Ehrlich replied: "Of course. But I will be especially obliged for any attention and assistance that you can bring to bear on this subject. As I indicated, I have been obsessed with but one object since my youth. When I visited my older cousin, the researcher, Carl Weigert, he permitted me to observe cells through the microscope for the first time. I was amazed to note that not all of the cells were stained to the same extent. Some were deeply stained while others were barely visible. After meditating on this, I theorized that this phenomenon is connected with the selective relationships of choice between the stain and cells, manifested by the readiness with which the stain was absorbed. The differences in affinities explained why it was that only certain dyes would form linkages with specific cell elements. I have devoted my life's work to defining the mechanism responsible for the specific affinity of cells for various coal tar derived, chemically pure dyes."

Chuckling, Sigerson interjected: "I see by your fingers, that the human dermis has an affinity for every color of dye possible. You seem to have defined those conditions perfectly."

"Yes, that is indeed the case," Ehrlich replied "People are afraid to touch anything in my laboratory for fear of acquiring the same nonspecific stains. However, my thoughts on the specific affinity of different dyes, at lower concentrations, of course, have led me to espouse theories that have met with cool receptions from my peers. After many years of painstaking research, I have come to the conclusion that chemical compounds, such as dyes and drugs, have specific side chains that fit, as do keys in a lock, into specific receptors in bacterial and mammalian cells."

Sigerson removed his recently lighted cigar from his mouth and stated: "Such is the situation that I found myself in several years ago. Using a similar chain of logic, I was able to devise a reagent with which I can easily detect the presence of human hemoglobin in a solution of only one part in one million. When I presented this finding to the professors at the laboratory in which I was working, they refused to accept my premise nor my efforts as worthy of pursuing towards an academic degree. Seeing that I was to be thwarted by the narrow-mindedness of academe, I left the laboratory and initiated an independent study of chemical phenomena."

After taking another sip of wine, Ehrlich replied: "The same fate befell me at my previous location. After many dialogues with the newly appointed director, I had no recourse but to do the same. I also set up a private laboratory, until Dr. Koch recruited me for collaboration in his facility. In my laboratory I investigated the relationship between dyes and nerve cells. Again, the same high degree of specificity. I was also able to demonstrate that methylene blue had a much higher affinity for malarial parasites than cells of the human organism. The veracity of my observations, the very specific affinity of dyes for various tissues and organisms, has been supported by my more recent studies with the very concentration dependent interaction of toxins and their antitoxins. Thus, we have at least two independent classes of chemical interactions that support my hypothesis."

Looking ever more keenly at his companion, Sigerson said: "Splendid! I have always thought that when you follow two separate chains of thought, as you have done with chemical dyes and antibodies, you will find some point of intersection which should approximate to the truth. Taking your theories to the ultimate conclusion, if you were to appropriately modify the side chains of the various coal tar derivatives, you would be able to synthesize compounds that could kill microbes such as sleeping sickness and syphilis without damaging the cells of the body."

Ehrlich excitedly replied, "Exactly my thoughts! It is very inspiring to find someone who follows my theories and reaches the same conclusions! I even have devised expressions to define the ideal relationship. Those compounds with a high attraction to parasites I refer to as having high parasitotropy and those with weak effect on mammalian cells as having low organotropy. The index of these two factors expresses the relative medical utility of such compounds. A compound that attacks invading cells such as bacteria, fungi, parasites, or even cancer cells could be classified as a chemotherapeutic agent. I will try to devise drugs that are highly selective for disease cells on one hand and inactive against those of the host on the other -- a Magic Bullet if you will."

"I commend you on your interests and the very fine work that you have done. I can only hope that you will be able, with the assistance of Dr. Koch, find a cure for the illness that afflicts the wife of my very best friend." Then, tearing off his false beard and wig, revealing a moderately short haircut and clean-shaven face, the tall gentleman, known to Ehrlich only as Herr Sigerson, leaped over the table and quickly ran from the scene, leaving as his parting exclamation: "I must go quickly now! The game is afoot! If you value your life, do not under any circumstance tell anyone that you saw me." And then he was gone forever.

This conversation was forever etched into the consciousness of Professor Ehrlich. Long had he mused about the one man who, in his earliest struggles with the scientific establishment, both understood and encouraged him. Finally, he smiled. " Now I know, I know," he thought to himself as he glanced down at the two books that he had acquired to help him alleviate the long hours that he would be required to endure on the train back to Berlin. Their titles were: *Späte Rache* and *Das Zeichen der Vier*.

Some may think that this account is fanciful. There are some who would doubt the actual existence of either Sherlock Holmes or Paul Ehrlich, or even both. Regardless, there is no doubt that Dr. Ehrlich, through hard work, intelligence, and creativity brought forth a new science of chemotherapy which was destined to revolutionize, eventually, the strategies by which new drugs are discovered. Salvarsan, or generically arsphenamine, was in use from 1910 until penicillin replaced it over 30 years later. It was not until the late 1930s that another scientist followed in Ehrlich's footsteps and introduced the next class of anti-infective, the sulfonamides. Both the inventors of the sulfonamides and the developers of the useful application of penicillin acknowledged the contribution that Paul Ehrlich's efforts had on theirs. The fundamental underpinning of all modern immunology and medicinal chemistry, especially the theory of receptors, all derive from the initial concept of Ehrlich's creative research.

Who is to say that Ehrlich's bent for deductive reasoning and meticulous observation did not stem partly from his love of the stories about Sherlock Holmes, as penned by Sir Arthur Conan Doyle, another creative physician of note? There have been numerous accounts of Ehrlich's obsession with the Sherlockian adventures. When Sir Arthur learned about this, he sent his picture, along with a signed note, to the world renowned scientist. Thus, the writings may have had an impact on the world far beyond that which has been previously deduced.

Literature Referred to and Recommended:
1.   Baring-Gould, William S. *The Annotated Sherlock Holmes;* New York: Clarkson N. Potter, Inc., 1967.
2.   Bäumler, Ernst (Edwards, Grant translated by); *Paul Ehrlich Scientist for Life;* New York: Holmes & Meier, 1984.
3.   Blau, Peter E. Scuttlebutt from the Spermaceti Press; Washington, DC: The Spermaceti Press, April, 1994.
4.   Hardwick, Michael. *The Complete Guide to Sherlock Holmes;* New York: St. Martin's Press, 1986.

5.　　　　Redmond,　　C. *A　　Sherlock　　Holmes Handbook;* Toronto: Simon & Pierre, 1993.

Further Reading:

1.　　　　Caplan, Richard M. "Why coal tar derivatives at Montpellier?" THE BAKER STREET JOURNAL (NS), 39, (1989), 29.
2.　　　　Moss, Robert A. "Sherlock Holmes, Paul Ehrlich, and Salvarsan" in THE BAKER STREET JOURNAL (NS), 44, (1994), 20.
3.　　　　O'Brien, James F. "What kind of chemist was Sherlock Holmes?" in CHEMISTRY & INDUSTRY, 7 June 1993, 394.

Acknowledgments:
I must acknowledge, with sincere gratitude, the fortitude and patient assistance of my wife Sandie, who corrected the poor grammar and punctuation in the original manuscript, in spite of the fact that she has absolutely no interest in the subject matter - neither chemistry, chemotherapy, nor Sherlock Holmes.
I am also grateful to the chemist and fellow seeker of scientific truth, Samuel M. Gerber, BSI, for responding so very nicely to my request for information on the state of synthetic organic chemistry in 1893, and for sending me copies of relevant articles concerning the chemical skills of Mr. Sherlock Holmes.

Sherlock Holmes: The Education of the World's First Forensic Scientist

Published in *The Hounds Collection* Vol. 10, May 2005, p 66-72 and *Sherlock Holmes Magazin* Fall Issue, No. 13, pp 12-15 (German Translation)

Introduction

There is ample published material to support the assertion that Sherlock Holmes was the world's first forensic scientist or criminalist. He was the very first individual to apply the Methods of Scientists to the solution of criminal cases and other mysteries.[1] In this treatise, I will attempt to show how his education and life experiences led to this evolutionary process.

Several books and articles attribute the invention of forensic science to Mr. Sherlock Holmes, often attributed to the Literary Agent, Sir Arthur Conan Doyle. According to Richard Safferstein, Ph.D., "Sir Arthur Conan Doyle had a considerable influence on popularizing scientific crime-detection methods through his [sic] fictional character Sherlock Holmes. It was Holmes who first applied the newly developing principles of serology (see Chapter 12), fingerprinting, firearm identification, and questioned document-examination long before their value was recognized and accepted by real life criminal investigators."[2] As support, Dr. Safferstein quotes the text at the beginning of *Study in Scarlet* (STUD), in which Mr. Holmes expounds upon the importance of the "Sherlock Holmes Test for Blood" as the "most practical medico-legal discovery for years."

In his 1983 book, the editor, Samuel M. Berger, Ph.D., BSI, included an entire chapter that identifies Sherlock Holmes' contributions to the development of forensic science. Dr. Berger discussed the Sherlock Holmes Test for blood in relation to tests that were available during that era. He concludes with the statement: "Perhaps the story *A Study in Scarlet* by Conan Doyle gave impetus to the development of improved methods in blood identification." [3] I'm certain that we would all concur in that claim. Articles by chemists James F. O'Brien [4] and Christine L. Huber [5] may be consulted for in-depth evaluations of the revolutionary blood test devised by Sherlock Holmes.

In her more recent book, Judy Williams discusses how the careful, well-contrived methods worked out by Sherlock Holmes led to the development of the modern science of forensics.[6] She sums up his contribution to the scientific method of crime detection as follows: "He did not solve his cases by inspired guesswork or intuition, but by a combination of careful examination, hard work and logic, just like the present day forensic scientist, to arrive at a conclusion based more often than not on a balance of probabilities pointing to the guilt or innocence of the suspect."

It would be very inappropriate to claim that Sherlock Holmes was the very first person to use a scientific approach to the solution of criminal cases. However, he was the first to formalize his experiments and observations into a scientific discipline as early as 1881. As indicated by Mr. Holmes himself in *A Study in Scarlet*, there was already a guaiacum test available for that use. [7] Thus, the concept, at least, had already been formulated. In addition, although Mr. Sherlock Holmes had the practice of "beating the subjects in the dissecting-rooms with a stick" to see how long after death bruising can be manifested, he was not the first to engage in this practice. According to Mr. Owen Dudley Edwards researches, "this was actually a forensic medical experiment carried out by Christison in Nov. - Dec. 1828, to discover if the bruises on the sole corpse obtained by the police . . . were caused by accidents in packing the deceased. [7] Christison "used a number of animal and human corpses and struck them at various carefully timed intervals to determine whether bruising could be induced subsequent to death."

Then, there is the pioneering work of Dr. Joseph Bell, as exemplified in the TV production that was shown on the Discovery Channel on Oct. 5, 2004. *Sherlock Holmes the True Story:* "Who is Dr. Joseph Bell? [8] As stated on their web site, think Sir Arthur Conan Doyle, pipe smoker, funny hat. Sherlock Holmes wasn't simply conjured up by the author. No indeed. The fact is, one of the most recognizable figures in all of literature was based on the personality, physical appearance, and diagnostic genius of a little-known Edinburgh doctor." Although Dr. Bell used his scientific expertise to assist the Edinburgh police in solving cases of murder, he did not develop his researches into a new scientific discipline. Nor did he enlarge the field of inquiry by exploring new scientific methods of analysis. For this, we must give full credit to Sherlock Holmes, the world's first forensic scientist.

It was not until 1893, a full seven years after the publication of STUD and 12 years after Sherlock Holmes formulated his famous test for blood, that the very first book published on this subject appeared. [9] Hans Gross organized his information into a book titled *Handbuch für Untersuchungsrichter* in which he first used the term "Kriminalistic." However, not being a scientist, he did not contribute new research to the field in the manner associated with Sherlock Holmes . . .

Education in the Early Years

Three cases, very well documented by John H. Watson, M.D., provide most of the evidence required to piece together the evolutionary and educational processes that resulted in Sherlock Holmes originating the scientific discipline, forensic science and criminalistics: *The Gloria Scott* (GLOR), *Musgrave Ritual* (MUSG), and *Study in Scarlet* (STUD).[10-12]

The available evidence appears to support the theory that Mr. Sherlock Holmes was home-schooled as a child, via a personal tutor on his parent's estate, and through extensive travel. After all, he was the scion of a "family of country squires who appear to have led the same life as is natural to their class." [13] The fact that his grandmother was French, "the sister of Vernet, the French artist," would have provided excellent inducement for the family to frequently travel to Europe and for Mr. Holmes to become fluent in her native tongue during that time. According to Sherlock Holmes himself, he "was never a very sociable fellow, Watson, always rather fond of moping about in my rooms and working out my own little methods of thought, so that I never mixed much with the men of my year." [10] I suggest that had Mr. Holmes received an education at one of England's prestigious public schools, his aversion to social contact would have been beaten out of him by his classmates. A further support for his solitary upbringing is the fact that he never participated in team sports. "Bar fencing and boxing, I had few athletic tastes," Sherlock Holmes declared. Then, as I will later demonstrate, Mr. Holmes did not matriculate in a university until he was 20 years old, in 1874. Had he followed the standard path, such as that attributed to his contemporary Dr. Arthur Conan Doyle, he would have initiated his college career at an earlier age, perhaps 17 or 18. [14] I suggest that he delayed his entry into the world of higher education due to a lack of enthusiasm for a disciplined plan of study that he would have had to follow at any major college. As we see later, he never accepted that requirement. However, since the son of an aristocratic family must do something in life, he was obligated to go up to university, and go up he finally did. Of course, there are many other possible reasons for his late entry into the university, such as illness or a need to stay at home to help care for a sick relative. One could also speculate that he spent time with his French relatives studying art and music or that he entered the world of the theater as a sign of Bohemian rebellion. However, I suspect that the initial explanation fits his lack of desire to follow any standardized path of study. He resisted until he had no other choice, perhaps under the threat of disinheritance.

When Were His College Years?

First, let us speculate on the years in which Mr. Holmes pursued his collegiate, intercollegiate, and post-collegiate education. Most evidence suggests that Mr. Holmes began his collegiate career at the late age of 20. In GLOR, Sherlock Holmes established that he spent two years in college during which he befriended Victor Trevor. According to Baring-Gould, GLOR took place in 1874.[10] It goes without saying that almost everyone agrees that Sherlock Holmes was born in 1854, making him 20 years old at the time of this episode.

During GLOR, after having spooked the elder Trevor by an episode of observation and deduction during a visit to his estate, Sherlock Holmes left to return to London. According to Mr. Holmes, "All this occurred during the first months of the long vacation. I went up to my London rooms, where I spent seven weeks working out a few experiments in organic chemistry." Thus, even during his tenure at a university, Mr. Holmes was engaged in chemical experimentation. The Canon is silent as to whether these were original research problems or assigned studies, but they set the stage for his becoming an individual researcher later in life.

Later, during the activities described in MUSG, Mr. Holmes had not seen Reginald Musgrave in four years.[11] This encounter was dated as 1879 by Baring-Gould, when Holmes was 25 years old.[15] Counting back, it is logical to calculate that this reunion took place four years after Holmes' second collegiate year.

Prior to MUSG and after leaving college in 1876, Sherlock Holmes "had rooms in Montague Street, just round the corner from the British Museum, studying all of those branches of science which might make me more efficient." This self-study began in 1876, and continued through 1881 when Holmes and Watson, paired at last, took up their famous quarters at 221b Baker Street. From that time on, Sherlock Holmes was able to continue his studies as well as the chemical researches that he had, for some unspecified time, performed during his tenure as a student at St. Bart's and initiated during his first year at an unspecified university.

What University Did He Attend?

Based on his elevated status in society, it appears obvious that Sherlock Holmes attended one of the two more prestigious and ancient universities in England, Oxford or Cambridge. After all, he was a member of the upper class, and that is where upper-class students were sent. Sherlock Holmes' status is evidenced in several ways. For example, he insisted on being referred to with the prefix *Mister* before his name when addressed by Count Silvius. This is clearly the mark of a member of the gentry.[16] Further, Mr. Holmes always used the first-class carriage when traveling by train. In that era, "most people accepted their place in the class hierarchy" and chose the class of railroad cars accordingly.[17] It would be unseemly for a middle-class individual, regardless of income, to do so. And finally, as stated before, Mr. Holmes was descended from "country squires who appear to have led the same life as is natural to their class." [13] In addition, only Oxford or Cambridge would have been appropriate for the son of a wealthy land owner such as Mr. Trevor, and it would be unthinkable for someone with the social status of Reginald Musgrave to attend a lesser institution. [19]

However, beyond that, we cannot go. "Dozens of scholars" have attempted to determine which of these ancient universities can lay claim to Sherlock Holmes.[18] Even the elegant researches of the noted author and Sherlockian scholar Dorothy Sayers were unable to provide a definite conclusion.[19]

There have been several attempts to define Sherlock Holmes' major course of study and therefore his college and university without any success.[18, 19] I would suggest that Mr. Holmes refused to commit himself to a specific course of study, regardless of the college he chose to enter. He had not chosen his field of endeavour and, as he himself stated, was "always rather fond of moping in my rooms and working out my own little methods of thought"[10] I am certain that this lack of attention to a specific course of study would not enamour him to his tutor.

I suggest that at the beginning, Mr. Holmes attended college at the strict desires of his forebears. As a member of the upper class, but not the eldest son who would inherit the estate, he was expected to attend university and establish himself in an appropriate profession such as the military, law, clergy, medicine, or university don in the same manner that his older brother, Mycroft, became an accountant for the British government. [13] At the same time, he would have been expected to make contacts with other members of his college for future networking opportunities. These, no doubt, actually did come into play during the years of his active professional life, helping explain the large number of highly placed individuals who came to his quarters seeking assistance. The only record of a specific academic interest that we have is in chemistry. As we learn in GLOR, Sherlock Holmes spent part of his long vacation in London performing "private chemical researches."[11] That he was not engaged in a normal scientific curriculum can be derived by observing Dr. Watson's later critique of Mr. Holmes' scientific knowledge.[12] Had he done so, we would expect a more general knowledge of various aspects of science in addition to chemistry. However, we learn from "Sherlock Holmes -

his limits, that his knowledge of astronomy was nil; botany - variable except for poisons; geology -- practical but limited; and anatomy - accurate but unsystematic." Thus, it appears quite likely that he only paid attention to those subjects which interested him.

The Great Epiphany

The situation changes abruptly in the long vacation of 1874. Sherlock Holmes discovers his true purpose in life, a reason to learn and study. It all happened during Mr. Holmes' first visit to the estate of his painfully acquired friend Victor Trevor.[11] We owe a sincere debt of gratitude to Trevor's father whose very utterances will forever be regarded as the impetus which led Sherlock Holmes from his life of indecision and lassitude to a remarkable career as a scientific detective. We all recall the elder Mr. Trevor's words that should be engraved on a monument for all to see: "I don't know how you manage this, Mr. Holmes, but it seems that all of the detectives of fact and fancy would be children in your hands. That's your line of life, sir, and you may take the word of a man who has seen something of the world."

And then came the words from Sherlock Holmes that will forever change the history of forensic science and scientific crime detection. He turned to Dr. Watson with a sense of purpose and remarked: "and that recommendation, with the exaggerated estimate of my ability with which he prefaced it, was, if you will believe me, Watson, the very first thing which ever made me feel that a profession might be made out of what had up to that time been the merest hobby." There we have it, the epiphany that set Sherlock Holmes on the course to be the world's foremost consulting detective and the world's foremost protagonist of scientific investigation.

Continuing Education

After leaving college, Mr. Holmes sets out a program of self-study to prepare himself for his chosen vocation. As he related to Dr. Watson, "When I first came to London I had rooms in Montague Street, just round the corner from the British Museum, and there I waited, filling in my leisure time by studying all of those branches of science which might make me more efficient."[11] No doubt, Mr. Holmes also began, at that time, the chemical researches that took him to the chemical laboratory in St. Bart's as well. Although it was possible for Sherlock Holmes to take examinations for a degree at London University or University College, I do not think that this ever came to pass. After all, into what standard discipline would there be an examination that would be commensurate with the studies that Sherlock Holmes imposed upon himself?

Uniquely, *Study in Scarlet* documents the later stages of scientific education that prepared Sherlock Holmes for his lifelong career.[1] Young Stamford, who appears briefly only to disappear forever after that, utters the very first descriptions of Mr. Sherlock Holmes. Stamford tells us that Sherlock Holmes is "a little queer in his ideas -- an enthusiast in some branches of science." Additionally, "He is well up in anatomy, and he is a first-class chemist; but as far as I know, he has never taken out any systematic medical classes. His studies are desultory and eccentric, but he has amassed a lot of out-of-the-way knowledge which would astonish his professors." And, Sherlock Holmes "beat the subjects in the dissecting-rooms with a stick . . . to verify how far bruises may be produced after death." Here we have a young man, who, we will eventually learn many cases later, has attended, but probably never graduated from, one or the other of England's two most prestigious universities, Oxford or Cambridge. Currently, we find him at a medical school, not studying medicine but pursuing a variety of scientific disciplines that we will find out later, will prepare him to approach the solution of criminal activities in a scientific

178

manner. Clearly, Sherlock Holmes was a man ahead of his time. What seemed odd then is very common now. Basic science departments in medical schools, in addition to providing professional education for future physicians, supply academic graduate and postdoctoral training to research scientists leading to a Ph.D. degree or equivalent. In fact, most of the research funding in such departments supports the work of graduate students and postdoctoral fellows. The innovative academic program that Sherlock Holmes created for himself in the Victorian era is not unlike that received by scientists in toxicology and forensic science. But, Sherlock Holmes was the first.

[1] Heifetz, Carl L. *A Study in Scarlet* Yields to the Methods of Sherlock Holmes, Scientist, *Wigmore Street Post Office*, Issue Number 12, Summer 1998, p 18-21,24 and *The Hounds Collection* Vol. 5, April 2000, p 13-17.

[2] Safferstein, Richard, Ph.D. Chapter 1, History and Development of Forensic Science In: Criminalistics An Introduction to Forensic Science. 7th Ed. Prentice Hall, Upper Saddle River, New Jersey, 2001, pp 2-3.

[3] Gerber, Samuel L. Chapter 3.A Study in Scarlet Blood Identification in 1875 In: Chemistry and Crime. From Sherlock Holmes to Today's Courtroom. American Chemical Society, 5th printing, 1992, pp 31-35.

[4] O'Brien, James F. What Kind of Chemist was Sherlock Holmes. Chemistry and Industry. 7 June 1993, 394-8.

[5] Huber, Christine L. The Sherlock Holmes Blood Test. The Baker Street Journal. 37 (4) (Dec.) 1987, 215-20.

[6] Williams, Judy. Chapter 1. Sherlock Holmes and the History of Forensic Sciences. In The Modern Sherlock Holmes. Broadside Books Ltd., London, 1991, pp 13-16.

[7] Edwards, Owen Dudley Ed., *A Study in Scarlet*. Oxford University Press, Oxford, 1993, page 143.

[8] http://www.ctvtravel.ca/shows/?mode=1&id=281

[9] DeForest, P. R., Petraco, N., and Kobilinsky, L. Chapter 4.Chemistry and the Challenge of Crime In: Chemistry and Crime. From Sherlock Holmes to Today's Courtroom. American Chemical Society, 5th printing, 1992, pp 45-63.

[10] Doyle, A. C. The "Gloria Scott," 373-385 In: The *Complete Sherlock Holmes* by Arthur Conan Doyle, with a preface by Christopher Morley, Doubleday and Company, Garden City, New York, single volume, 1988.

[11] Doyle, A. C. The Musgrave Ritual, 386-397 In: *The Complete Sherlock Holmes* by Arthur Conan Doyle, with a preface by Christopher Morley, Doubleday and Company, Garden City, New York, single volume, 1988.

[12] Doyle, A. C. *A Study in Scarlet*, pp 15-86 In: The *Complete Sherlock Holmes* by Arthur Conan Doyle, with a preface by Christopher Morley, Doubleday and Company, Garden City, New York, single volume, 1988.

[13] Doyle, A. C. "The Greek Interpreter," pp 435-446 In: The *Complete Sherlock Holmes* by Arthur Conan Doyle, with a preface by Christopher Morley, Doubleday and Company, Garden City, New York, single volume, 1988.

[14] Rodin, A. E. and Key, Jack D. Chapter 1, Student and Practitioner, pp 3-77 In Medical Casebook of Doctor Arthur Conan Doyle, Robert E. Kreiger Publishing Company, Inc., Malabar, Florida, 1984.

[15] Baring-Gould, William S. In: *The Annotated Sherlock Holmes*. Vol. 1Clarkson N..Potter, Inc., New York, 690 pages.

[16] Doyle, A. C. "The Adventure of the Mazarin Stone," pp 1012-22 In: The *Complete Sherlock Holmes* by Arthur Conan Doyle, with a preface by Christopher Morley, Doubleday and Company, Garden City, New York, single volume, 1988.

[17] Mitchell, S. Chapter 2 The Foundation of Daily Life: Class, Tradition, and Money. In Daily Life in Victorian England. Greenwood Press, Westport, Conn.

[18] Klinger, L. S. "The Gloria Scott" In The New Annotated Sherlock Holmes Vol. I, pp 501-527, Norton and Co., New York, 2005.
[19] Sayers, D. L. Holmes College Career In *Sayers on Holmes*, pp12-21, The Mythopoeic Press, Altadena, California.

Sherlock Holmes - Typical Research Chemist

Letter Published in *The Holmes Front*, Issue #5 August 1999

In the recent edition of the Baker Street Journal, the eminent scholars Wayne and Francine Swift provided a very interesting and well researched article defining the characteristics of the various "Associates of Sherlock Holmes."(1) Although I generally agree with their analyses of Sherlock Holmes contemporaries, I regret that I must thoroughly disagree with their contention that Mr. Holmes was a physician. Looking at the table provided on page 30 of their essay, they submit as their only proof the evidence that they have extracted from a prior work by Dr. Gideon Hill. Indicated therein are Dr. Hill's interpretations of the various steps that Sherlock Holmes uses in solving the problems that are presented to him. These are listed as "Making the appointment, Patient's statement of medical history and present situation, Physical examination by the physician, the diagnosis, Physician explains to the patient, and Lab studies ordered."

I contend that this is a serious misinterpretation of Mr. Holmes' mode of operation, and I would like to counter with evidence that clearly demonstrate that in personality traits and modus operandi Mr. Holmes was a prototypical research chemist. I will support my thesis with evidences regarding the fact that he was trained as a research chemist, had the peculiar life style of a research chemist, and finally, approached the solution to mysteries using the methods of a research chemist.

Let us first regard his training. In the beginning of *Study in Scarlet*, while discussing his proposed new apartment mate with Mr. Stamford, Watson queries: "A medical student, I suppose?" To which Stamford clearly replies: "No -- I have no idea what he intends to go in for. I believe that he is well up in anatomy, and he is a first-class chemist." I reiterate: When asked if Holmes was a medical student, Stamford didn't say "maybe" or "I'm not sure." Stamford said "No." That's good enough for me. Why would he lie or try to cover up the possibility that Sherlock Holmes was a medical student when he clearly had no reason to.

Now let us look briefly at Sherlock Holmes personality. In my opinion, nobody acts the way Sherlock acts except for research chemists. Believe me, I know. I have worked with many chemists in my more than 28 years in the pharmaceutical industry, and nobody acts the way they do - crazy, just like Sherlock Holmes. Once they have an idea for a chemical series, they work night, day, and weekends on their syntheses. I can still see them clearly, their stained and tattered laboratory garments half engulfed in their safety hoods watching crystals form, filtering, stirring, centrifuging, distilling, adding smelly and mysterious ingredients to their flasks, making photographs of thin layer chromatographic plates, and scribbling illegible entries, and scribbling illegible entries into their laboratory notebooks. Finally, they hand-deliver small vials of their product to be evaluated for biological activity, along with handwritten copies of their submission forms. Then they come back the next day asking for results of tests that they have been informed over and over again will take at least two weeks to complete and report out. In the interim, they brood. They sit in desultory fashion reading journals, writing patents, filing piles of accumulated data sheets, all the while waiting impatiently to determine whether their new side chains are worthy of further pursuit or not. Not for them the orderly life of the microbiologist: working through the day to set up the cultures that, thankfully, must be left to their own devices in overnight incubation before any readings can be made. Not for them the way of the biochemist who set up their reagents or extractions for overnight processing in a beta scintillation counter or sample changer. No, they will work tirelessly to produce their products and undergo serious ennui until they are finally informed of the results obtained with their precious products. Can anything be more reminiscent of Sherlock Holmes actions?

Finally, let us refute the thesis of the Swifts and Dr. Hill that Sherlock Holmes used the methodology of a physician. I believe that over the years I have provided sufficient detailed evidence to support my contention that Mr. Holmes used the methods of scientists to solve his cases (2). The steps that make up the "method of scientists" are summarized as follows: (I) Clearly state the **PROBLEM** in its simplest form. (II) Gather all of the **DATA** that you can find on the subject. (III) Be very diligent to **OBSERVE** everything, no matter how unrelated it may appear at the time. (IV) Read and master all of the available **KNOWLEDGE** on the subject to see what data has previously been reported. (V) Sift through all of the data, current and reported, and attempt to **DEDUCE A TENTATIVE HYPOTHESIS** and **WORKING MODEL** that reasonably fits all of the available information. (VI) List further needed information, observations, and experiments that may refute or support your hypotheses. Seek **EXPERIMENTAL PROOF** and **ADDITIONAL OBSERVATIONS** and determine if the results fit or point a reformulation of the hypothesis. (VII) With all data in hand, **PUBLISH** your observations, results, hypotheses, and conclusions in an appropriate format for others to read, challenge, and confirm. To the lay observer, these processes appear identical to those listed in the first paragraph supporting the view that Sherlock Holmes acted as a physician. And, in many cases they are indeed virtually identical. Physicians apply all of their observations to define a previously described medical condition. The scientific researcher, on the other hand, explores and defines the unknown. Thus, unlike the last step in the Swift/Hill sequence (Lab studies ordered), research scientists such as Sherlock Holmes are actually performing experiments to test or reject the validity of their hypotheses.

In the spirit of scientific inquiry, I would welcome any attempts by the readers of this thesis to provide any solid evidence to refute the excellent evidence provided herein.

(1) Swift, Wayne and Francine. "The Associates of Sherlock Holmes" BSJ (NS), vol. 49, no. 1 (Mar 1999)
(2) Heifetz, C. L. "Staying Focused," *Communication* (a publication of the Pleasant Places of Florida), No. 173 New Series, Volume 1, Issue 5, pages 3-4; Heifetz, C.L. 1998. The Scientific Detective Solves the Sign of Four. *The Wigmore Street Post Office*, Issue Number 11, Spring 1998, p 3-9; Heifetz, C.L. 1998. A Study in Scarlet Yields to the Methods of Sherlock Holmes, Scientist *The Wigmore Street Post Office*, Issue Number 12, Summer 1998, p 18-21,24;Heifetz, C. L., Sherlock Holmes Scientist Solves A Case of Identity, *The Wigmore Street Post Office* in press.

The Case of the Jewish Pawnbroker
or How Sherlock Holmes Got His Violin

Published in *Plugs and Dottles* January 1996, Issue
Number 208, p3;
and *The Basin Street Journal* March 2002, Volume 1,
Number 1, p 8-9; Practice Notes, The Friends of Dr. John
H. Watson, Feb. 2013, pages 8 - 9..

Dr. Watson has briefly related, in his account of *The Adventure of the Cardboard Box*, how Mr. Sherlock Holmes acquired his valuable and so loved Stradivarius violin. In this well-known narrative, which is documented on page 894 of the "Doubleday Edition" of *The Complete Sherlock Holmes*, the following statement appears, "We had a pleasant little meal together, during which Holmes would talk about nothing but violins, narrating with great exultation how he had purchased his own Stradivarius, which was worth at least five hundred guineas, at a Jew broker's in Tottenham Court Road for fifty-five shillings."

Recently, the phone lines have been abuzz with several theories that have been espoused by members of "The Hounds of the Internet" regarding Jews in the Canon and how it was that Mr. Sherlock Holmes got his Stradivarius so cheaply by putting one over on the unwitting Jewish pawnbroker. To set the record straight once and for all, let me tell you the real "emmus" about that deal. I got it from my second cousin, Moishe the bank president, who comes from a long line of money lenders and pawnbrokers. In fact, one of his ancestors even loaned money to Dr. Watson's older brother on a watch deal. But that's another story.

Anyway, according to Moishe's recollection from talks at a family meeting, one day Sherlock Holmes was disguised as an orthodox Jewish money lender and pawnbroker. Why, we don't know. The kibitzers say that he was trying to entice Moriarty's henchmen to use his services to fence some hot diamonds. True? Who knows, but it sounds good. Anyway, Mr. Holmes, dressed in orthodox Jewish regalia -- yarmulke, tsitsis, full beard, black hat and coat, all the stuff -- goes walking by the local shul just when the shamus is trying to round up one more guy for a minyan. Can Sherlock Holmes refuse? No Orthodox Jew would think of it. In fact, he would be honored by the invitation. How Mr. Holmes bluffed his way through the mincha I don't know. What an actor!!! Anyway, the pawnbroker, Schmulie, sees this new guy as a catch for his older, still unmarried daughter Rachel. What son-in-law material! A prosperous frume Jew new to the area, who has not yet a wife found? So Schmulie brings his new found friend over to his shop for a look see and for Rachel to check him out on the sly. What does Holmes spot but the rare Strad just sitting there big as life. Holmes' eyes light up when he sees the fiddle and Schmulie's mind starts clicking. You get the picture? Schmulie ain't no fool. He's been in business for a long time, and his landsman, Karp the Gypsy fiddler, last week set him straight right away on the real value of this instrument. But, since Schmulie only advanced a fraction of its value on the fiddle, he considers it a good investment to keep the new guy happy and around. Guess who helps Sherlock Holmes with his purchase, flashing her smile and bright teeth, Rachel, who else? She takes a shine to this guy right away. Guess who is oblivious to what transpires, the usually hep Sherlock Holmes. Well, at least Sherlock Holmes gets a deal on the fiddle and the shamus has enough guys for the minyan. Schmulie, what does he get but a good laugh at himself when he reads about the episode in the *Strand* in 1893? And Rachel realizes that there is nothing wrong with her charms. This guy doesn't go for any dames, except that uppity Jewish babe from New Jersey, Irene the opera singer. All's well that ends well.

I hope that this lays to rest all of the fruity notions of how Sherlock Holmes took the Jew pawnbroker to the cleaners.

The Importance of The Contribution of Dr. Watson to the Development of Forensic Science

Published in *The Friends of Dr. Watson 2006 Essay & Pastiche Competition* (tied for 2nd place)
and *Communication* No. 270, 11 (2): 5-6, 2007.

There can be no dispute regarding the fact that Sherlock Holmes was the world's leading proponent of the application of scientific technology to the solution of criminal cases. In fact, several books and articles support this assertion.[1-3]. Further, there is no dispute that, until fairly recently, the Sherlockian Canon represented the most complete compilation of examples of scientific criminal investigation.[4]

How then, one would ask, did Dr. Watson make a significant contribution to the development of forensic science? After all, he was not the scientist. Sherlock Holmes was the scientist. Watson didn't develop a blood test, Sherlock Holmes did that. But, had it not been for the writings of the good doctor, the world would have been deprived of this important contribution to the literature of scientific crime investigation. Perhaps an analogy will help support my assertion. Centuries ago, a normal sized Hebrew youth slew a gigantic Philistine by bopping him with a well slung stone to the forehead. That might have been big news at the time, but who would have known about it today if the anonymous author of the famous biblical account had not inked the narrative on a roll of parchment. The same example that has been stated about the Hebrew Canon may also be proposed for the Sherlockian Canon. Who would have known about the scientific propensities of the world's first consulting detective had his exploits not been publicized by his faithful side kick, Dr. Watson? Think of what the scientific world would have been deprived of had Dr. Watson not been on the job.

From the very beginning of the Sherlockian chronicles, we can see that Dr. Watson was obsessed with the use of science in the solution of criminal cases and proclaiming this assertion to the public at large whenever the opportunity presented itself. From the very origin of the Sherlockian saga, in *Study in Scarlet*, we see Watson remarkably focused on the scientific aspects of Sherlock Holmes' career. Did Watson really need to point out the content of his conversation with Stamford? Did he really need to proclaim the fact that Sherlock Holmes beats subjects in the dissecting room with a stick "to verify how far bruises may be produced after death"? This is quickly followed by a long discourse upon the Sherlock Holmes test for blood. Later, in the very next chapter, Watson provided us with a list titled "Sherlock Holmes -- his limits." This tabulation reads like a syllabus for a modern college program in forensic science. Watson was far ahead of his time. Then in Chapter 3, we are treated to Watson's description of the appropriately careful *in situ* examination of the corpse before sending it on to the morgue. Following this, Watson carefully describes how Holmes examined the room with minute care, utilizing a tape measure and magnifying glass to assist his observations. Watson then describes how the result of his examination, which had amused the police, provided a description of the murderer and the sequence of events leading to its final commission of the crime. Then, in Chapter 3, we are treated to Sherlock Holmes' careful analysis of boot prints and, as revealed in Chapter 4, the rut made by the carriage as it arrived at and left the scene of the poisoning of Stangerson. Further, in Chapter 3, Holmes chastised the police for not assuring the integrity of the murder scene, a primary objective in appropriate crime scene investigation.

These few examples, from *Study in Scarlet*, serve as a brief introduction to what will eventually become a textbook in forensic science presented within the vehicle of interesting mysteries. Perhaps another author than Watson would have neglected the scientific aspects of the cases, focusing on the action and adventure. An incomplete list of Sherlock Holmes' other important contributions to scientific crime detection would include the use of dogs to track chemical trails, characterization of tobacco ash and identification of cigarettes and cigars, identifying and preserving foot prints with plaster of Paris, and tracing people's comings and goings based on the use of splotches of mud on their clothing.

One might assert that Watson was only discussing the cases in which he was involved, and that the scientific aspects were merely an incidental part of the discourse. Then why is it that Watson included laboratory experiments that Holmes performed having nothing to do with the case under discussion? Simply put, Watson went out of his way to insert as many references to Holmes' application of scientific technology as possible. Why? To promote their utilization by the "official police."

Let's look at some examples in which Watson refers to methods of scientific criminology having nothing to do with the case under his review at the time. At the beginning of "The Adventure of Shoscombe Old Place," Watson encounters Holmes peering through a low-power microscope. Seeing Watson, Holmes declares "It is glue, Watson." According to Watson's account, he laughed and queried "Does anything depend on it?" To which Holmes responded that it proves that the cap found at a murder scene was worn by a picture-framer who habitually handles glue." Then, referring to a prior case, Holmes stated "Since I ran down the coiner by the zinc and copper filings in the seam of his cuff they have begun to realize the importance of the microscope."

Then, we have the experiment involving litmus paper in "The Naval Treaty." Alluding to an unreported case, Watson reveals how the diagnosis of murder relied on whether litmus paper changed color. According to Holmes,

"If this paper remains blue, all is well. If it turns red, it means a man's life." Those of us with scientific backgrounds cry out for further explanation. But, regardless, it provides another hint from Watson concerning Mr. Holmes' scientific approach to criminal investigation.

And in "Copper Beeches," Holmes told Watson that "I had better postpone my analysis of the acetone." What was that all about? Was he analyzing samples to see the source of a poisonous dose of a lot of acetone, or was he determining if a mysterious death was caused by slow starvation, in which ketone bodies would appear in the urine? We may never know. However, it is interesting to note that Watson insisted on inserting this irrelevant material into his discourse.

These examples, and many more that could be cited, serve to demonstrate that Dr. Watson was focused on those aspects that demonstrated how Mr. Holmes pioneered that use of scientific investigation in the resolution of criminal problems. He cited many examples where they were not relevant to the case at hand, to include them among his many examples, and he lovingly described the scientific aspects of Mr. Holmes' cases whenever he could. Thanks to Dr. Watson, we have a compilation of thorough and interesting demonstrations of the activities of a scientist who turns his mind to crime detection. There is no doubt in my mind that Dr. Watson, through his exciting narratives, intended to educate the police and the public at large with the proper use of technology in the pursuit of justice.

1. Gerber, S.M., Ed. *Chemistry and Crime*, 1983, American Chemical Society, Washington D.C., 2. Wagner, E. J. *The Science of Sherlock Holmes*, John Wiley & Sons, Hoboken, N. J.
3. Heifetz, C. L. Sherlock Holmes: The Education of the World's First Forensic Scientist, *The Hounds Collection* Vol. 10, May 2005, 66-72.

4. *The Complete Sherlock Holmes* by Arthur Conan Doyle, with a preface by Christopher Morley, Doubleday and Company, Garden City, New York, single volume, 1988.

The Missing Stradivarius

Published in *The Formidable Scrap-Book of Baker Street*, 1997, Classic Specialities Books, Cincinnati; *Baker Street West 1*, .12 (1): 14-20, (Winter) 2006

To the few relaxed diners enjoying a late, mid-Sunday morning breakfast in the revolving restaurant that towers over the Renaissance complex and overlooks the Detroit River, the day promised to be without any noteworthy events. As the viewing window turned to reveal Atwater Street below, all appeared to be normal. The nondescript, old, red brick warehouses and small manufacturing plants lining the northern side of this most southern street of the city of Detroit were deserted, with the exception of a few security guards and one or two type "A" executives getting an early start on the week to follow. The parking lots were virtually empty and no automobile traffic could be seen.

However, this day in 1995 promised to be a momentous one for Emile Vernet. As the tall, thin, blonde-haired man in his mid-20s rose from his customary corner table, a look of resolve covered his strong, hawk like face. After lighting his ever-present pipe, he donned his customary cloth driving cap and carefully wrapped his white silk scarf around his neck. The turtle-necked sweater, suede leather windbreaker, and buttoned driving gloves completed his appearance as an aficionado of the British sports car era of the mid-1950s. He carefully checked for onlookers before taking the private express elevator to the personal parking corral. Mr. Vernet completed the picture of elegant affluence as his British racing green Lotus Elan roared out into the waiting street. The trip was not a long one as the sleek sports car approached one of the old warehouses and disappeared through a door that briefly and noiselessly revealed itself in the back side of the building.

As Emile's eyes became accustomed to the dim interior light of the huge, concrete-floored main room, an expected scene was revealed. In the far right-hand corner of the red brick wall, a few empty cartons supported a broom and dustpan. In the center were twenty to thirty very large wooden pallets holding what looked like machinery covered by clean tarpaulins. And covering the entire left hand wall were uniformly arrayed boxes whose labels indicated the presence of such mundane items as wheel locks, mufflers, nuts and bolts. All in all, it had the characteristic look of a reasonably busy facility awaiting Monday's shipment of goods for temporary storage. Emile walked to the opposite wall, advanced to the corner, and carefully lifted the face of a brick to reveal an electric panel with myriad lights and control switches.

"It will not be necessary to announce your presence, Emile, or to ring the bell," a slightly British-accented voice gently sounded through quadri phonic speakers embedded in the wall. "The door to my studio is open. Please do come in. Due to a series of events, and the messages from my stalwart agents, I fully anticipated and prepared for your very welcome visit."

"Cut the Sherlock Holmes routine Uncle! You do not need to impress me with your sleuthmanship. Stick to your painting and leave the intrigues to James Bond or The Saint," the younger man replied. I only came here to tell you that I have been successful in my quest for Grandfather's violin that I initiated at your request."

With that, a large door slid open to reveal a square brightly lit and well equipped artist's studio. Oil canvases and water colors lined one 45-foot wall, while the wall opposite served as a backdrop to a series of bronze and marble statues. The works spanned all time frames and styles, from neo-classic to incomprehensible abstracts. Most noteworthy was the fact that they all bore the names of different artists, none the name of the person to whom Emile

Vernet addressed his comments: "I see that you have sold several pieces since last I was here. I trust that they brought in a pretty penny. I do admire your creativity, but cannot comprehend why you insist on never using your real name. You have made many pseudonyms famous by now. Is it not time to reveal your heritage and allow the world to revere yet another great Horace Vernet?"

"Dear Emile," the older man responded, "Someday soon, you will realize why our family has kept our identity secret all of these years. We have many enemies that have pursued us over the generations. If they understood who we really are, our usefulness would cease. Besides, since our cadet branch of the Vernet family has been in the United States, we have been going by the surname of Vernor, although our British cousins have retained the French pronunciation, but have decided to end the name with an 'er' rather the 'et' of our French ancestors."

"Well Uncle, enough of this silly genealogical discourse. I merely came to you to tell you that I will soon have in my hands the violin that once belonged to my grandfather, and which was missing all of these years."

"Most interesting, Emile, please tell me how you were able to accomplish this. But first, let us go into the parlour and relax with an early pre-lunch aperitif, if that does not shock your often too-conventional sensitivities."

Both men walked through yet another opening in the wall that led to a sumptuous drawing room with a large billiard table and a well-equipped bar.

"Uncle, it is still too early for me to imbibe alcoholic beverages, but I would be pleased to enjoy one of your fine cigars and a cup of coffee imported from one of your South American plantations."

With this dialogue, the two men sat across from each other in luxurious bronze leather recliners enjoying their respective drinks, the younger man his huge mug of life-instilling highly caffeinated coffee and the older with his

196

very dry sherry. Both drew heavily on their massive, dark brown double corona cigars, after which Emile commenced a continuation of their conversation, "I did as you suggested, Uncle. I scoured all of the English and French language newspapers and musical publications that I could get my hands on, from the date of the loss of the instrument to the current year, even though that meant many miles of travel to locate some of the less available sources. Eventually, I subscribed to a broad gamut of representative publications, and constantly perused the Internet. I followed all of the news services for any sign that might prove useful. Then, one day the break came. There was a small article in the *St. Petersburg Times* of January 8 of this year. The item stated that more than 1,000 stolen violins and cellos were found in the home of a second-hand dealer in Paris. The instruments were on display at an exhibition space on Avenue Montaine."

"So, Emile, you went to Paris to look for the violin."

"No Uncle, I did not want to tip my hand. Even though I do not believe all of your tales about ancient enemies, I thought that to satisfy you it would be better that I go through an intermediary. Thus, I contacted our old friend Inspector François le Villard. I believe you stated that our families have had a relationship going back several generations, and that he could be trusted completely."

"Good plan, Emile; although you do not believe me, it could have been a carefully planned effort to reveal our current identities and locations. These people are very clever, and they will stop at nothing to take their revenge on us."

"Yes, so I have heard before, from my poor dead father, and now from you. Anyway, I went to France and made Montpelier my headquarters. We have old and dear friends in that beautiful city. That is where I first examined the beautiful Stradivarius brought to me personally by M. Le

Villard. I examined it and the case very carefully with the powerful hand lens given to me by Father. Some very pertinent clues revealed that I was on the right track."

"My dear nephew, how did you proceed?"

"Well, I knew that it would be necessary to convince M. Le Villard that I could describe features of the violin that only its true owner would know. Once I had enumerated these features in advance, he allowed me to examine the instrument to determine if they were indeed present."

"And Emile, I trust from your claim of success that you were able to predict very special features of the instrument that only its true owner would know. I am curious as to what you found."

"As I predicted to M. Le Villard, there were several almost imperceptible scratches under the strings and on the inside of the case. The hand lens revealed four lines of scratches. Each line bore several numbers followed by some letters that I was at first unable to decipher. Upon further inspection with the lens, the numbers revealed themselves to be several dates during the late 1870's. Also, as I expected, the script was in the Jewish language. These supported my predictions that the violin had been purchased from a pawnbroker of the Jewish persuasion. Needless to say, M. Le Villard was flabbergasted by my uncanny ability to describe the instrument, and without further ado he handed it to me for my further disposition. It is very nice to have friends in important positions, is it not, Uncle Horace? "

"Is that the only evidence that you have?" asked the uncle.

"Not exactly," the nephew replied. "I also directed his attention to the interior of the instrument. As I had predicted, there was a large accumulation of rosin inside. That could only have come from holding it flat, say on the knees, while bowing. That was the last piece of evidence that the Inspector required."

"Were you satisfied as to the authenticity of the instrument? How do you know that our enemies, in whom you do not truly believe, did not disguise another violin to trap you? All of this information could have been garnered from well-recognized literary sources. "

"Interesting question. I brought the violin back to Detroit and had it subjected to chemical analysis to complete its authentication. I assure you that I know the chief chemist very well. Here is the report of the analytical laboratory for your edification. I am now completely certain that we have finally located our precious family heirloom that we were deprived of for all of these many years." And with that, the younger man handed the laboratory report
to his uncle:

PRIVATE CONSULTING ANALYSTS,
INC.
No job too large---No job too small!!!
P.O. Box 221, Oak Park, MI 48237

Chemical analysis of the following object: One
Stradivarius violin

Procedures: *Scrapings of the interior of the object were carefully made to avoid any alteration of the violin. The material thus derived was separated in five (5) equal-weight samples which were dissolved and analyzed according to standard protocol 5789.21 (see addendum for detailed procedures).*

Results: *It would appear that said object resided for many years in a chemical laboratory. Analysis of the obtained samples revealed the presence of small amounts of the following compounds: several unidentifiable vegetable alkaloids, several closely related coal-tar derivatives, bisulphate of baryta, several unknown hydrocarbons that proved to be very difficult to dissolve, a variety of acetones (ketones), and traces of hydrochloric acid, iodoform, carbolic acid (phenol), amyl nitrate, prussic acid, and vitriol.*

Comment: The presence of these chemicals indicates that this instrument was possessed by an individual who performed a variety of chemical experiments over a prolonged period of time. It is highly unlikely that such a mixture of compounds could have been obtained in recent times, since many of the organic compounds are not listed in any compendia and are, thus, very obscure. We thus conclude that this is a unique article unlike any other. It is interesting to note that most or all of the items extracted from the scrapings were predicted in the request for service. For an additional fee of $50,000, we can provide more extensive analyses in an attempt to define the chemical structures of the unknown substances.

Certification: I certify that the above report and attached addenda are accurate and that the analyses have been performed as described   J. H. Watson, Ph.D.

Please make all checks for services payable to Private Consulting Analysts, Inc.

"My dear nephew let me present you with the violin that you have so nicely discovered and identified."

"Uncle!" exclaimed the now excited younger man, "How could you possibly have possession of the violin!? Where did you get it!?"

"Well, my dear nephew, I too have a few tricks up my sleeve. I am the Private Consulting Analyst known to you as Dr. John H. Watson. The gentleman you know as an agent for that firm is an employee of mine in our consulting detective agency. His real name is not Mr. Barker, as you thought. That was only a little joke of mine. Now that you have passed the final test to join the family business, I will be able to explain the significance of the names Watson and

Barker, and the true identity of the original owner of the violin, and the name of our long-time nemesis."

With that, the older man handed the precious violin to his stunned nephew and escorted him into a chamber whose opening appeared in the floor in response to a low whistling sound from his pursed lips.

"Once this was a secret chamber utilized by the bootleggers who brought their cargo across the River from Walkerville. There is also a passage leading under Atwater Street to an old abandoned dock several feet out into the water. This room is now my secret headquarters. Come take a look. I expect that you will be spending a lot of time here now that you will be the fourth generation in the family agency that was started by my first-cousin thrice removed. It is unfortunate that your father did not live to see this day. However, you will have the opportunity of helping me to finally avenge his untimely death at the hands of our enemies, by bringing them and their minions to justice."

"My dear Uncle, I think that I would like that drink now. A nip from the Tantalus and gasogene, that I note to be in possession of the side table in your hideout, would be very welcome indeed."

[The scene switches to Sherlock Holmes' retreat in Sussex sometimes after 1903]

Do come in, Watson. I am so happy that you have finally had the chance to come again to my refuge in Sussex. Your visits are much too infrequent. But you could not have come at a more propitious time. Please help yourself to a cigar and the fruits of the vine that I have only now opened for our enjoyment."

"But Holmes," said the good doctor, "I note that you have three wine glasses on the table. Is this to be a reenactment of our adventure regarding Sir Eustace Brakenstall?"

"No, my good fellow. I know how curious you are about my relatives. I have desisted in introducing you to any more since the time that you revealed this private information about my grandmother in the narration involving our Greek friend Mr. Melas. However, since you have agreed to not produce any more narrations of our adventures together, I feel that it will now be appropriate for you to meet my cousin's grandson, Michael Verner. He will be here soon to share the wine. You might recall his father, Dr. Verner, who bought your practice."

"So, Holmes, it really was as I suspected. I thought that I was too fortunate in selling my declining practice for such a good price. Why did you trick me that way?"

"I knew that you eventually would see through my subterfuge and realize that I was behind the entire transaction. I so missed my partner, and had a very difficult time concentrating on the boring intervals between challenging cases without you to prod me into action on the mundane activities required to keep up my activity logs and reference works. Also, you took the death of your wife very hard, and I knew that the activity would bring you back out of your state of funk. Some of our best cases, and, I might say your very interesting accounts, came after that diabolical transaction. I hope that you can forgive me for tricking you once again. But wait, here comes my distant cousin. Let me introduce him to you."

Now entering the room was a 25-year old blonde-haired man, but as tall, thin, and hawk faced as his older cousin, wearing a fashionable tweed hunting suit with the obligatory knickerbockers and deerstalker cap. Mr. Holmes continued, "Come in Michael. I would like you to meet my old friend and comrade in arms, Dr. John H. Watson. Watson, this is my young cousin Michael Verner of whom I was speaking. Michael, please come join us in some fine claret while we discuss the violin that you will soon possess."

At that comment, Dr. Watson's eyes looked at the customary resting place of Holmes' prized Stradivarius.

"Watson, I can tell by your expression that you are surprised that I am willing to part with my musical companion that has both plagued and charmed you over the many years of our association. As you mentioned in the preface of your most recent book, I now suffer from rheumatism and am no longer capable of doing justice to such a fine instrument. Michael is an accomplished musician and, in addition to many other activities, will carry the tradition that I began many years ago."

References

Anonymous. *The St. Petersburg Times.* St. Petersburg, Florida. Sunday, January 8, 1995.

Doyle, Sir Arthur Conan. *The Complete Sherlock Holmes.* Garden City, New York: Doubleday.

Doyle, Sir Arthur Conan. *The Memoirs of Sherlock Holmes,* in *The Oxford Sherlock Holmes,* first ed., Ed. Owen Dudley Edwards. New York: Oxford University Press, 1993, 282-3.

Doyle, Sir Arthur Conan, *The Sign of Four, in The Annotated Sherlock Holmes,* first single

volume ed., Ed. William S. Baring-Gould, New York: Clarkson N. Potter, 1986, vol.

1.15.

Goodrich, William D. *The New Good Old Index*, Dubuque, Iowa: Gasogene, 1994.

Tracking With Aniseed And Its Other Uses

Based on a Presentation at the fall gathering of the Pleasant Places of Florida
Discussion of Sherlock Holmes Mystery - *The Adventure of the Missing Three-Quarter*
November 18, 2000, Palm Harbor, Florida
Published in *The Holmes & Watson Report*, 5 (1): 26-32, (March) 2001; and The Hounds Collection Volume 9, 2004, p 1-5.

Imagine if you will, the chaos that would result if a star football player such as Warren Sapp, defensive star of the Tampa Bay Buccaneers, were missing just before he was scheduled to play in the Superbowl. Well, it doesn't hurt to dream, does it? Anyway, the fans would go nuts; the gamblers would have a field day if they found out. In despair, Sapp's teammates would seek out the best private consulting detective available.

This hypothetical situation is not without precedence. Consider the story that we are analyzing today. Documented by Dr. John H. Watson, such a similar event occurred in Victorian London. Godfrey Staunton, star three-quarter of the Cambridge Varsity rugby team was missing under mysterious circumstances the day before their big rugby game with Oxford. To whom should the distraught teammate Cyril Overton turn? Sherlock Holmes, of course. Where is Mr. Staunton? What happened to him? Things appear very dark for the young man. The obvious impression is that Mr. Staunton has either been kidnapped or has otherwise met with foul play. The case takes Holmes and Watson to the city of Cambridge in search of the missing athlete. Staunton's location appears to be associated with the mysterious comings and goings of the wily Dr. Leslie Armstrong. What is the doctor's hold over Godfrey Staunton? Why does he not permit Sherlock Holmes to see him? Try as he might, Mr.

Holmes is stymied in his efforts until he tries one last tactic. Using his hypodermic syringe, he sprays the wheels of Dr. Armstrong's carriage with aniseed, and later, with the assistance of the olfactory apparatus of the draghound, Pompey, is able to locate the hideout of the two gentlemen in question. The mystery is cleared up as we find Mr. Staunton mourning his just-deceased secret wife, and Sherlock Holmes and his erstwhile antagonist shake hands as they reach a friendly understanding.

Legendary Canine Olfactory Skills: In Sherlockian lore, we have several instances in which the scenting ability of a dog has a major impact on the outcome of Sherlock Holmes' cases. In *The Adventure of Shoscombe Old Place*, the Shoscombe spaniel recognized the fact that the "old woman" in the carriage was not his mistress, who was already deceased. Previously, the dog had accurately detected his mistress's scent among the bones in the family crypt.

There is also the mysterious attack by the wolfhound Roy on his master Professor Presbury in *The Adventure of the Creeping Man*. The dog did not make a mistake. According to his lights, and his great olfactory sense, the creature he attacked was not the professor; he attacked the simian scent that resulted when Professor Presbury utilized the "serum of anthropoid" supplied by H. Lowenstein.

We must also take cognizance of the "dog who did nothing in the night time," in *Silver Blaze*. This non-event led Sherlock Holmes to understand that the culprit who spirited away the prize horse was scented as the dog's master himself.

And finally, and most relevantly, who can forget the great dog Toby in *The Sign of Four*? This dog led Holmes and Watson on a merry chase throughout London following a trail of creosote that had been laid down by the Andaman Islander, who had accidentally stepped in this material in Mr. Sholto's attic.

Why Did Sherlock Holmes Choose Aniseed?: In *The Adventure of the Missing Three-Quarter*, Sherlock Holmes had many more options available than he did in the *Sign of Four*. Instead of being limited to creosote, he could choose whatever scent he wanted. From the shelf, he chose aniseed over all of the many other lures as his scent of choice, and a draghound as his tracking tool. This combination of *apparati* would probably seem obvious to Mr. Holmes' contemporaries, but was a mystery to me. Why did Mr. Holmes choose aniseed over all other available spices, and why did he select a draghound? What is a draghound? As we shall see by the following discussion, such a strategy was the most obvious and effective one available at the time, and would have required no explanation for his contemporary readers. We will also discover why aniseed was very available to Mr. Sherlock Holmes.

What Is Aniseed?: Let us first consider the various definitions of the term "aniseed":

(1) According to one Internet website, "aniseed" is a 4-piece band from Melbourne, Australia. Blending an eastern influence with soaring guitars, Aniseed is renowned for passionate scintillating live shows. The critically praised debut CD "Carnival" is out now!"

(2) A more likely definition comes from the *Grolier Encyclopedia* which states that, "Anise, *Pimpinella anisum*, is an annual herb of the carrot family, cultivated for aniseed, its small, fragrant fruits. Aniseed is used as a flavoring in baked goods. Its essential oil is used to flavor licorice candies, cough drops, liqueurs such as absinthe and anisette, and some tobacco blends. Anise is native to the eastern Mediterranean but is cultivated today in southern Europe and North and South America."

(3) According to Jack Tracy's good old book *The Encyclopedia Sherlockiana*, aniseed is "the aromatic seed of the Mediterranean anise plant, or a derivative of this seed that Holmes sprayed upon the hind wheel of Leslie Armstrong's

brougham, so that Pompey might follow it (MISS)." Also, his definition reveals that the derivatives of aniseed may also be referred to by that name. Since it is unlikely that the seeds themselves could be sprayed on to the wheel and adhere thereon, one might consider that in this case the alternate definition would apply. Thus, the material squirted through the syringe was most likely anise oil, a substance prepared by the compression of aniseed.

So now we know what aniseed is and are reminded of how Sherlock Holmes utilized this substance to locate Dr. Armstrong's hideout, and thus, Mr. Staunton as well.

But the second question still remains. Of all available scents to guide his canine associate, why did Mr. Holmes choose aniseed? There are certainly many other, more pungent spices from which to choose. Why not creosote? After all, it worked with Toby.

Aniseed Drives Dogs Nuts!: I am immensely indebted to Ms. Mary Vivit, who provided the first major clue, in response to my query over the Hounds of the Internet regarding this topic. She supplied very important information that she had derived from *Rodale's Illustrated Encyclopedia of Herbs*, a book that was not available in any of my local libraries. To quote directly from page 16: "What catnip is to cats, anise is to dogs; they love the scent of this herb. For drag hunting, a sack saturated with oil and dragged across the countryside provides a scent for foxhounds to follow. In greyhound racing, the artificial hare is scented with anise." Probably everyone in England at that time was familiar with anise and drag racing. What would have been more obvious at the time for Mr. Holmes than to use this pleasantly scented herb?

Jack Tracy's definition of draghound supports this explanation. To quote: "Draghound, a hound trained to follow an artificial scent, usually that of a bag of aniseed dragged along the ground, which is substituted for a fox in riding to hounds. Holmes called Pompey "the pride of the local draghounds." (MISS)

Is Drag Racing Still Practiced?: How civilized of the British! Having the dogs trail an herbal scent through the woods seems much more humane than having them chase a poor fox to death. That is true, from the rider's perspective and that of the fox. However, the dogs and horses probably would probably not note this difference. Do you wonder if this still counts as a real hunt? I did. Do some of the guys still wear red jackets and blow their horns? Can you still "ken John Peel with his horse and his hounds in the morning?"

Well, it turns out that you can! In response to my query over the Baker Street E-Regulars List and the News Group alt.fan.holmes, I received several replies in the affirmative, indicating that drag hunting is popular throughout the English-speaking world.

Alex Parker wrote, in one reply: "Yes people do still drag hunt -- I've done it myself in the last 6 months. Everyone wears the "proper" clothes and follows all the traditions and in my opinion it is better than a proper hunt (I've done both). It is more structured, and less cruel to animals (e.g. foxes) involved. As to the specific breed of dog, I can't remember I'm afraid!"

Someone identified only as Josh responded with: "Well, I can give you a little information, for I am slightly familiar with the practice of drag hunting. People indeed do still "drag hunt," but as far as I know they no longer call it "drag hunting." If the updated practice has a new name I can't tell you what it is. However, while growing up in central Pennsylvania I witnessed a neighbor who would regularly train hound dogs or beagles through the use of various bags containing scents. No one associated with my neighbor in PA would take part in anything remotely like the traditional drag hunt, e.g. red jackets, horns, etc. But, I believe the great majority of the dogs he used were beagles, simply trained by him through the use of scented bags. He would drag the bags along the ground and through a wooded area and then hide them somewhere...like in a hole, or on a tree, or under brush, etc., and then the dogs would be released. He would put barbed wire inside the bags so the dog would learn not to bite down too hard when bringing the prey back to him."

Spurred by these replies, my own Internet search revealed that drag hunting is even practiced in Northern Florida at "Misty Morning Hounds." For those wishing to try this activity, their address, phone number, and E-mail address are: 9243 SE CR 2082, Gainesville, FL 32641; (352) 375-0800; <info@mistymorninghounds.com>. For more detailed information, their beautiful website may be found at "http://mistymorninghounds.com/." According to their home page: "Misty Morning Hounds is a private drag pack in the Ocala-Gainesville / North-Central Florida area. The Hunt was organized in 1995 by Alexis and Walter Macaulay, MFHs, with the drafting of 7-1/2 couple of Foxhounds from the Middlebury Hunt in Connecticut. The Hunt became registered in 1997 by the Masters of Foxhounds Association and then Recognized in 1999. Hunt country encompasses roughly 40,000 acres of mostly public land owned or managed by the St. Johns River Water Management District, the Florida Game & Freshwater Fish Commission, and Georgia Pacific, as well as several private farms. Hunting is twice a week from October through March. Jumping is not required and typically there is a tally-ho wagon for non-riding spectators. A limited number of field hunters are available for hire."

Other sites for information and photos on Britain's current drag hunts are: http://www.necdh.co.uk/ (North East Cheshire Drag Hunt), drag-hunting in South Africa at http://www.capehunt.atfreeweb.com/ (Cape Hunt & Polo Club); and the USA http://www.horse-country.com/hunt/woodbrook.html (Woodbrook Hunt Club) and http://www.smithtownhunt.org/ (The Smithtown Hunt).

Where Did Sherlock Holmes Get the Anise?: But I digress. Now that we have established that anise is the perfect olfactory tool to encourage Pompey to track down the brougham, where did the anise come from? I have searched my spice racks, accumulated over 41 years of marriage, without finding one trace of aniseed or anise oil. My wife assures me that she has never, ever used this substance, even when we were in a gourmet club in Ann Arbor, Michigan. As a retired pharmacist (active from 1957 to 1964), I do not recall one instance of a prescription requiring the use of anise, and this was back in the old days when we actually made medicines. I also never encountered it while studying pharmacognosy, even though we were required to learn about many obsolete herbal and botanical remedies that hadn't been used for over 30 years.

Uses of Anise: A review of the literature reveals that anise has a long and storied past as a useful substance. In addition to tracing missing rugby players, aniseed has had many applications in the household and in industry. These include foods, medicines, alcoholic beverages (such as absinthe, pernod, ouzo, raki, arak, anisette), tobacco blends, bait in mouse traps, greyhound racing, and potpourri. Thus, it is very likely that aniseed was easily available to Sherlock Holmes in the kitchen, at a bakery, the local chemist, or pet shop.

Uses of Aniseed and Anise Oil in Food Preparation: Even today, aniseed is widely used to flavor pastries; it is the characteristic ingredient of a German bread called Anisbrod. Aniseed and anise oil are often used alone or with other herbs to flavor many foods and beverages. Foods include roast pork, duck, fish and vegetable dishes, cookies, marinades, candies, dried figs, game, soup, sweet spices, desserts, salads, vegetables (carrots, spinach), and stewed fruit. The website "Women.com" states that: "among the cafe set, anise is the herb most likely to be invited to cocktails. From Greek ouzo to French pastis to Italian sambuca, anise lends its distinctive flavor to some of the world's most sophisticated libations -- but the herbally hip know that this plant has as important a place in the medicine chest as it does in the liquor cabinet."

According to "MotherNature.com," 1 fl.oz of Anise Mature Seed, is available from Herb Pharm in 2 - 3 days for only $6.15.

Medicinal Uses of Aniseed: Aniseed and anise oil have several medicinal uses. It makes a soothing herbal tea and has been used medicinally from prehistoric times. The essential oil content is about 2.5 percent, and its principal component is anethole. According to the most authoritative source, Youngken's *Textbook of Pharmacognosy*, the dried ripe fruit of *Pimpinella anisum* can be used medicinally as a stimulant, carminative, and flavoring agent. The average dose is 0.5 Gm. or 8 grains.

Other published applications are as a laxative and in mouthwash. More extensive claims include its use in coughs, flatulence, respiratory infections, asthma, indigestion, and insufficient lactation. It is used externally for lice, scabies, and as a chest rub for bronchial complaints. Romans used aniseed to make a early version of a wedding cake called *mustaceum*. After a heavy meal, such as that eaten at a wedding, it was eaten as digestive aid.

There is even scientific support for the medicinal use of anise. A popular ingredient in cough drops, anise contains the chemicals creosol and alpha-pinene, which have been shown to loosen mucus in the bronchial tubes and make it easier to cough up. The after-dinner ingestion of anise-flavored cordials, containing the chemical anethole, help relieve gas and settle a queasy stomach. Anise contains the compounds dianethole and photoanethole, which are chemically similar to the female hormone estrogen. Thus, drinking anise tea appears to help lactation and relieve menopausal distress.

References:

Artists direct network website

Bown, Deni *Encyclopedia of Herbs and their Uses by Deni Brown Dorley Kindersley*, New York

Doyle, Sir Arthur Conan *The Complete Sherlock Holmes* Doubleday, Garden City, New York

Garland, Sarah *The Complete Book of Herbs and Spices* Readers Digest, Hong Kong 1995

Kowalchik, Claire and Hylton, William H., Editors *Rodale's Illustrated Encyclopedia of Herbs* Rodale Press, Emmaus, Pennsylvania 1998

Meals for you.com

MotherNature.com

Tucker, Arthur O. *In Grolier Interactive Reference Suite*, Danbury, Connecticut 1999

Women.com

Youngken, Heber W. *Textbook of Pharmacognosy* Blakiston, Philadelphia 1950

Watson's Finest Moment

Prepared for *The Formulary,* The Journal of the Friends of
Dr. Watson
April 17, 2006

The "sacred" Canon reveals many excellent instances
that may fulfil the object of this essay -- to describe the finest
moment in the life and career of John H. Watson, M.D.
Could it be the time that he stood bravely on the deck of
the *Aurora*, revolver in hand, facing down the dangerous
Tonga and his poisoned dart in *The Sign of Four*, or, in the
same adventure, when he walked, alone and unprotected, late
at night through a dangerous part of London seeking Toby?
How about the time that he steadfastly acted as a British jury
in "The Adventure of the Abbey Grange?" The list is
virtually endless.

Although many other episodes could be cited as
exemplifying the subject of this discourse, I maintain that the
best exemplar was the occasion in which Dr. Watson agreed
to share Baker Street quarters with Mr. Sherlock Holmes.

Look at the circumstances that would have mitigated
against this decision. Watson was weak and weary from his
horrible experiences. His leg and shoulder ached constantly,
forcing him towards excessive drink. His constitution had
been weakened by a case of enteric fever. He was probably
also suffering from post-traumatic stress disorder. And, no
doubt, his nerves were very highly susceptible to anxiety,
admitting later to "keeping a bull pup." Yet, he agreed to
share a suite with a man described as a very sinister
companion; a man who greeted him with a mysterious
statement concerning the fact that he had been in
Afghanistan, a statement which could put most men's nerve
on edge, and then ran around yelling about some test for
blood.

It is indeed a tribute to Dr. Watson that he must have seen some very positive outcomes associated with a future relationship with the "mad scientist" whom he had just met.

Let us consider the serious consequences had Dr. Watson not decided that it would be in his best interests to share rooms with this eccentric gentleman. Just imagine, we might never have heard of Sherlock Holmes. His personal reticence would have dimmed whatever other records there were of his accomplishment. Think of it: The world would never have been the same; we would all have been deprived of the main focus of our scholarly pursuits.

Let us all sing the praises of Dr. Watson, and his finest moment -- the beginning of an adventurous life for Dr. Watson and all of us who relish Dr. Watson's accounts.

Also from MX Publishing

MX Publishing is the world's largest specialist Sherlock Holmes publisher, with over a hundred titles and fifty authors creating the latest in Sherlock Holmes fiction and non-fiction.

From traditional short stories and novels to travel guides and quiz books, MX Publishing cater for all Holmes fans.

The collection includes leading titles such as *Benedict Cumberbatch In Transition* and *The Norwood Author* which won the 2011 Howlett Award (Sherlock Holmes Book of the Year).

MX Publishing also has one of the largest communities of Holmes fans on Facebook with regular contributions from dozens of authors.

www.mxpublishing.com

Also from MX Publishing

Our bestselling books are our short story collections;

'Lost Stories of Sherlock Holmes' , 'The Outstanding Mysteries of Sherlock Holmes', The Papers of Sherlock Holmes Volume 1 and 2, 'Untold Adventures of Sherlock Holmes' (and the sequel 'Studies in Legacy) and 'Sherlock Holmes in Pursuit', 'The Cotswold Werewolf and Other Stories of Sherlock Holmes' – and many more……

Also from MX Publishing

"Phil Growick's, 'The Secret Journal of Dr Watson', is an adventure which takes place in the latter part of Holmes and Watson's lives. They are entrusted by HM Government (although not officially) and the King no less to undertake a rescue mission to save the Romanovs, Russia's Royal family from a grisly end at the hand of the Bolsheviks. There is a wealth of detail in the story but not so much as would detract us from the enjoyment of the story. Espionage, counter-espionage, the ace of spies himself, double-agents, double-crossers...all these flit across the pages in a realistic and exciting way. All the characters are extremely well-drawn and Mr Growick, most importantly, does not falter with a very good ear for Holmesian dialogue indeed. Highly recommended. A five-star effort."
The Baker Street Society

www.mxpublishing.com

Also from MX Publishing

The Missing Authors Series

Sherlock Holmes and The Adventure of The Grinning Cat
Sherlock Holmes and The Nautilus Adventure
Sherlock Holmes and The Round Table Adventure

"Joseph Svec, III is brilliant in entwining two endearing and enduring classics of literature, blending the factual with the fantastical; the playful with the pensive; and the mischievous with the mysterious. We shall, all of us young and old, benefit with a cup of tea, a tranquil afternoon, and a copy of Sherlock Holmes, The Adventure of the Grinning Cat."
Amador County Holmes Hounds Sherlockian Society

www.mxpublishing.com

Also from MX Publishing

The American Literati Series

The Final Page of Baker Street
The Baron of Brede Place
Seventeen Minutes To Baker Street

"The really amazing thing about this book is the author's ability to call up the 'essence' of both the Baker Street 'digs' of Holmes and Watson as well as that of the 'mean streets' of Marlowe's Los Angeles. Although none of the action takes place in either place, Holmes and Watson share a sense of camaraderie and self-confidence in facing threats and problems that also pervades many of the later tales in the Canon. Following their conversations and banter is a return to Edwardian England and its certainties and hope for the future. This is definitely the world before The Great War."
Philip K Jones

www.mxpublishing.com

Also from MX Publishing

The Detective and The Woman Series

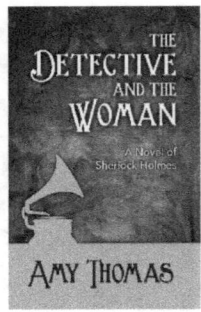  

The Detective and The Woman
The Detective, The Woman and The Winking Tree
The Detective, The Woman and The Silent Hive

"The book is entertaining, puzzling and a lot of fun. I believe the author has hit on the only type of long-term relationship possible for Sherlock Holmes and Irene Adler. The details of the narrative only add force to the romantic defects we expect in both of them and their growth and development are truly marvelous to watch. This is not a love story. Instead, it is a coming-of-age tale starring two of our favorite characters."
Philip K Jones

www.mxpublishing.com

Also from MX Publishing

The Sherlock Holmes and Enoch Hale Series

The Amateur Executioner
The Poisoned Penman
The Egyptian Curse

"The Amateur Executioner: Enoch Hale Meets Sherlock Holmes", the first collaboration between Dan Andriacco and Kieran McMullen, concerns the possibility of a Fenian attack in London. Hale, a native Bostonian, is a reporter for London's Central News Syndicate - where, in 1920, Horace Harker is still a familiar figure, though far from revered. "The Amateur Executioner" takes us into an ambiguous and murky world where right and wrong aren't always distinguishable. I look forward to reading more about Enoch Hale."
Sherlock Holmes Society of London

www.mxpublishing.com

Also from MX Publishing

Sherlock Holmes novellas in verse

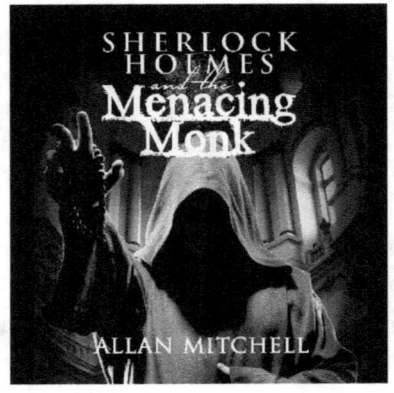

All four novellas have been released also in audio format with narration by Steve White

Sherlock Holmes and The Menacing Moors
Sherlock Holmes and The Menacing Metropolis
Sherlock Holmes and The Menacing Melbournian
Sherlock Holmes and The Menacing Monk

"The story is really good and the Herculean effort it must have been to write it all in verse—well, my hat is off to you, Mr. Allan Mitchell! I wouldn't dream of seeing such work get less than five plus stars from me…" **The Raven**
Also from MX Publishing

THE VATICAN CAMEOS
A SHERLOCK HOLMES ADVENTURE

"An extravagantly imagined and beautifully written Holmes story"~ NY Times Bestselling Author LEE CHILD

RICHARD T. RYAN

When the papal apartments are burgled in 1901, Sherlock Holmes is summoned to Rome by Pope Leo XII. After learning from the pontiff that several priceless cameos that could prove compromising to the church, and perhaps determine the future of the newly unified Italy, have been stolen, Holmes is asked to recover them. In a parallel story, Michelangelo, the toast of Rome in 1501 after the unveiling of his Pieta, is commissioned by Pope Alexander VI, the last of the Borgia pontiffs, with creating the cameos that will bedevil Holmes and the papacy four centuries later. For fans of Conan Doyle's immortal detective, the game is always afoot. However, the great detective has never encountered an adversary quite like the one with whom he crosses swords in "The Vatican Cameos.."

"An extravagantly imagined and beautifully written Holmes story"
(**Lee Child**, NY Times Bestselling author, Jack Reacher series)

Also from MX Publishing

The Conan Doyle Notes (The Hunt For Jack The Ripper) "Holmesians have long speculated on the fact that the Ripper murders aren't mentioned in the canon, though the obvious reason is undoubtedly the correct one: even if Conan Doyle had suspected the killer's identity he'd never have considered mentioning it in the context of a fictional entertainment. Ms Madsen's novel equates his silence with that of the dog in the night-time, assuming that Conan Doyle did know who the Ripper was but chose not to say – which, of course, implies that good old stand-by, the government cover-up. It seems unlikely to me that the Ripper was anyone famous or distinguished, but fiction is not fact, and "The Conan Doyle Notes" is a gripping tale, with an intelligent, courageous and very likable protagonist in DD McGil."
The Sherlock Holmes Society of London

www.mxpublishing.com